I0761450

Death on a Scottish Train

Also available by Lucy Connelly

The Scottish Isle Mysteries

Death at a Scottish Christmas

Death at a Scottish Wedding

An American in Scotland

Death on a Scottish Train

A SCOTTISH ISLE MYSTERY

Lucy Connelly

NEW YORK

Books should be disposed of and recycled according to local requirements. All paper materials used are FSC compliant.

This is a work of fiction. All of the names, characters, organizations, places and events portrayed in this novel are either products of the author's imagination or are used fictitiously. Any resemblance to real or actual events, locales, or persons, living or dead, is entirely coincidental.

Published in the United States by Crooked Lane Books, an imprint of The Quick Brown Fox & Company LLC.

Crooked Lane Books and its logo are trademarks of The Quick Brown Fox & Company LLC.

Library of Congress Catalog-in-Publication data available upon request.

ISBN (hardcover): 979-8-89242-191-1
ISBN (ebook): 979-8-89242-192-8

Cover design by Jim Griffin

Printed in the United States.

www.crookedlanebooks.com

Crooked Lane Books
34 West 27th St., 10th Floor
New York, NY 10001

First Edition: October 2025

The authorized representative in the EU for product safety and compliance is eucomply OÜPärnu mnt 139b-14, 11317 Tallinn, Estonia, hello@eucompliancepartner.com, +33757690241

10 9 8 7 6 5 4 3 2 1

To my lovely readers, thank you so much for everything.

Chapter One

I frowned at the beautiful silvery, sequined dress hanging in my wardrobe. After a long day of seeing patients, the last thing I wanted to do was pull on my Spanx and dress up in 1930s' garb for a Friday-night party on a train. Most of my Friday nights were spent on the couch watching UK mysteries. I preferred it that way.

We were at the end of tourist season in the small town of Sea Isle, Scotland, and with the increase of tourist injuring themselves in surfing and boating accidents, it was the busiest time of year for the practice.

Guilt edged its way into my brain. I'd promised my friends I'd be there for them, and I didn't want to let them down. That, and I had spent a small fortune on my outfit.

Come on, Em. Let's do this.

After dressing and taking a quick look in the mirror, I went downstairs. I lived and worked in a 400-year-old church and while it had its quirks, I'd grown to love it.

I headed to the kitchen to make myself a quick espresso. Nothing like a jolt of caffeine to get me through the evening.

My phone dinged with a message from my bestie, Mara. She ran the Pig & Whistle pub with her grandparents just down the hill on the corner. And she was the main reason I'd been rooked into participating in tonight's festivities on the newly refurbished Scottish Storytellers' Train.

The locomotive hadn't run in the last fifty years, but Mara and a group of volunteers had helped to refurbish it, and it would be a new connection between Sea Isle and Edinburgh twice daily. I liked the idea of that, so I didn't have to drive on the wrong side of the road in the city.

It was one thing to handle a car on Scottish country roads here in town. Quite another in a bustling metropolis like Edinburgh.

Tonight was the big launch of the train and a chance to show off their hard work.

Mara's text stated the shuttle would be ready in twenty minutes to take us up the mountain to the refurbished station.

I texted back that I'd be there.

I sipped my espresso and stared out the back window in the kitchen, which had a lovely view of the cemetery in my yard. Over the past year, since I'd moved to Sea Isle, I'd come to appreciate the history and beauty of the church, even if it was sometimes a bit drafty in the cold Scottish winters.

By the time I finished my coffee and put my hair in a messy bun at the nape of my neck, I only had five minutes to make it to the shuttle.

When I opened the front door, I nearly slammed into my assistant, Abigail. There was no way I would have survived my first year in town without her. She helped at the practice and kept my world running.

"You look gorgeous," I said. Her beautiful, heart-shaped face was framed by red ringlets, and she wore a black-sequined dress that showcased her petite figure.

Her cheeks turned a rosy shade. After growing up in a rather difficult environment, she was beyond shy and never knew how to take a compliment. She was amazing, though. In addition to everything she did for me, she looked after her adorable brother, Tommy, who was on the spectrum and absolutely brilliant.

"Thank you," she said shyly. "You, too, Doc Em."

"Did you get Tommy sorted?"

"Aye, he's with Ewan's housekeeper making cookies. Then she's going to play one of his video games with him. That woman is a saint."

Ewan Campbell was the laird, local assistant chief constable, and mayor; he looked after Abigail and Tommy like they were family. He and I butted heads more often than not, but even I had to admit he was a decent guy. And he cared about the people in Sea Isle like they were all related.

"We should get to the pub," she said.

I picked up a lacy shawl that matched my silver dress. Even though it was summer, Scotland nights were chilly.

Sea Isle had two parts of the town. There were the beachside pubs and stores, and then up the mountain a mile or so, was another quaint part of the town with more shops and restaurants.

I'd grown to love the place and the people, even though the winter had been harsher than anything I could have imagined. Everyone promised I'd become accustomed to the constant grayness and bone-chilling cold. That hadn't happened yet.

By the time we made it down the half-block to the shuttle, the van was nearly full.

"Yay, you're here," Mara said as she checked our names off a clipboard.

"You look gorgeous," I said. She was dressed in a red fringed dress that was more 1920s than 1930s, but it fit her figure perfectly.

"Same to you, my friend. What is it you Americans say? We clean up well."

I nodded.

After a short ride up the mountain, we arrived at the quaint station.

"It's like something out of a storybook," Abigail whispered beside me. The outside of the station was an Italianate style with elaborate woodworking details on the roof, handrails, and door.

I nodded in agreement.

"You all did a fabulous job," I said to Mara as we exited the shuttle.

"It was a huge group effort," she said. "I'm just the bossy one who keeps things running. Though, after all this work, I'm glad it's done, and I can hand everything over to the station master."

She was a force to be reckoned with and gave a great deal to the town of Sea Isle. Like Ewan, she never complained about any of it.

I'd come from Seattle and never experienced the kind of community pride people here had. It was lovely to live in a place where the residents genuinely cared for one another.

The station was a mix of old stone with ornate trim and fixtures. Most of the buildings in town were several hundred years old, and this was no exception. Lights had been put up to show off the intricate architecture.

"It's so pretty," Abigail whispered beside me.

"The committee worked very hard on making it feel like something out of a storybook," Mara said.

"It's absolutely that," I added.

"You two go on, I have to check off the guests as they come in and make sure we have our storytellers."

The building was cozy inside and had been beautifully decorated with ornate wooden benches. There were maps of Scotland on the walls, along with various train memorabilia.

A ticket window was on the right side of the entry and a small coffee and tea cart in another corner. Tonight, a server was handing out flutes filled with champagne.

I took one and mingled a bit with the other guests, many of whom were patients of mine. After about a half-hour I followed the crowd through the other set of doors to the train.

The locomotive had been completely refurbished and was dark hunter's green, with cream trim, and gold lettering on the side that read: The Scottish Storyteller's Train. It reminded me of the pictures I'd seen of the Orient Express. Traveling on that train was on my bucket list. But this beautiful train, at least from the outside, would give it a run for its money when it came to beauty.

What made this train different than any others in the world were the volunteer storytellers. Tonight, there would be several—one in each car. But on regular trips, there would be one volunteer, whose voice would be piped through the train. On each trip back and forth, they would regale the passengers with a bit of Scottish history and folklore.

As we stepped onto the train, I nearly gasped. It really did remind me of pictures I'd seen of the Orient Express. The woodwork had intricate detailing, and the interior fabrics, in shades of green and cream, were incredibly plush.

The chairs were luxurious loungers. A pair of them sat on each side of beautiful ebony tables. On each table was a small Tiffany-styled lamp, and there were electric sconces in between the huge windows.

"Wow," I said.

"It's a movie set," Abigail said.

"You took the words right out of my mouth. I had no idea it would be this fancy."

"I'm glad we are dressed up, or I would feel out of place," she said.

I put my arm through hers and squeezed. "You always look beautiful."

She shook her head. "You're being kind, but thank you."

"Oh, Abigail. Someday you'll see yourself the way the rest of us see you. Come on, let's check out the rest of the train."

There were four passenger cars and a dining one, each one fancier than the last. It wasn't at all what I'd been expecting. The committee had outdone themselves.

After grabbing some hors d'oeuvres from the dining car, we found our assigned table. The program we'd been handed when we boarded said that we would stay put, and the storytellers would change every half hour or so.

It wasn't long before the train lurched into movement, and Mara and our favorite baker, Jasper, sat down across from us.

"Em and Abigail, you look beautiful," he said. "Isn't this exciting?"

Now that I was here, I was eager to see what came next. "It is, and you are adorable in your chef's whites," I said.

He did a fake bow, and we laughed.

The first storyteller began to speak: "I'm Elspeth Bell, and my story tonight is about the haunted moor where the Elfin Knight wanders through eternity." Her tale involved missing people who were believed to be captured by the Knight, most of them never to be heard of again.

She was lively and fun and kept the audience at the edge of their seats. One of the things Mara had done was to audition the storytellers, and if Elspeth was any indication, she'd done a fabulous job.

When Elspeth finished her yarn, she received a standing ovation from the crowd.

Not long after, a new storyteller came in, and a woman I didn't recognize came up to Mara and whispered something.

She frowned, and then pulled out her clipboard.

"But he signed in at the station," Mara said to the woman.

The woman shrugged. "We cannot find him anywhere."

"What's wrong?" I asked.

"I'm missing one of my storytellers," she said. "I have him checked off, so I know he was at the station, but Sheila says they've hunted throughout the train, and they can't find him anywhere."

"We'll help you look," I said. "Is there someone who can take his place for now?"

"Yes, Grandad is helping out in case someone was sick. But I cannot imagine what must have happened."

"Maybe he's in the loo?" Abigail offered.

"They checked there first," Mara said. "The train isn't that big. There aren't many places to hide. Not that he's hiding, but maybe he has stage fright or something."

"OK, let's check methodically, car by car. What's his name?"

"Donald Jacks," she said. Then she pointed to his picture in the program. He was older and slightly balding. He glared at the photographer as if he didn't know what a smile might be.

"OK. Let's do this," I said.

She and Abigail nodded. We started with the engine cab at the front of the train. Everything had been converted to electric so there were only two engineers. There was a storeroom for luggage just behind them, and we searched throughout.

So that we didn't disturb the storytellers, we waited to search each part of the train until after they'd finished and there was a short five-minute break for people to move around, and grab snacks and drinks.

An hour later, by the time we'd reached Edinburgh, the man was nowhere to be found.

"I don't understand," Mara said. "I remember seeing him at the station. He was on the shuttle with us. I checked him off." She held up her clipboard and pointed to the man's name.

"Maybe, you're right about the stage fright, and he never boarded the train."

She huffed. "Even so, that's so unprofessional of him. The very least he could do was let me know."

"Is there anyone at the station you can call? Maybe he just missed the train," I said.

"No. We locked up and everyone boarded the train. He's just missing."

I don't know why, but I had a bad feeling about this.

My stomach churned and that was never a good sign.

Had someone thrown the man off the train?

Chapter Two

OK, a man being thrown off a train was a bit of a reach, but he hadn't just disappeared. I trusted my friend. If Mara had marked him off her list, he had been around at some point.

"Do you think we should call Ewan?" I asked.

Mara bit her lip. "Let's don't bother him yet," she said. "I want to check the station first. I did try to text Donald, but he didn't answer."

"Maybe, he had stage fright. I would," Abigail said. "And he might be embarrassed by it."

"If he's run off, I'll have his head," Mara snarled. "I had every moment of this trip planned, and he's gone and ruined everything."

I put a hand on her shoulder. "Look through the window," I said. We were in the covered space between the train cars. "Everything is just fine."

From the faces of his audience, her grandfather had their attention.

"Well, I suppose you are right," she said. "Grandad has always been able to tell a great story. Still, the missing man was one of the ones we hired on a part-time basis. I can tell you he no longer has a job with us.

"It's strange because he helped so much with getting the train ready. He was a peculiar man, but had good ideas on how to recreate what had once been. Maybe, a bit hard-headed at times, but I cannot believe he would do this." She bristled.

Mara was so easygoing, nothing much phased her, but she was more than annoyed. I didn't blame her. Still, that churning in my gut meant something wasn't right. I'd long ago learned to trust that feeling. Especially, after I had solved a few murders.

There was a bit of maneuvering with the train when we arrived in Edinburgh, and they moved the engine to the front of the train once again.

While that commenced, small bites and desserts were served in the dining car. No one seemed to have noticed that one of the storytellers might be missing, which pleased Mara.

"Why does my granddaughter look like she wants to throw someone off the train?" her grandfather asked.

"One of the storytellers went missing, and that's why you had to cover."

"Ah. I wondered what had happened when they asked me to tell some stories."

"Abigail thinks the man was nervous and maybe ducked out."

"Could be," Mara's grandad said before moving on.

Jasper glanced down at me. "And what do you think? You have that look in your eyes."

"What do you mean?"

"The one that says there is a mystery you need to solve."

I laughed. "I had no idea I was so easy to read."

"Only to your friends. Do you think something bad happened?"

I shrugged. "I don't know about bad, but odd for sure. At the very least, he could have made an excuse that he wasn't feeling well before leaving."

"Maybe, it came on quickly," Jasper said.

Jasper made a good point.

On the way back to Sea Isle, Mara was notably fidgety. I could tell she was pretending not to worry, but she wasn't very good at hiding it.

I didn't blame her. People didn't just go missing. I hoped that the man had a bad case of nerves, and he was safe and sound at home.

On the way back, the stories all focused on Highland fairy lore, which Scotland was known for, along with its rich oral history.

While I didn't believe in fairies, people in Scotland talked about them like they were among us. It was part of the charm of living here and made for some wonderful tales. They had fairy stories for just about every moral lesson.

When the train made it back to the Sea Isle station, I stood next to Mara and Abigail doing my one job of the evening. We handed small gift bags to the travel writers and bloggers who had joined us for the ride.

Inside was a replica of the engine and a pamphlet that gave the history of the train.

As they disembarked, the guests had been extremely complimentary about the ride. And while everyone had told Mara it was a great success, the words didn't seem to help the lines of strain across her forehead.

Once the last passenger was off the train, she turned to Abigail and me. "Will you two help me search the station? I can't imagine he's still there. He's probably at home, but I won't sleep tonight if we don't check. I was angry earlier, but I'm worried now that something might have happened to him. No one was more excited about the train launch than he was."

"Of course," Abigail and I said at the same time.

"I'll help too," Jasper offered as he came up carrying some of the catering trays. "I've already offloaded most of my equipment."

She gave us a tight smile. "Thank you."

Inside the station, we each took a corner. While Mara searched the ticket booth area, Jasper checked the area with the tea and treats cart.

Abigail went into the restrooms, and I went through a door that led to a small office. I flipped on the light to find it empty and incredibly tidy. There wasn't a speck of dust or a paper out of place.

I was about to turn off the light and return to the center room of the station when I noticed a skinny door at the back of the office.

It was latched on the outside, and I undid it. When I did, something thumped inside.

Nerves clawed at my throat. As neat as everything might have been, it didn't mean there weren't mice hanging out. I wasn't a big fan of them.

I closed my eyes and whipped open the door. When I blinked, I was surprised to find a very dead man staring back at me.

"What in the . . ." I'd been expecting a mouse, not a corpse.

His eyes were wide open, and his toupee had slipped to the side of his head like a strange furry cap.

He was dressed in a trench coat, and a fedora had fallen down to cover his shoes. It must have been a costume of sorts harkening back to the days of 1930s film noir. The sickening scent of vomit and death had gathered around him in the tight confines of the broom closet.

Why had he gone into the closet to throw up? It didn't make sense. Nor did the bluish tint to his lips or the yellow haze in the whites of his eyes. It appeared he'd been quite sick in the small closet.

His pupils were dilated, and rigor had just begun to set in, so he had to have been killed in the last few hours. Though I'd need to take an internal temperature to be more accurate.

"Em, where are you?" Mara called out.

"Uh. In the office," I said. "Don't come in here, though. I don't want to contaminate the crime scene."

"Crime scene?" Mara screeched. "What? No. Please tell me he isn't dead. I've had such awful thoughts about the man tonight."

"Well, I don't think you were alone. He appears to have been quite ill, but I need my kit."

"On it," Abigail said. I never really had to ask her to do anything. She was incredibly adept at anticipating anything I might need. Whether that was coffee or the tools of the trade.

"I'll drive her down and back, I've got my delivery van," Jasper offered. "I don't suppose it was from natural causes?"

"I can't comment," I said. "You know how Ewan is, and speaking of whom, I need to call him." But the answer was no.

"Is it the storyteller?" Mara asked.

"I think so."

"Let me look. I can handle it. I promise," she said.

I wasn't so sure about that, but we would need some form of identification one way or another.

"Stand at the door and lean in," I said. I glanced back to find her doing what I'd asked. I moved so she could have a clear view.

"Is that him?"

Her hand flew to her mouth. "Yes," the word came out as a whisper. "That's Donald Jacks."

"OK, I'll call Ewan."

I'd been surprised he hadn't been on the locomotive. But Mara had mentioned a few days ago that he had business in Edinburgh he couldn't get out of, so he had to miss the inaugural trip for The Storytellers Train.

I couldn't help but wonder what kind of business that was.

I pulled my phone out of my pocket.

Ewan picked up on the second ring. "What's wrong?" he asked worriedly.

"Why do you always assume something is wrong?" I asked.

"You only call if you're about to be killed or if you found a dead body."

He was probably right about that.

"It's a body," I said. "I found him at the train station in a broom cupboard. Mara has identified him as one of the storytellers. He never made it onboard. We thought he'd chickened out, but that isn't true."

"Right, I'm fifteen minutes out. I'll call the station and send my team over."

"OK, Abigail and Jasper have gone to collect my kit."

"I don't suppose it was natural causes?" He sounded hopeful.

"Unfortunately, I don't think so. The cupboard was latched from the outside. Though, until I have some gloves and can examine the body, there isn't much more I can tell you. Other than that, from the time Mara signed him in until now, it has been about four hours. As I said, I can thoroughly examine him once I have my kit and get him back for autopsy."

"Right. Stay there, and I'll see you soon."

It wasn't as if I was going anywhere, but he hung up before I could give him a smart retort. I liked Ewan, and I believed he, at the very least, appreciated my talents as a doctor, but we were always awkward with one another.

"What did he say?" Mara asked.

"That he's on his way and is sending his team over."

"I can't believe this happened. This could ruin everything we've tried to do with the train. And yes, I know how selfish that sounds."

I shrugged. "It is understandable. You and the committee have worked very hard to make this something that would benefit the town."

"How could it even happen? You saw how crowded it was in the station when everyone arrived. And we all boarded at the same time."

Since I'd been carrying an evening bag, I didn't have the notebook that I normally had on my person. I opened my phone again and hit record. Ewan might not appreciate it, but he was the one who taught me that it was important to get the facts quickly after something happened. Peoples' memories weren't as reliable the more time passed.

"Can you tell me everything you remember about him?"

She was used to my prying. She left the office door and went to sit on one of the benches in the main room of the station.

"He was a part-timer we hired for weekend work," she said. "I think he said he was an accountant or something like that, and storytelling was a creative outlet for him."

"Right. And you saw him come in when?"

"He arrived with the first shuttle with us."

I hadn't noticed him, but there were lots of people I didn't know in the van.

"All of the storytellers were asked to come in a half-hour before everyone else so we could sort out the schedule, and they all knew what to do.

"I checked him off with the others. He was supposed to be on the second rotation and was telling 1930s detective stories set on trains."

"Do you remember seeing him get on the train?"

She shook her head. "I was working by the front door at the station as guests came in and I marked them off. Once he went past me, I don't know what happened. Two of the other volunteers were passing out the programs. We can ask them if they remember seeing him."

"We will. So, after you checked him in, you don't remember seeing him?"

"No. I can't believe someone killed him here. I mean, the place was packed. How did that even happen?"

I chewed on my lip. "I have no idea. Once Abigail gets here, I can start examining the body, and that will help us create a better timeline."

"You think he was murdered, don't you?"

I sighed.

"Please, tell me. I saw him in the closet."

"Again, I can't say for sure until I've sorted him and the scene."

There was a bustling at the door. Some of Ewan's officers filtered into the station.

One of them was Henry, who was Abigail's boyfriend. He was a kind soul but also a good policeman.

"Doctor, Ewan said you had a suspicious death," he said seriously.

"We do," I said. "I'm waiting for Abigail to return with my kit. Do you by chance have some gloves on you?"

"Aye." He pulled out a box from the backpack he carried and handed it to me.

"Once I examine the body, I'll need your techs to go over the scene. Though, you know Abigail will be pulling prints and hopefully some DNA as well."

"Yes, ma'am."

"We're here," Abigail said as she hurried through the door. "I brought you a suit to wear," she said. "I dinnae think you'd want to get your nice dress messed up."

She'd already changed into jeans and a sweater, or jumper, as they called them here.

I took the hazard suit and booties from her and went into the restroom to change.

When I came back out, my attention was drawn to the center of the room where Ewan stood. He was dressed in a tuxedo, looking extremely attractive in his tall-dark-and-handsome way.

My throat went dry. Wherever he'd been, he'd had to dress up. Was he on a date?

I sighed. Why should I care?

I wasn't ready to examine that answer quite yet.

When Henry nodded toward me, Ewan turned the full force of his gaze on me.

He looked like something out of some gorgeous men's magazine. It wasn't fair for a man to be that handsome.

I cleared my throat.

He held up a hand. "Tell me everything."

Chapter Three

Since anyone who might have been a suspect was long gone, Ewan decided to help Abigail and me with the initial examination. Once that was done, we'd transport the body to my office.

"Before we go in, Mara, we'll need a list of the guests. Give that to Henry, please." He turned to his team. "It's late, but first thing tomorrow we'll work on narrowing down the suspects. That is, if Dr. Em says it is a suspicious death. We'll look for connections between the victim and the other guests."

I was fairly certain the victim hadn't stuck himself in a broom closet, but Ewan worked with evidence and was never a fan of assuming anything.

"Henry, I need a full workup on the deceased tonight. Get his information from Mara."

"Yes, sir," Henry said.

After suiting up, Ewan followed Abigail and me into the small office area, made tinier by his enormous presence.

He understood the drill and handed Abigail evidence bags as I went about the initial examination.

"Temp tells me he died just before the train took off," I said. "And rigor has begun settling in, which will make it difficult to move him in his current position."

Some parts of the job were not very glamorous, including scooping up some of the sick for testing.

Thank goodness for mint-scented masks. I'd had Henry as well as Abigail order them not long after solving our first case.

I poked and I prodded.

"What are your initial thoughts?"

"From the outward signs, I'd say anaphylactic shock."

"What makes you say that?"

"Blue tinge on the lips and the yellowing of the eyes," Abigail said, as she closed one of the evidence bags.

I smiled, and Ewan looked from me to her.

My assistant's eyes opened wide. "Sorry. I said that out loud, didn't I?"

I chuckled. "You did. And you're right."

"So, it's possible it could be he just ate or drank something he was allergic to, and this isn't murder."

"I seriously doubt he stuffed himself into the closet and then latched it from the outside. And I find it suspicious that he would get sick and not remove himself from it. Which means he may have been unconscious when that happened."

"So," Ewan said, "someone poisoned him, and he couldn't move. Then they put him in a closet."

I shrugged. "Until I can run toxicology, I can't confirm any of that. All I can say right now is it does look like anaphylactic shock."

"So, someone gave him peanuts or something?" he asked.

I glanced back at him. "Ewan, I have no idea what he was allergic to so I can't say. The only thing I can tell you for certain is he's been dead for at least three hours. Like I said, I can give you more specifics once we get everything back to the lab and tested."

I found some fibers on his coat and put them into the small Petri dishes we used for evidence. I could feel Ewan's frustration rolling off of him, but I tried to ignore it.

I wasn't certain his frustration was from us finding a dead body. Where had he been before joining us? While he was always quite serious, tonight he had an edginess that I'd never seen before.

By the time I'd finished gathering evidence, I was stiff from bending down so much that Abigail helped me to stand.

"From the state of rigor, your officers will have trouble moving him out of that narrow closet," I said.

"We'll take care of it," he said. "And we'll have the body to you in less than an hour."

I stifled a yawn. It had been a very long day. Unfortunately, it was about to be a long night as well. I never liked to leave a body before we'd gathered all the evidence. That was based on the experience of the first time I'd had to do my coroner's job, and the killer had stolen the body out of the makeshift morgue at my practice.

"I can do the rest alone," I told Abigail.

"I'm too wired to sleep, and Tommy is cared for at Ewan's. I'll be helping you run the labs," Abigail said in her matter-of-fact way.

I'd learned from experience that it was no use arguing with her. Also, she was twice as fast as I would ever be with the equipment we had. In my defense, she had a great deal more experience with it.

When we walked out of the office, we found Mara curled up on one of the benches with her eyes closed.

I touched her shoulder, and she jumped.

"You're OK," I said. "Why didn't you go home and go to bed?"

She cleared her throat. "I know it isn't my fault, but I feel responsible. I mean, I'm head of the committee who pulled this event together."

"You aren't responsible," Ewan said from behind me. "It may not even have been murder."

Her eyes went wide. "Really? So, he put himself in that cupboard?"

I covered my laugh with my hand. She made a good point. One I'd mentioned earlier.

"Right. We need a key," he said. "We'll close up after we've finished. You head home."

Mara glanced at me.

"Abigail and I are heading back to my practice. There's nothing more we can do here."

"OK," Mara said as she followed us out.

Jasper was asleep in his van.

"Why is he still here?" I asked.

"He thought we might need a ride back down the mountain," Abigail said.

"More than likely he wanted in on the gossip," Mara added.

He jumped when Mara opened the passenger side door.

"Are you finished?"

"For now," I said climbing into the back of his catering van. "Do you mind giving us a ride down the mountain?"

"That's why I'm here."

"I said it was because you'd want all the juicy facts about the case," Mara said.

He chuckled. "Well, I'm a part of the Dr. Em Scooby gang, so yes." That's what my friends started calling themselves after helping with my first case almost a year ago.

We'd been through a lot together since then, and they were more like family now.

"True," I said. "But you know how Ewan feels about sharing information on cases."

He started up the van. "But it isn't like I'm going to say anything."

That was true. The man could keep a secret.

"Did you by chance know the deceased?" I asked him.

"Do you have a picture?"

Abigail leaned forward and showed him a picture from the digital camera she used for crime scenes.

He made a face in the rearview mirror, before pulling out of his parking spot. "Oh. My," he said. "He does not look good. No. I dinnae think I've ever seen him before."

Abigail sat back, and then Jasper maneuvered the van down the mountain.

"Any idea how he died?" he asked.

"I'm curious about that as well," Mara said.

Abigail and I glanced at one another.

"I do not even have to turn around to know you two are looking at one another," Mara said. "Maybe Jasper and I can help if you give us something to go on."

"This stays in this van," I said.

"Promise," Jasper and Mara said at the same time.

"I better not hear a word has leaked at the pub."

Mara sighed. "I've never said a word about your cases to anyone outside our group. But that doesn't keep people in our small town from talking. My guess is half the town already knows something bad happened."

She wasn't wrong. The grapevine in Sea Isle was a quick one. That was one of the many things I'd learned about small-town living.

As a doctor, I knew more than I wanted about most of my patients. Of course, I never said a word because of confidentiality. That didn't stop my patients from gossiping about their neighbors as that was the town's main form of communication.

As we made our way down the mountain, I explained that he may have died from an allergy.

"Did he mention anything to you, Mara?"

She shook her head. "Since we were doing small plates and desserts only, we didn't have dietary restrictions. We tried to have a good mix."

"Do you have any idea what caused the reaction?" Jasper asked. "I'd hate it if something I prepared killed him." He'd provided petits fours and macarons for the event.

"I don't think you have to worry," I said. "From what I could see, he never made it onto the train. So, whatever caused the reaction was most likely ingested before he arrived or inside the station."

"But all we had in the station was the champagne," Mara said. "Maybe, he was allergic to alcohol."

"Could be," Abigail relayed. "But wouldn't he know not to drink it? I think the Doc is right. Whatever reaction he had was caused by something either before or just after he got here. His time of death, which she'll be able to be more precise about once the labs come back, will most likely show when he ingested whatever it was."

I smiled. Abigail was a flower who had blossomed over the past year. She was confident about her skills, as she should be. She was a marvel.

"So, he was allergic to something but that doesn't mean someone killed him," Mara said.

I didn't blame her for wanting the case to be murder-free. I'd feel the same way if I'd worked as hard as she had to launch the Storytellers' Train.

"We'll see," I said. "We have a lot more testing to do."

"That doesn't sound good." Mara sighed.

"It will be OK," I said. "No one is going to blame you."

"And who knows," Jasper said. "Some people might want to take the train even more if they feel like their lives might be in danger. I mean, there is a reason there are so many murder shows and podcasts."

"Not. Helping," Mara told him.

We pulled up at the corner behind the pub, which was just down from my home and practice.

"Get some rest," I said to Mara. "I promise to share what we find out tomorrow. Just please . . ."

"I know. Don't say anything in public."

I nodded.

Jasper drove us up the small hill to my home.

"Thanks for the ride," I said as I helped Abigail move my kit out of the van.

"Promise you'll let me know if you find anything out?"

"I will," I said.

* * *

As soon as we made it inside, I headed for my coffee machine. It was going to be an even longer night, and I needed a brain boost.

While I made coffee, Abigail headed to the back of the practice to start the lab testing. The town was remote and sometimes we were cut off from the outside world. Ewan had made certain the practice was equipped for anything that might happen. We had more up-to-date equipment than many small hospitals in America.

Abigail was a marvel and had taught herself how to run all the machines. I trusted her more than I would any other lab tech.

By the time I had the autopsy suite set up, Ewan and his team arrived with the body. They had to roll him in the cramped position he'd been in because of rigor.

As Abigail took more samples from him and cut his clothes off, I began lining up my tools.

The other officers left, but Ewan stayed behind to help. At some point he'd changed into a cable-knit sweater with dark jeans and boots. Mara and I called it his working uniform.

"You don't have to be here," I said. "I'm sure you're exhausted."

"As are you," he said. "And I remind you that as the Assistant Chief Constable, I must be here to oversee the findings."

He told me that every time, but I wasn't sure it was true.

That said, I didn't question him. He'd been through this so many times with us that we all worked like a well-oiled machine.

Abigail handed him the chain of evidence clipboard. He recorded things as we went about our business.

Almost an hour later, I made my first cuts. And it was easy to see why the victim had died. His windpipe was closed off, and his lungs had signs of extreme irritation. As did his heart, which showed signs of the same sort of stress.

"Any idea what could have caused such a reaction and failure so quickly?" Ewan asked.

"We'll know more when the tox screens are done," I said.

I glanced at Abigail, who checked her watch. "Another couple of hours," she said.

After that, we worked quickly and efficiently. Ewan logged things down, as Abigail put things in evidence bags or helped me with the weighing and measuring.

We finished in the early hours of the morning. By that time, all I could think of was going to bed.

"Everyone go home," I said as we covered the body. "We can look at all the tests in the morning. But I need some sleep."

"You do look dead on your feet." Ewan nodded.

"Uh. Thanks."

"I can stay and run more tests," Abigail said.

"No. You need to rest as well. Just lock everything up in the lab. We'll take a look at the results later on. I promise to send over the reports first thing to you, Ewan."

I didn't bother stifling a huge yawn, as I nearly shoved them both out the front door.

But even though I was exhausted, I couldn't resist checking some of the labs that I knew would be finished.

I headed through my practice and back to the lab.

Almost all of the machines were still running. But something dinged on the main computer. When I brought it up, it was the first part of the tox screen.

I frowned. "That's odd."

I headed back to the autopsy room. I still had work to do.

Chapter Four

The next morning came way too soon, but I was curious about the lab results Abigail had run over night. I wanted to see if they came to the same conclusion I had the night before.

After a quick shower, and dressing in my favorite jeans and dark purple sweater, I headed downstairs. I grabbed a quick cup of espresso and headed through the hall to my office.

Abigail was already at her desk in the reception area.

"Why am I not surprised to see you here?"

"Because you knew I'd be just as curious as you are about the tests."

"Did anything of interest come up? Other than the histamine profile?"

She raised her eyebrows. "You already looked?"

"Only at the ones that were completed last night. I went over the body but did not see any kind of puncture wound."

"So, he ingested the bee venom and must have been highly allergic, according to the reports."

"Someone must have put it in his food or drink."

"Except the only thing in his stomach was some French bread and tomato soup," she said. "I'm testing the contents again for a more specific profile."

"Good," I said. "But there was significant swelling of his lips so the venom must have passed through them at some point. I looked at the brochure picture of him from last night. He had quite thin lips in the photos. But as we saw, his mouth was swollen."

"I'll keep testing. Maybe, we'll find the answer there. Still, if someone was trying to kill him, there are easier ways."

"True."

My stomach made a horrible grumbling sound, and we laughed.

"I'm going to head down to the pub for a quick bite to eat. Do you want me to bring you anything?"

"I had breakfast with Tommy. He's here by the way, out in the back doing end-of-summer plantings."

Her brother was an incredible horticulturalist and kept my gardens around the old church beautiful. He knew more than most in the business who were twice his age.

"It's Saturday; if they have any of the blueberry scones left, I'll bring you some."

"I wouldn't turn one away." She and Tommy loved the scones that Mara's grandmother made.

I made the short jaunt down the hill. It was a cloudy day, and even though it was summer, the temperature was chilly. That didn't seem to matter to the Scots who swam and surfed in the frigid waters off the coast of Sea Isle even when it poured rain. I would never understand it. I could barely stand to put my feet in the water.

"Morning," Mara said from behind the bar. Even though it appeared clean, she wiped down my favorite spot at the bar.

As I made my way through the pub there was an audible hush of the crowd.

"Any news?" Mara said a little louder than necessary.

"Nothing yet. Tests are inconclusive," I said just as loud.

The patrons went back to chatting.

This was a game we played anytime I had a new case. People in town were always curious, and the pub was often the best place for someone to hear the latest craic, as they called it.

"Really?" She leaned in and whispered the word.

I nodded. "Nothing conclusive yet. Abigail is continuing to run tests."

"I still feel guilty for having such horrible thoughts about the man, and he'd been dead the whole time."

"No one blames you. As far as you knew, he didn't show up for work."

"Do you think it's murder?"

I shrugged. "Like you said last night, he probably didn't stuff himself in that cupboard and lock the latch."

She glanced over my shoulder. "What can I get you this fine morning, Doctor?"

Customers must have taken notice of our hushed tones.

"Full Scottish," I said. "And if there are any blueberry scones left, a few of those to go."

While I ate, I tried to think of ways the bee venom could have entered the dead man's system. If it had been in his food, which he would have eaten elsewhere, the attack would have happened before he even arrived.

It would have gone straight into his bloodstream. It was possible, if he had a glass of champagne when he arrived, it could have been in there. But it would have been quite dicey for the murderer to pick the right glass.

"Mara, did anyone leave out the front before we got on the train?"

She shook her head. "I was the last on board, and locked the front doors since everyone in the building was on the train. We didn't want to leave it unattended."

That meant the killer had most likely been on the train. I shivered.

I didn't remember seeing champagne listed among the contents of his stomach, but I'd come down here before reading the full report.

I'd just finished my breakfast, when my phone dinged.

I think I found the source. It was a text from Abigail.

"Is everything OK?" Mara asked.

My face must have given something away.

"Some more of the tests came back. I need to go."

She handed me a paper bag. "There are blueberry scones, and I threw in a couple of chocolate ones for you."

"It's like you read my mind. Thanks."

"Let me know if you learn anything," she whispered.

I nodded.

I was well aware the rest of the pub had quieted down when they'd seen us whispering. Even though Mara wouldn't say anything, people here had a way of finding things out. But that information wasn't coming from me. I had no desire to face the wrath of the ACC.

Abigail was still at her desk when I made it up the hill. I put the sack of scones on her desk. The door opened behind me, and I turned to tell whoever it was we weren't open. Though, we were always open for emergencies, but it was Ewan coming in behind me.

He held up a hand as if to say hello, and then turned his attention to Abigail.

"What did you find?" he asked.

"I discovered how the bee venom entered his system."

"Bee venom is the cause of death?" he asked and the surprise on his face said it all.

"Yes, but we couldn't find an injection site on the body," I told him.

Abigail lifted the evidence box lid and pulled out a plastic baggie with what looked like lip balm.

"One of the reasons his lips were so swollen was because he used this balm." She held it up.

"Is bee venom one of the ingredients? They use it in all sorts of cosmetics and creams these days."

"They do?" Once again, Ewan appeared shocked.

"Yes," I said. "It has great healing properties. That is unless you are allergic to it. So, why would he use something that he was allergic to?"

"That's how we know it was murder," Abigail said. "It is in the balm, but it isn't listed as one of the ingredients."

"So," I said, "he used something that was poisonous to him without realizing it. Given the histamine reaction throughout it body, it had to be a pretty hefty dose."

"It was. I'm still running those tests, but we saw his lungs and heart. It was enough to do some damage."

"I need to know who manufactures that lip balm," Ewan said. "That at least gives us a starting point with the investigation."

That surprised me. "There were cameras at the station, I thought you might start there to see who went into the office with him. I can check out the lip balm angle."

Ewan frowned. "Yes, well, the cameras were not operational yet. The security team is working on them next week. They were just up for show according to the station master."

"Oh, that is disappointing. Have you spoken to any of the guests?"

"I divided my team to talk to all of them this morning. They'll be canvassing everyone who was there last night. I stopped by to see if you had any other leads for me, and you didn't fail me."

"I'd like to come with you, if that's all right. I'm wondering if maybe the balm was mislabeled. I doubt he ended up in that cabinet on his own, but with that sort of reaction, he may have been disoriented and thought he was going into a restroom or something. And maybe the lock just fell into place."

I never liked imagining there were killers running around our sweet town. It made me and everyone else very nervous.

"Ever the optimist," Ewan grumbled.

"Not really. I just think it's an odd way to kill someone." I read the side of the balm. The company was a small one owned by one of my patients. She made lotions and potions, and I even used them.

She was a single mom and one of the kindest people I'd ever met. There was no way she would have killed someone. She didn't do this.

Or did she?

Chapter Five

Since the store where the lip balm was sold happened to be a half a block from the pub, we walked there. The sun had peeked out and the air warmed slightly. Still, it was cold.

Of course, that didn't keep the surfers and visitors from the beach. There were chairs and umbrellas, and a few brave souls were out in the waves.

"I'll never understand how the Scots can handle the frigid water here." I said the words more to myself and then pulled my kelly green sweater tighter around me.

"We are acclimated to the chill from birth," Ewan said nonchalantly. He wore a short-sleeved shirt and jeans. The cold didn't seem to bother him at all.

"I believe you. I thought the water would be much warmer this time of year."

"It is by several degrees, just not by Caribbean standards."

I laughed. "It's the same in the Pacific Northwest, but not quite as cold as it is here. I can't imagine surfing in either place. And I'm surprised I haven't had any cases of hyperthermia."

"We Scots are tough," he said, and then smiled. "It is probably different if you've grown up playing in the sea since you were a wee one."

I grinned. "Maybe so."

The storefront had a sign that read Kiara's Lotions and Potions hanging over the sidewalk. I had visited the store many times. Her natural products were amazing for the skin. And she'd staged the place to look like an old-timey apothecary. With lots of wood and glass, and the walls painted navy, it was a cozy place to shop.

What I loved most of all were the scents of the products. She had everything from chocolate to strawberry smells.

When Ewan opened the door, the bell rang over it like a cheery hello.

"Morning, Doc," she said when I walked through. Then she frowned when she saw Ewan. "Is everything OK, ACC? Are you two out shopping on this fine day?"

Scottish people said that sort of thing even when it was raining.

"Morning," Ewan and I said at the same time.

"Everything is fine," he said. "I have a few questions about your products and one of your customers."

She'd been filling out paperwork on the counter, but she put down her pen.

The store was filled with glass jars, flowers, herbs, and various products for every kind of skin and hair. The place smelled like a lovely garden and was one of the most relaxing stores I'd ever been in.

With her maxi dress, Kiara looked like some kind of bohemian princess. Her son, Max, was eight. He was seated at a small desk behind the counter, working on some kind of word puzzle. He was a quiet boy who did well in school and had an intellect far beyond his years. I tried to never pick favorites when it came to my patients, but he was one.

We had the most interesting conversations about everything from dinosaurs to airplanes when he came in for his appointments. He always had a different book, which made broaching those topics a bit easier on my part. His wisdom went far beyond his young years. And he was very even tempered.

"Kiara and Max, it is good to see you," I said.

Max glanced up and gave me a short wave. Then he went right back to working on his puzzle.

"I'm guessing that you aren't here for more product since you just bought some a few weeks ago," she said appearing worried.

I shook my head and motioned toward the front of the store. "Let's talk up front," I said so that her son didn't have to hear any unsavory details. Not that Ewan would share that much.

"What's going on?" she asked.

Ewan nodded toward me.

"Right. I don't know if you heard, but there was a death last night at the train station."

Her brows drew together. "I'm sorry. I've missed the town gossip, I suppose. We were running late this morning. Like most kids, Max doesn't like getting up early in the summer." She smiled. "He's always a bit slow getting out of bed. So, what happened?"

"Well, we discovered something quite odd when I was doing the autopsy last night."

She frowned again. "Oh?"

"Was Donald Jacks a customer of yours?"

She pursed her lips. "The name sounds familiar. I can check my records."

"I'll ask you to do that in a moment," I said. "We will need to know if you sell any products with bee venom?"

"Bee venom? No. It does have healing properties, but too many people are allergic. I try to keep my products simple, so they can be used by as many people as possible."

I pulled out the evidence bag with the lip balm.

"Can you give me an idea of the ingredients in this?"

Her eyes went wide. "Oh. No. It's in one of those baggies you see on television. What happened?"

"I can't say until we finish the investigation, but we do need to know the ingredients," I added.

"It's fairly simple. Coconut oil, peppermint oil, and a bit of wax. I don't use any sort of preservatives because they can cause cancer. I'm very careful. I promise you." She wrung her hands, and her eyes were watery.

I hated that we upset her, but we needed to know.

"Please don't get upset. We are only curious about the ingredients. I just need to make sure. You don't use bee venom?" I asked.

She shook her head. "No. Like I said, too many people are allergic, and I'm looking for a wide audience of women, men, even kids.

"Do you have any idea if maybe this batch was mixed up or perhaps a mistake was made?" I asked.

She shook her head. "While I have bees at home, it is only for the honey. And that is for personal use only. If there was bee venom in the lip balm, it didn't come that way from my shop. And I wouldn't use something like that for lips. Though, it can help lips look like they've had collagen. But many peoples' lips are often too thin and sensitive for something like that. I refuse to use anything that might be deemed harmful, no matter what the latest trends might be."

"What kind of products would you use it in?" I asked. "I mean, I know you don't, but if you could give us some ideas of things you've seen bee venom used as an additive."

She shrugged. "Under eyes, or maybe some lotions for the face. As I said, it can help with collagen production. But there is too big a risk for allergic reactions. I'm telling you that I would never use it. Maybe some bigger manufacturers might get away with it, but those products would be mass-produced and come with warnings."

"Do you have any idea how they extract bee venom?" I asked.

She rubbed her forehead. "I remember when it first became popular, I did some research. They use some sort of electric current and a special glass. I can't quite remember the exact method, but it was fairly complicated. I don't have the equipment or the knowledge, even if I wanted to do it. If you're wondering how to get it—my guess is it would be fairly easy to find on the internet. So just about anyone would have access."

Oh. That wasn't great. Just about anyone meant we could have way more suspects than we had imagined. Though, it would have to be someone with the knowledge of the allergy, and the cleverness to put it in the lip balm.

"Let me check my records, and I can let you know what he bought. It will only take a minute as everything is on the computer."

We followed her back to the counter.

She typed a few words into her computer and then nodded. "Right, he's who I thought. He bought six lip balms. I remember him saying he liked to keep them around his house and office."

She pushed more buttons. "He was a repeat customer. That was the third set of six he'd bought. He also picked up a lotion with tree tea oil for his dry skin and scalp."

"And none of them had bee venom," Ewan said.

She sighed, and I didn't blame her for being exasperated with us. She'd already answered that same question several times. But Ewan was always thorough. "As I mentioned, I don't use it in any of my products. If it was in that balm, then someone tampered with it."

Ewan and I glanced at each other knowing what the consequences were of what she'd just said.

Not only did we have a murder, but a premeditated one.

"Thanks for your help," I said.

She bit her lip. "This is terrible to say, but once it gets out about how he died, it is not going to be good for business. I don't know what I'm going to do. It's all I can do to keep up with things as it is." She glanced worriedly at her son. "This is our livelihood."

"Dinnae worry," Ewan said. "No one will hear anything from us."

She pursed her lips. "You know how this town is, though. It's bound to get out if that's how he died." She whispered the last bit.

"Like Ewan said, we don't release that sort of information until everything involving the investigation is completed. That said, method of death will most likely be poison. We will be very careful how that is stated in the reports."

She blew out a breath. "Really?"

"You've helped us a great deal with our line of inquiry. Please don't worry." Ewan reached out and shook her hand.

She nodded and smiled but I wasn't sure she believed us. I felt guilty for causing her to worry. She had enough on her plate.

As we left the shop, the sun came out in full view. I welcomed the bit of warmth it provided.

"Well, that will help narrow down the suspect list," I said.

"Will it?" he asked.

"Yes. We only have to find out who at the party ordered bee venom. I bet Henry could figure that out somehow using the computer."

"Except, we dinnae know for certain the murderer was at the party."

He wasn't wrong. "I forgot. You're right. He could have been poisoned before he ever walked into the train station, and become disoriented after applying the lip balm, perhaps one too many times. But

I still stand by the fact it looked like he was stuffed into that cupboard. I suppose he could have done it to himself if he was out of his mind. There were no contusions on the body, which I admit would be strange if someone put him in there." I snapped my fingers. "Unless he was already dead. Those bruises might not show up as clearly."

"Do you need to head back to your office?" Ewan asked. "I'm going to meet Henry at the victim's home. Do you want to go with me?"

I stopped. It was so unusual for him to ask me to help. Usually, I had to beg to be included.

"What's going on?"

He paused with me on the sidewalk. "What do you mean?"

"You never let me be involved in the active investigation. I usually have to figure things out on my own."

"Well, I decided that perhaps it is best to involve you so that you don't find yourself in a predicament like the last few cases."

"None of that was my fault," I said. That sounded weak even to me. I wasn't great about keeping my nose out of police business, and my life had been threatened more than once. While trying to investigate on my own, I sometimes found myself in jeopardy.

As one does.

"Where is his house?"

"Up the mountain. Once we finish up there, we'll head to his office."

It was my day off, but I had nothing better to do. Besides, it beat trying to find a way to sneak in on my own later. Easier to walk through the front door with Ewan.

"OK, I'm in."

* * *

A half-hour later, we were in a neighborhood near the big library in the middle of town. There were rows of small brownstone houses on a tree-lined street. The main street in downtown Sea Isle was only a few blocks away, along with the train station. So, the victim had most likely walked there.

Our small town had CCTV cameras along the main avenues. And I was curious about something.

“Did you see him walking to the station on CCTV?” I asked as we climbed the steps.

“He walked there alone,” he said. “From what we could tell on the cameras he came from the direction of his home. His executive assistant said he’d left work early to go change into his costume for the evening. So, that checked out on the timeline.”

“OK. I guess it was too much to ask that the killer might have been walking with him forcing him to use lip balm.”

He chuckled.

One of Ewan’s officers stood by the door and nodded as we went by. Henry was in the main living area searching through bookshelves.

“Find anything?” Ewan asked.

“No sir. Nothing out of the ordinary. I have bagged and tagged the lip balms we found. I also found some shaving items and lotions we took into evidence.”

“Good. Let’s have those tested by the Doc and Abigail. Take them down when we’re finished here.”

“Yes, sir.”

I pulled a pair of gloves from my bag and headed for the bathroom. Even though it sounded as if Henry had done a thorough job, I wanted to double-check. The accountant wasn’t one of my patients. I was curious if he had any prescriptions.

As I passed by the kitchen, it was noticeably tidy. All the rooms were quite stark and clean. I wondered if perhaps Jacks had OCD. Nothing in the home appeared out of place.

The bathroom was no exception. I wondered if he kept it this way or if he had a housekeeper, who cleaned for him.

I was lucky that Abigail was OCD when it came to neatness, she kept the practice and my house tidy. Even though, I’d offered more than once to have cleaners come in and take care of it. She had acted offended, and I had given up trying to help out. She didn’t like the way I loaded the dishwasher or hung my clothes in the closet either. It was easier to let her do things her way.

As I went through the deceased man’s bathroom, I was surprised by just how clean it was. The medicine cabinet was empty, except for some shaving cream, the tree tea oil, and toothpaste. He didn't have any prescriptions. Nor did he have an epi pen.

I found that odd. Most people with that sort of allergy would keep one nearby and on their person.

"Henry?"

"Yes, Doc?"

"Were there any medications in the cabinet in the bathroom?"

"No, ma'am. There were some vitamins, though. I have them bagged for Abigail. They are in a box in the entry with the loo label."

I went to find the box. He was right. There were no prescriptions.

I needed to speak to his physician to make certain about the allergies and to find out if he'd had any other illnesses.

I found several items including the lip balms. There were vitamins sometimes used to treat anxiety and depression. Which made me wonder if he'd been having some kind of trouble with his mental state.

Most people were these days. Or at least, we were all a bit more open about mental health. Even the stubborn Scots who did not like to show any sort of weakness.

"I'll search the database to see if I can find out who his primary doctor was."

"Sounds good, Doc."

After putting the lid back on the box, I went in search of Ewan. He was in the main bedroom, of which there were two.

"Find anything interesting?"

He shrugged. "The bed was made."

"He seemed like a tidy sort if the rest of the house is any indication."

There was a neat stack of books, most of them historical fiction, on his bedside. Some of them were about Scottish lore, and there were a couple of detective novels. They were from the 1940s or so, which I remembered were the kind of stories he was supposed to tell on the train.

"Hmmm."

"What?" Ewan asked as he perused the closet.

"Nothing much. I just remembered that Mara said he was going to tell old-fashioned detective stories on the train. Some of the books on his bedside are exactly that. The sort of thing Humphrey Bogart might star in back in the day.

"I thought it odd that he'd choose that subject when there is so much Scottish folklore around here," I said. "Maybe he liked the idea of the costume."

Ewan shrugged. "Mara wanted to interest all sorts of people to ride the train," he said. "I sat in on one of the committee meetings a few months ago. They were trying to round up an eclectic group."

"True. I remember her saying that. He was a fastidious man, who used a lot of lip balm and was worried about his dry skin. That isn't much for us to go by."

"And he was an accountant, who also worked as an investment counselor. Could be one of his clients wasn't happy about his work. People can be strange when it comes to their money."

"Quite true. Money is one of the main reasons for murder."

"When we finish here, I'm heading to his office."

"I'll come with you," I said.

The victim lived a very tidy and clean life. But murder was messy, and there was almost always a motive.

We just had to find what instigated this one.

Chapter Six

As we headed out, Ewan received a call. He sounded frustrated. When he hung up, he paused on the sidewalk.

"The trip to the victim's workplace will have to wait. I need to take care of something first."

"Is everything OK?"

He shoved a hand through his hair. "A land dispute between two hot-headed neighbors who do not have an ounce of sense between them."

"Oh?"

"Aye. They are brothers and are always fighting over something."

I smiled. "Family."

He shook his head. "These two seemed to have become sworn enemies. We get a call a week about something. Unfortunately, I seem to be the only one who can deal with them."

"You go ahead," I said. "There is something I want to check on the tests we ran. Come and get me when you're ready to go to the victim's office."

"No, I'll drop you off. That way you don't have to wait for one of the shuttles."

In the summer, shuttles ran between the seaside and the town center every half hour or so. It cut down on traffic.

A few minutes later, he pulled up in front of my office.

"You'll come get me before you head to his workplace?"

"Aye. I'll text when I'm on the way."

"OK, thanks for the ride."

Inside, Abigail was at her desk.

"I was about to call you. We have a possible fracture in room one. A roller blading accident."

"Is it a kid?" Children doing crazy dangerous things were some of our most repetitive clients at the practice. Funny, it was the same when I worked in emergency in Seattle. Kids always seemed to think they were invincible.

She hid a laugh behind her hand.

I was confused. She seldom laughed and especially not when a medical case was involved.

"Not exactly." She cleared her throat and straightened her shoulders. Then she handed me the tablet we used to update our patient info and to make diagnoses.

My eyes went wide. I shook my head. "I can't believe it."

I headed into room one. Sure enough, there sat Lulu. She was the owner of the shop where I bought most of my clothes these days, and she was my friend Angie's aunt. I adored her.

Lulu had her own sense of style and it worked for her. Today she was dressed in hot pants, which probably hadn't seen the light of day since they were popular in the 1970s.

"When I mentioned you should get some exercise at your last appointment, I meant walking," I said, as I shut the door.

"You didn't specify, and walking is boring," Lulu said. She also wore her trademark blue eyeshadow. Her shop on the main seaside boardwalk had vintage and modern clothing and other gifts. It was one of my favorite places to shop.

"I didn't think I needed to specify," I said. "Pool aerobics might have been a better choice."

"All that is boring. Besides, I was doing just fine. The town needs to fix the sidewalks and make them more level." She huffed. "I'll be speaking to the mayor about that. He'll be lucky if I don't sue."

She wouldn't sue, but I felt sorry for Ewan the next time she saw him.

I turned so she didn't see me smile.

"And do not start with that woman of a certain age business, lass. I'm not that old."

"Even I would not dare to pick up a pair of skates," I said.

"We'll luv, you aren't me. And I used to do it all the time when I was younger. I'm good at it. And it's easier on the joints than walking."

"Not if you break said joints," I grumbled.

"I'm certain it's just a sprain."

I gently probed her wrist with my fingers.

She winced.

The deep contusions were already forming, and it was swollen.

"I'm going to have Abigail take some X-rays. Even a hairline fracture can cause a great deal of pain if it doesn't heal properly."

She sighed.

I pushed the button on the tablet for Abigail to come in, and she came through the door a few seconds later.

"I want full posterior, anterior, and lateral views," I said. "And let's get these skates off her. I have some slippers she can borrow to get home."

I pointed my pen at her. "No matter what the tests say, no more roller blading. Before you decide what you want to try next, come by and check with me first."

"Well, I wanted to do one of those stripper pole classes, but there are none in the area."

A strangled sound came from Abigail, who had knelt to take off the skates.

I had to turn away again to hide my laughter. I cleared my throat. "Well, maybe we can go over the activities available at the senior center. They have a wide selection."

"Old people stuff," she mumbled.

Abigail helped her off the table and took her back to the lab where we kept our machines.

By the time we'd put a cast on the fracture I'd suspected, Lulu's normally tan skin had gone a bit pale.

"Abigail is going to make sure you get something to eat, and then will take you home. No lifting anything—not even a glass of water—with that hand. If you want it to heal the right way, you better listen."

The older woman rolled her eyes. "Fine, Doc. But I don't need any help. Been taking care of myself since before you were born."

She was extremely independent, which was why we would be following up daily with her.

"Just the same, Abigail will make certain you eat and get home safely. Doctor's orders. And you need to call Angie and tell her what happened."

She rolled her eyes, and for the third time in twenty minutes, I had to hide my laughter.

* * *

A half hour later I received a text from Ewan that he would be tied up for some time. While I could have gone over the evidence we'd already collected, I was curious to find out more about the deceased.

I clicked onto the file share program that Henry had set up for me at the police station. They didn't have much in the file that I didn't already know, but there was a business address. Even though it was Saturday, I wondered if someone might be at the office.

I doubted it, since work–life balance was much better here in Scotland than it was in the States. With the exception of myself, who was open for emergencies twenty-four/seven, few people worked weekends, unless they were part of the tourist trade. Many of the people who lived here worked four-day weeks.

I had to admit it was a much healthier lifestyle and even corporations had learned the value of giving people time off to reset and rest. I didn't think that would ever happen in the States, where we were much more driven by the idea that success meant hard work. Whoever worked the most was the winner.

But that was incredibly unhealthy.

I was curious about the accountant's work life. Even though I'd promised to wait for Ewan, I decided to take a chance and drive up the mountain. Maybe I'd be lucky and someone would be there.

Worst case, if the office was closed, I could go by the bread maker's and pick up some sourdough. And maybe pick up some new novels from the bookstore.

When I arrived at the stone building a block down from the police station, I realized it was several offices in one space. The front door was open.

Inside, I found a board that listed the accounting offices located on the second floor.

When I arrived, the door to the office was open.

"Hello." I said tentatively. There were bustling sounds inside.

What if it's the killer?

I pulled the mace I carried out of my bag.

A smart person would have called the police. But I knew Ewan and his team were busy.

I cleared my throat. "Hello?" My voice squeaked.

Heavy footsteps headed toward me. I held up the mace and steadied myself ready for an attack.

"Doc?" Henry asked as he came around the corner. "What are you doing here?"

The tightness in my chest released, and I blew out a breath.

"I came to see if I could get a better sense of the victim's work life. Maybe I could glean who would want the man dead."

"So you've decided it was murder?" Henry asked.

I nodded. "It was anaphylactic shock, but I can't imagine he would have poisoned himself."

"Couldn't he have eaten something that caused his death?" Henry must not have had access to our reports so far. Ewan meant what he said about trying to keep things close to the vest. Not that sweet Henry would ever say anything on purpose that might hurt the case. He was a great officer.

"No." I didn't see any harm in him knowing, since he was the one investigating. "Abigail updated the reports this morning. The bee venom was in his lip balm. We checked with the maker of the balm, and they don't use the stuff. So someone must have put it in there. I wanted to check here and at his home to see if there were more tubes that might have been affected."

And to see if there were any clues to who might have killed him. I was not sure exactly what I thought I might find, but it was worth looking.

Whenever I started a case, I had no idea where the evidence might lead, but I had this deep-seated need to find out. It turned out my real-life love of mystery novels and television shows had come in handy when I moved to Scotland.

I'd been a reluctant coroner when I'd first arrived in Sea Isle a year ago. But the need to solve cases had become a part of me that I'd never known was there. It was my job to speak for the dead, and I took the responsibility seriously.

"I came by to look through the files and to collect his computer," Henry said. "I'll be searching all of the offices for information. The partner gave me permission to go through anything that wasn't personal client files. I have a warrant with the judge for that."

There was an offer in his voice. Henry really was the sweetest.

"Do you mind if I help out?" I asked.

"No problem."

"Don't you need to check with Ewan?"

He shook his head. "The boss says to keep you informed. You might as well be here."

I wasn't so sure that was exactly what Ewan meant, but I was grateful to the young officer. "Thanks, Henry."

We worked in silence. After putting the computer equipment in the box he'd brought, he went through some of the bookshelves that lined all three offices.

I donned a pair of gloves and went through the victim's desk.

"Have you spoken with anyone who works with him?" I asked. I found more lip balms and put them in an evidence bag and marked them on the log Henry was keeping. "Also, I'm taking these to the lab for Abigail to check. I marked them on the evidence log."

He nodded. "I spoke with his partner, Mr. Burns. He is in Edinburgh for an event. He left early last week to take some vacation. He's speaking at the event but plans to come back in a few days."

"OK, so he wasn't here when his partner died. Still doesn't absolve him from possibly tainting the lip balms."

"True. But he wasn't the one who put him in the closet at the train station. I followed up on his alibi, and it's solid."

"There is that."

Ewan had mentioned something earlier that made me curious. "What if it's an angry client?"

"We're looking into that," Henry said. "In addition to being an accountant, he did a lot of family planning and financial advising. There is a chance if he lost money for one or more of his clients, they could have wanted him dead."

"True. Money is . . ."

"One of the top motives." He finished my sentence.

I'd said the same thing earlier. Great minds and all that.

I continued to go through the desk. There was something weird about the spacing of the top right drawer. The drawer from the outside looked larger than the inside actually was.

I took everything out and found a false bottom.

"That's strange," I said.

Henry turned toward me. "What did you find?"

"A secret space in this top drawer."

"Anything interesting?"

I pulled out a stack of letters that had been rubber-banded together.

I took the band off. Then I opened one of the letters.

My eyebrows rose.

"What is it?"

I turned the first letter so Henry could see it.

The message was typewritten.

You stole my money. You will die.

"Well, that looks like motive," he said.

"If only they'd taken the time to sign it," I joked. OK, it wasn't funny but it was true.

Henry grunted.

I opened a few others. Many of them were the same tone. Someone was quite upset with the victim.

"I wonder if we've found our killer?" I'd just said the words when there was a noise in the front office.

Henry pulled out his baton as he inched to the door of the victim's office. He held out his other hand to tell me to stay.

He needn't have bothered. I was frozen to the chair.

Chapter Seven

I found my courage and picked up a brass tiger-shaped paper weight from the desk. My hand shook, and I forced myself to calm down. This kind of situation called for a clear head. We might have to move quickly. Henry held his baton at the ready and stealthily made his way around the door.

"Police," he shouted.

There was a scream and a thunk.

I peeked around Henry's shoulder. A woman with red hair stood near the desk in the front office with a deer-in-the-headlights expression in her eyes. All around her were items that had been on the desk. She was dressed in white twill shorts and a pink T-shirt that appeared to be a couple of sizes too small. Or maybe that's the way she liked to wear them.

"What are you doing in here?" she shrieked. "I'm calling the police."

"As I mentioned, I'm with the police," Henry said patiently. He was always the calm in any storm. "Can I get your name please?"

"Catherine Allan, I'm the executive assistant for the owners, Mr. Jacks and Mr. Burns. How did you get in here?"

"The building manager let me in," he said. Then he held up a piece of paper. "I spoke to you on the phone yesterday, and again this morning. I advised you that I have a warrant to search the business and home of Mr. Donald Jacks."

She frowned. "Right. You're the one who told me he died. I just didn't expect anyone to be here today. Besides, why would you need to look through his things? What has he done now?"

"Has he had trouble with the police before?" I asked before Henry could say anything. I glanced at him and made my "I'm sorry" face. I hadn't meant to butt in, but my curiosity often got the best of me.

She glanced at me and appeared surprised that someone else was in the room. She frowned. "We've been under investigation with Revenue Scotland because of him." She shook her head. "Not that he's done anything wrong, mind you." She swallowed hard and stared down at her feet.

It appeared she said that last bit to cover herself. Why was that?

"Shouldn't you have waited for my boss to be here?"

Henry opened his mouth, no doubt to explain, but I put a hand on his arm and stopped him.

"As the officer said, we do not need anyone's permission. Do you usually work on Saturday?"

She sighed. "No. I realized I forgot to email one of Mr. Burn's clients that he is out next week. He is at a seminar and had to change his flight."

"Oh, why is that?" I asked.

She stared at me curiously. "Are you with the police as well?"

"I am the coroner."

Her eyes went wide. "Coroner? Was his death suspicious?"

"Perhaps, you'd like to take a seat," Henry said. He motioned toward her desk.

She frowned. "I need to know what's going on. Why is there a coroner here?"

"We will get to that," Henry said. "When was the last time you saw Mr. Jacks?"

She shrugged. "He left early yesterday. He was attending some event on the new train in town, I think. I don't know if you are aware, but he was a freak about trains. He talked about them constantly. I often tuned him out.

As if she'd realized what she said, her hand flew to her mouth and her eyes went wide. "Anyway, he said he was doing a performance. He asked if I wanted to go, but it sounded like something stuffy, and I had a hen party to go to last night."

"And what time was that?"

"The hen do?" She rubbed her head as if she were still feeling the effects of her night out.

"No, when you saw the vic—Mr. Jacks."

"Around three in the afternoon. Is everything OK? I don't understand why there are so many questions. Didn't he die of a heart attack or something? He never took very good care of himself."

She appeared genuinely worried. But we'd been tricked by sincerity more than once. Until they were proven innocent, everyone who knew the deceased was a suspect.

Part of my skepticism came from working in the ER in Seattle for way too long. People always wanted to make themselves look better than they truly were. They often lied about their health or the meds they took. Many of them didn't mean to lie, it was just human nature.

Then there was the other end of the spectrum of people who lied about pain to get drugs to feed a habit.

I had my reasons for being suspicious, though I tried my best to see the good in people.

"Where was your hen party, and how long were you there?" Henry asked.

Her eyes went wide again. "You are asking me for an alibi, aren't you?"

"Please, answer the question," Ewan said as he came into the office. He flashed his ACC's badge.

"I—uh." She looked between the three of us. "Do I need a solicitor?"

"Did you do something wrong?" Ewan asked.

I hid my smile behind a cough. He had a way of taking control of situations and making people nervous.

"No. I've never been questioned by the police. I dinnae know how these things work."

"Right," Ewan said. "You are not under arrest. These are only preliminary questions to help set our scene for the death of Mr. Jacks. We're trying to ascertain your whereabouts last evening to see if you had any contact with him. Perhaps you may have noticed something that might help us with our inquiries. If you could give us the details, please."

She appeared confused, as if she were trying to understand Ewan's doublespeak. Everything he'd said was true, but designed so that she wouldn't be suspicious.

I didn't blame him. Lawyers complicated things and came with their favorite phrase: no comment. That sort of thing never helped with our inquiries.

"I left right after Mr. Jacks, which is why I came back today. I wanted to get home so I had time to get ready last night, and I forgot to send the emails changing appointments for Mr. Burns," she said. "We were in Edinburgh at The Witchery. We all went in and rented one of the fancy suites and had the party catered so we dinnae have to worry about getting arrested for being drunk and disorderly like happened at Samantha's do."

None of us had any idea who Samantha was, but it didn't matter. I had heard about The Witchery, though. I'd looked it up online after hearing someone talk about it at the pub. It was a cool sort of gothic hotel, and the rooms were not cheap. The hotel was on my list of places to check out.

"I left around ten this morning when I realized what I'd forgotten to finish at work. Now, can you please tell me what happened?"

Even though her story sounded true, Henry or Ewan would be following up on her alibi. They never left a stone unturned.

"Mr. Jacks died last night at the train station," Ewan said. "It is an ongoing investigation so that is all I can say at the moment."

She fell back into her office chair. "I can't believe he's really dead. If you're asking so many questions, then it wasn't a heart attack? That's what I assumed." The surprise was evident in her voice.

"The coroner is still running tests," Ewan said. "When did your boss Mr. Burns leave for his business trip?"

"He's been in Edinburgh all week. He has an event. He left from his home. Should I call him?"

"I already have," Ewan said.

"But he didn't tell me. Why wouldn't he call me?"

"I asked him not to." Ewan wrote something in his notebook. "Is there anyone who was upset with Mr. Burns or Mr. Jacks?"

She leaned her elbows on her desk and put her head in her hands. "I do not know. This is . . . I drank a great deal last night. I cannot think."

"I'll ask again: were their clients happy?"

She sat back in her chair and shrugged. "When you are dealing with money, few people are happy."

"I want to make certain that I understand the business," I said.

Ewan just loved it when I interrupted.

"You do accounting for clients but also financial planning and investments, as well. I'm from America and those things are usually done by different professionals there."

"We provide both services out of this office, which is why clients are not always happy with us. Though, according to Mr. Burns, Mr. Jacks had been off his game for some time. His investment strategies have landed our company in a bit of trouble."

"That's why you're being investigated by Revenue Scotland?" I asked.

"Aye," she said. "Though, I'm an assistant. I send out invoices and take calls. I'm not a financial expert like my bosses. I dinnae really understand what they do, or why they are under investigation. You'll need to speak to my boss about that."

I wasn't so sure I believed her. I had a feeling she knew much more than she let on.

"I cannae believe he's dead. We were only talking yesterday afternoon. Well, he was talking about his train ride. I only half listened. I was waiting for him to leave so I could get ready for the party. I feel so guilty for wishing he would just hurry up and go."

"Do you remember if he was taking anyone with him to the event?" I asked.

"Like a date?" She laughed hard.

"Why is that funny?" Ewan asked.

Her eyes went wide, and the smile dropped off her face. "I—uh. He was into trains and acting. He did some community theater. But I've never seen him go on a date.

"He's the opposite of Mr. Burns, who has a different woman on his arm every week—even though he's married." She gasped and once again put a hand to her mouth. "I mean. Uh. I cannae believe I said that out loud. He's going to kill me."

Well, that was good to know. I had a feeling Ewan would most definitely be following up with that line of questioning.

"What was Mr. Jacks like as a boss?" I asked.

"I shouldn't speak ill of the dead, but he was a tough one. Nothing made him happy. What's that word people use for grumpy men?"

"Curmudgeon?" I offered.

She nodded. "Never happy with anything and seldom had a kind word for me or Mr. Burns. He made fun of me every time I made a mistake. He wasn't exactly a people person, if you understand what I mean. In my opinion, he had no business being someone who dealt with our clients."

"That is strange," I said. "Why did Mr. Burns allow him to work with the clients?"

She shrugged. "He always said people appreciated someone who wasn't very emotional when it came to investing. That they liked a bit of a cold fish. I'm not so sure about that."

"Is there anyone you can remember in particular who might have been angry with him?" I asked.

Ewan glanced at me, but he didn't appear angry. She'd seemed to relax since I started asking questions.

She shook her head. "We had some unhappy clients when several of his investment choices dinnae pan out the way he had expected. We received some nasty calls. And I heard him talking to Mr. Burns about some threatening emails."

Ewan motioned toward Henry, who held up the laptop.

"Was there anyone who might have been angry enough to cause him harm?" Henry asked. I was surprised he spoke up. When Ewan was around, Henry usually deferred to his boss. But it was a good question.

"I can make you a list," she said.

A list? Oh. No. That meant more suspects.

* * *

While Henry boxed up the evidence from the office and took it back to the station, I followed Ewan out of the building.

"Can I come back with you to the victim's home?"

"How did you know that is where I was going next?"

"You asked Henry for the warrant."

"You are observant, Doc." He smiled and, like always, my stomach did something twisty inside. His smile had that effect on me.

"I always feel like two sets of eyes are better than one. You had to rush off, so we didn't finish looking at all the rooms. I'm available."

"Henry will be meeting me there when he's finished at the station."

I sighed. "Please, don't make me beg or force me to break into Mr. Jacks's home later."

He laughed. "You would, I'm sure."

I shrugged. "You've met me."

"Aye, I have."

"Besides, you let me go before, what's so different now?" I paused at his car.

"Fair point." He waved me to follow him.

"Aren't we going to his home?"

"It is only a few blocks away. If anything else needs to be boxed up, Henry will take care of it."

"Right." I felt dumb for forgetting.

Once we arrived, he pulled a small evidence packet from his pants pocket. There was a key ring inside. After trying a few, the last key finally worked.

"Hello, ACC," a woman said before we could go inside.

His shoulders stiffened for a second before he turned and smiled at the woman. "Hello, Mrs. Culbert."

She had gray hair that was cut short around her face. She wore a house dress with an apron over it and fuzzy house shoes. She was a patient of mine, but the one time she'd come in, she'd been in a church dress, hose, and black patent leather shoes.

I smiled at her, and she did the same back to me. "Doctor."

"Good to see you, Mrs. Culbert. I hope you are feeling well."

"I am. Thanks to you."

"Was there something you needed?" Ewan asked gently. I could tell he didn't want to chat; he was ready to just get inside.

"Nasty business," she said as she waved a hand toward Mr. Jacks's home.

"Aye," he said. "Did you know him well?"

I was curious, since the police hadn't shared any details, what she knew about her neighbor. And then I remembered this was Sea Isle. Word spread quickly here.

"Invited him over for a cuppa a few times, but he was always too busy. A hard worker that one."

"Have you seen anyone coming or going besides Mr. Jacks?" I asked.

She shook her head. "No. I cannae say he had many visitors over the years. I am a part of the neighborhood watch so I keep an eye on things, you know."

I bet she did. We'd been on the doorstep for less than a minute before she came out.

"He was quiet, except for the occasional train whistle," she said. "I had a word with him about that a few years ago. I'd only heard it occasionally after that and never after eight PM or so."

"So, no visitors?" Ewan repeated.

"Let me see. Maybe, his business partner on occasion but not in some time. I remember asking about him. He was a handsome one, and Mr. Jacks said he was his business partner.

"Then there was his assistant who would occasionally drop by with files. Though, why he couldn't walk across the street himself, I've no idea."

"When was the last time you saw one of them?" I asked.

"Thursday evening," she said. "I remember because the assistant went inside. Usually, she'd hand him the files at the door. She went in though, on Thursday. She didn't come back out for an hour or so."

As I suspected, Mrs. Culbert kept a sharp eye on things. I wondered why the assistant had taken so long. Were they having some sort of affair?

In the interview, she didn't seem as though she liked her boss much. Though she could have been trying to hide something. We'd need to question her again.

"Have you seen anyone suspicious hanging around here?"

She shook her head. "I would have reported them if I had. That's my job."

"Thank you for your diligence," Ewan said. "We need to search his home." With that he went inside.

"We appreciate your help," I said. "I need to assist the ACC with his investigation."

"He's a handsome one," she said. "Seems to have his eye on you. He watched you the whole time I spoke to him."

I'm sure my cheeks turned bright pink. The heat on them burned. "I—uh—he's a good officer," I said, quickly stepping inside.

Why was it people tried to make more of my relationship with Ewan than was there? Mara and Abigail were always giving me a hard time because Ewan seemed to find excuses to come over these days. Sometimes, it was questions about a case, other times it was to discuss things about the town. We were colleagues talking business and that was it.

Did he sometimes make me feel strange and warm? Yes. And did his compliments make me blush? Always. Did he stay after our chats and watch whatever mystery show I'd planned on watching? Every time. But that was just because we enjoyed the genre.

We'd always been awkward with one another, but over the past year a friendship of sorts had developed. I could admit that much. That, and we had an appreciation of each other's talents. I'd learned a great deal from him about investigating cases.

And he'd reluctantly grown to trust my instincts when it came to the medical side of things.

If I were honest with myself, I might have even admitted I enjoyed his company as we sat at my kitchen table drinking coffee and going over cases. But that was the extent of it.

After my past experiences, trusting men was still a problem for me. My late husband hadn't been a bad man, but he was duplicitous. And I'd been clueless to the very end.

I shook my head, as if wiping that cobweb of memory away. Inside, the air was a bit musty. To the left, in what might have been a parlor or dining room was a huge train set up. I couldn't believe I'd missed that before.

The pocket doors must have been closed. I moved into the room.

Our little town of Sea Isle had been brought to life in miniature. Even my church home was represented. "Wow," I said. "It is so life-like and so tiny at the same time."

"Aye. He put some work into this," Ewan said.

We walked around the table taking in the seaside shops and pubs, and then over the small hill in the middle was the part of the town that sat up in the mountains. The buildings and settings had been carefully crafted to match nearly exactly.

"I've never seen anything like it," I said. "Look at that, he's already recreated the Storyteller's Train." The locomotive was parked at the station, and both were exact replicas.

"Mara said he was a part of the restoration work," I said. "We should talk to the team of volunteers who were involved with the project. Maybe one of them saw something. Or, perhaps, he said something to them."

"Aye," Ewan said. "Henry spoke with them last night and earlier today."

"What kinds of things did they say?"

He shrugged. "I only glanced over the report. Most of those interviewed said the victim was quite enthusiastic about working on the train, as in that was all he talked about. He had been excited about being a storyteller part-time. He took it all quite seriously."

"Did any of them notice anything strange over the last week? I keep wondering if his lip balms had been treated, if perhaps he'd had milder reactions."

"I promise you Henry was quite thorough, and the reports are in the files you have access to. But to answer your question, I don't remember them saying anything like that. I only skimmed them a few hours ago. When Jacks wasn't talking about trains, he kept himself to himself."

"OK, good to know." Still, I would take a look at it later. It never hurt to have another set of eyes.

"So, he kept to himself and was a train enthusiast. Since he'd been looking forward to it, it's sad that he never had a chance to perform his stories."

"Aye," he said.

Set back from the main part of town was a small row of townhomes. I pointed to the one where he lived. "Is that a replica of him standing on his porch?"

"Could be," he said as we both squinted at the figure.

"I don't see anyone chasing him with knives or guns. That might have been helpful," I said.

Ewan grunted, probably to hide his laugh. He'd grown to understand my odd sense of humor. I don't know if he appreciated it, but he understood. It helped to make jokes during dark times. Otherwise, life would be unacceptably dreary and sad.

"I wonder if his heirs would be willing to donate this set up. It would be great to have it at the train station. There's that corner over to the right that's sort of empty."

When I looked up at Ewan, he gave me a perplexed look.

"What?"

"Do I have something on my face again." I did a cursory wipe around my mouth.

"No, you look perfect. I just thought that was a grand idea. I'll speak to his sister and lawyer."

Did he say I looked perfect? I nearly snorted. That absolutely was not true.

The other side of the stairs was a library and office. Many of the books had to do with the history of trains, and the others were accounting books.

Who knew there were so many books about numbers?

"Is it OK if I sit in his chair and go through his desk?"

Ewan nodded. He was going through the bookshelves. "And the warrant gives us free rein to look at any client files he brought into the residence."

"I'm curious about why the business is being investigated. Is the Scottish version like the SEC or IRS in the United States?"

"I'm not sure I could say, but they do not get involved unless they are certain a crime has been committed. I have a call out for when they get back into the office on Monday."

There were a few client files neatly placed in a rack on the corner of the desk. I pulled out my notebook and wrote down the names on the files. I glanced through them, but numbers had never been my thing.

I mean, I could do math, I had to do a great deal of it as a doctor, but accounting was a different universe in that regard.

When I tried to open the desk drawers, they were locked.

"Can I borrow the key ring?" I asked.

Ewan crossed the room and then pulled the evidence bag from his pocket. He handed it to me.

"Thanks. Do you think it's odd that he had client financial records out on his desk, but then locked the drawers?"

"That is odd," he said. "Did you see anything that might need to be flagged?"

I shook my head. "Just rows of numbers with no context. You'll need someone who is good at that sort of thing to look them over."

"Aye." He went back to searching through the shelves. I tried a couple of the smaller keys and finally found the one that worked.

There were some office supplies in the top drawers. It was odd that he locked those. Did he have a housekeeper? And was he worried that they might take something? The bottom ones held files. A couple I recognized as duplicates from the office.

While I didn't know what that meant, it seemed unusual that he would have duplicates made when the others were a block away.

I pulled the files out of the bottom right drawer to put in evidence boxes. Anything out of the ordinary could be an important clue.

There was a pop-up lever at the bottom of the drawer. I tried to get it up with my nails, but it didn't work. Then I pushed down on the lever, and the lid popped up.

"A secret hiding space," I whispered.

"What's that?" Ewan asked. I slid the lid out and picked up a laptop that had been hidden.

"Why would he hide his laptop like this?" I pointed to the false bottom and then the computer. "And why would he have two? There was one at the office, as well. I remember that Henry boxed it. That's weird right? Unless there is something on here he didn't want others to see."

I shivered. "I hope it is nothing disgusting," I said.

I opened the lid, and the machine turned on, but it was password protected. I told Ewan.

"One of my guys is good with all things computer related. He can figure it out."

"I want to try something." I typed in, trainspotting, and the screen popped open.

"How did you know the password?" He'd come around to the other side of the desk where I sat.

"I guessed. People pick their hobbies and pets. I read that in one of the FBI handbooks I've been studying on electronic theft. I made Abigail go in and change all of our passwords."

"You should do that every few months. Though, if you're like me remembering them can be difficult."

I nodded. "Abigail found an app to help with that. And we have extra authentications for the patient files and anything financial. I get a coded text."

"Smart. Let's take a look and see what the accountant was up to."

I opened several of the files. I'd been half expecting dirty pictures. But all that was there were train pics and what looked like client files. I recognized two of the names. They were the same as the ones on the desk.

"We need to ask the secretary about these," I said as I opened the computer file to see if it was the same as the paper one. "Or a forensic accountant."

"What is it?"

"I know nothing about accounting, but I understand enough to see that the numbers in the paper file and the ones on the computer do not match up," I said. I waved the manilla folder.

"Maybe, everything hadn't been logged." Ewan offered.

"Could be, except that it's nearly ten thousand dollars difference between the two on one of these accounts." I pointed to the differences.

"I'm not a forensic accountant, but that seems like a large sum to be so different in one quarter. And look, it shows as a loss here. But a gain on the computer."

I glanced up at Ewan. "Are you thinking what I am?" I asked.

"That our accountant might also be a thief?"

"You're going to need a forensic accountant to figure all of this out. But yes, that is the way it appears. I bet that's why Revenue Scotland are investigating the firm."

"I know a great accountant in Edinburgh," he said. "I'll call her."

Her? Why did I assume it was a man? And why did I even care?

Maybe, it was the excitement in his voice when he mentioned her.

Again, why would you care?

Because I liked Ewan. There. I said it. Maybe, not out loud but I admitted it to myself.

There was a knock on the door. Before Ewan could respond, it opened.

"Hey Boss, I brought help and some more evidence boxes," Henry said.

Before Ewan could answer, my phone rang. It was Abigail.

"What's up?" I asked.

"I have something you need to see," she said.

"Oh?"

"Easier to show you, than explain over the phone."

"All right. I'll be right there."

I couldn't imagine what it might be. It was an assumption, and I didn't have the proof yet, but I had a feeling the accountant had made someone very angry. As we'd said a few times, money was a big motivator. If someone had stolen my money, I would have wanted to get it back.

OK, I was a doctor, and I'd taken a do no harm oath. But I would be very angry if someone had embezzled from me.

While I couldn't be certain exactly what was going on with our crafty accountant, he'd definitely been up to no good.

I wonder what Abigail has for me?

Chapter Eight

As I was leaving the victim's town home, there were two fake ficus trees on each side of the entry, and I stopped. Henry, who was carrying out boxes, nearly bumped into me.

"What is it?" he asked.

"Look around," I said. I pointed to the train room and the office. Everything was neat and orderly. Not a book was out of place. I'd glanced in the kitchen and there were no dishes in the sink.

Ewan came to the entryway.

"What are we looking at?"

"Symmetry," I said. "Nothing is out of place, and everything is neat and orderly."

"Right, and?" Ewan asked.

"These trees are fake but are different heights."

They glanced at each other and then at me.

I shrugged. "So, you know how I love some UK mysteries? You've watched a few with me."

"Aye," Ewan said. "What does that have to do with trees and our case?"

"One is taller than the other. I saw an episode where the victim had hidden drugs under a fake tree like this. The detective noticed the different heights."

I leaned over to pull the tree from the pottery it sat in, but it was stuck. Ewan tugged as well, and it came loose.

In the bottom was a plastic garbage bag. I'd already taken off my gloves, so Ewan reached in and pulled it out. He sat it on the floor.

When he untied the bag, he opened it so we could see. Inside was cash and a lot of it. If the tops of the piles that had been rubber banded together were any indication, it was several thousand.

"How much do you think that is?" I asked.

Ewan flipped through some of the bills. They were all one-hundred-pound notes. "Tis difficult to say without counting but at least fifty thousand pounds."

I'm sure my eyes were the size of saucers. "That doesn't seem like something a man who invests money for a living would keep around. Unless . . ."

"Unless, what?" Ewan asked.

"He was getting ready to make a run for it," I said. "Maybe someone found out things didn't add up with his accounts. He knew he was under investigation."

Ewan shrugged. "Then why take the part-time job with the train? That isn't the action of someone running away. Perhaps, he was saving to invest in something else."

"Then put the money in a safe," I said. "He has to have one around here somewhere. I know you like evidence, but my gut says he was up to no good. Maybe he took the part-time job because he loves trains, and he was biding his time until he could make a getaway.

"I mean, think about it. As the government closed in on him, he could don his costume, hop on a train, and be at the airport in Edinburgh in a couple of hours."

"But someone got to him before he could do that," Henry offered.

I nodded.

Ewan sighed. "That is a scenario, but we deal with . . ."

"Facts," Henry and I said at the same time.

"Exactly," Ewan said.

"I bet you a pint at the Pig & Whistle he has money all over his home. That amount isn't exactly enough to run away from the life he had and start a new one. I have to go. Abigail has something she wouldn't tell me over the phone. But you need to check."

"Aye," Ewan said.

Maybe we needed more proof, but things were definitely not adding up with the accountant.

* * *

Henry gave me a ride down the mountain to my practice. He'd been instructed by Ewan to find out what Abigail had discovered in the tests. That was no problem for the young officer, since she and her brother were two of Henry's favorite people.

I put my bag on her desk. She was just coming down the hall from the lab.

"That was quick," she said.

"Henry gave me a ride." He came through the door as I mentioned him.

Abigail's cheeks turned a lovely shade of pink, which happened anytime he was near. She'd been through a great deal as a youth and wasn't terribly trusting when it came to men.

We had that in common.

But sweet Henry had all the time in the world when it came to Abigail and Tommy. I'd enjoyed watching their relationship blossom over the past year.

"The Doc said you had something new." Henry smiled at her, and she bit her lip.

"Yes, I decided since the lip balm had been treated with bee venom, I'd check the epidermis for signs that it might be on more than his lips. I tested patches for reactions and found that the venom wasn't only on the lips.

"If he used a moisturizer or shaving cream, it may be in those. We should check all of his toiletries. I'm surprised there wasn't some sort of skin reaction given his allergy. That part doesn't make sense to me."

"The concentration may not have been as strong," I offered. "We think the bee venom was injected into the balm, and the levels were quite high. But tainting something like shaving cream, if it comes in a can like most of it does, wouldn't be as simple.

"Henry, when I checked earlier there wasn't much in the way of toiletries in the bathroom."

"I'd already boxed everything, once the ACC said we were dealing with some sort of toxin."

"Ah. That makes sense. Can you find that box in evidence and bring it down for tests?"

"Yes, is there anything else?"

"Maybe a few articles of clothing. Look for things that are a bit worn."

"Why some of his clothes?"

"I'm curious how long this poisoning has been going on and if perhaps the killer had upped their game."

"How would they poison the clothes?" Abigail asked.

"I don't think the killer did, but I want to check. And they could have misted the bee venom on there. It's a stretch, I know, but I want to make sure.

"Again, the murderer most likely thought we would think it was just an allergic reaction. And they may have thought we wouldn't check the lip balm.

"We need to keep that part of the case quiet from the public." Though, we'd already spoken with Kiara who made the balm. I had a feeling she wouldn't say anything that made her business look bad. From the way she'd reacted, I didn't think she would want anyone to know we'd even spoken with her.

"It's a very odd way to kill someone," Henry said. "Using bee pollen. He dinnae seem like a man who would run around and tell people he was allergic. How would the killer even know?"

"Which may tell us that his murderer knew him well. Maybe it's even someone we've already spoken to. But you know your boss, and he's going to need proof, not supposition. If we can show other toiletries and such are tainted, we'll know it is someone who had access to his house."

I snapped my fingers. "That reminds me. He seemed to be a man who likes things tidy. There is nothing wrong with that, but I wondered if we might check to see if he has a cleaner who comes in to take care of things."

"Good idea," Henry said. "I'll ask the boss when I go back up."

The doorbell rang, and we all looked at one another. Then I checked the monitor by the door. After a few dangerous incidents where killers showed up at our door, Ewan had insisted on updating the security with cameras and monitors so we could always see who was on the other side of the huge oak doors.

It was Mara with a woman I didn't recognize.

"Is everything OK?" I asked as I opened the door.

"Yes," Mara said. "This is Kaitlyn Jacks, the sister of the deceased," she added quietly. "She has come to identify the body."

Mara gave me a face that said she had no idea what was going on with the woman and found her to be suspicious.

We didn't need anyone to identify the body. Mara and Ewan had already done that.

"She drove in from Glasgow when she was notified about her brother's death."

Ewan had mentioned that he had a sister when I asked if the train set could be donated. There hadn't been any pictures of her in his home. Though, other than trains, there hadn't been many personal affects downstairs.

"I stopped into the pub for a late lunch and asked where I might need to go next," the woman said. Dressed in a power suit of gray, with a white blouse, she appeared to be someone who was used to getting what she wanted. She had that air about her. "I was going to try the police station, but Mara says my brother is here. I'm ready to take him home."

"I see. We can prepare him so you can see him, but I'm afraid we are several days away from releasing the body. His death is under investigation."

Kaitlyn's eyes narrowed. "Do you mean to say someone killed him?"

"As I said, his death is under investigation at the moment. Until we are finished, I cannot release the body."

The woman's eyebrows went up. There was something about her that was off-putting, and it wasn't just her attitude. She acted like someone who felt that dealing with her brother's death was an imposition.

We all mourned in different ways, but she didn't appear at all sad.

"I wish the ACC had made that clear. I will be having words with him. All he said was that my brother had an allergic reaction and died."

It didn't seem right to say, yes, because his death was suspicious but that was all Ewan could admit.

"Right. Until all the evidence is gathered and processed, we need to keep him here."

"We would be happy to make the arrangement for transport when we are done," Abigail spoke up. She and Henry had been watching the conversation from the waiting room.

"Won't you come in," I said. "Abigail, can you please prepare Mr. Jacks so that his sister can see him?"

"Yes, ma'am." She took off.

"I need to get back," Henry said and left quickly for the door. He was probably headed straight to Ewan to tell him about this latest development.

"I have to get back to the pub, as well," Mara said. "You are in good hands with the doctor."

"Can I offer you coffee or tea?" I waved toward the coffee and tea bar we kept stocked in the waiting room. During regular business hours, we also had fruit and protein bars available for the patients.

That was something quite different from working in the ER, where it was diagnose the patients and move on as quickly as possible. Here, going to the doctor was an event, and we tried to make patients as comfortable as possible.

"No. I had lunch at the pub. If my brother died of an allergic reaction, why is his death being investigated? I do not understand."

That was a very good question and a tricky one for me. "We are not one hundred percent certain how the reaction happened. So, we are running tests to determine that."

"Do you think someone killed him?" She appeared shocked by the idea.

"As the ACC said to you, we're investigating all possibilities. I really can't say until we are done. If you would like to take a seat, I'll see if I can help Abigail get him ready for you."

We'd done a full autopsy, which meant several cuts to cover. Abigail had stitched him earlier, but it took more than that to make the body presentable.

In the autopsy lab, she was scurrying around.

"I'm about done," she said. "I wanted to put away any logs or tests we still have out so she wouldn't see them."

"Smart thinking." I helped her clean up, not that there was much to do. Abigail kept everything neat. It was a matter of putting away anything that might have encouraged the sister to have more questions.

As we came out of the autopsy room, Tommy came in the back door. He was dressed in khaki shorts and a T-shirt with one of his favorite video games.

"Hungry," he said to Abigail.

"I made you some lunch," she said. "Do you want to eat in the kitchen or the garden?" There were several benches in the garden where he liked to sit when he wasn't working.

"Garden," he said. He was a young man of few words. Not that he didn't have the vocabulary. He did. He was quite bright. But he was never one to prattle on about anything except flowers, and sometimes video games.

He was a lover of nature and preferred to be out in it no matter the season.

"Go on out, and I'll bring it to you, but wash your hands first."

"I'll handle our guest. You take care of Tommy."

She smiled at me. "Thanks."

I did one last check of the autopsy room and then went to get the sister.

She sat ramrod straight in one of the chairs. Her brunette hair in a tight bun at the nape of her neck. I wondered what she did for a living.

"Are you also an accountant?" I asked as I led her through my home and kitchen to the autopsy suite.

"No," she said. She didn't offer any other information.

OK, then.

I put in the combination that opened the door and led her inside. Once the door was shut. I slid down the sheet to the neck.

"Why does he look like that?" she asked.

His lips were still misshapen and an odd color, but other than that he appeared normal. "The reaction made his lips and face swell a bit."

"The only thing he was allergic to was bees. How was he stung?"

"As I said before, we are still investigating."

"You're a country doctor. Doesn't it make more sense for a medical examiner in the city to take a look?"

The words didn't hurt my feelings. If I were someone from outside looking in, I might have asked the same.

"I'm the former head of ER at a Seattle hospital in the States. I've only been here a year. Part of my new duties is that I've taken on the role as coroner. All of my findings are sent to the medical examiner in Edinburgh. I can assure you that your brother is being well looked after."

"Oh," she said.

"Would you like a moment alone with him?"

She shook her head. "No. I just needed to see for myself that it was actually him."

I pulled the sheet back over his face. Then I followed her out the door and shut it.

"When was the last time you saw your brother before today?"

She stood in my kitchen looking anxious to leave. "I don't understand why that would matter."

"We are trying to find out if anyone might have heard or seen something before he died." I prayed Ewan wouldn't kill me for spilling the tea as Mara liked to say.

Her shoulders stiffened. "Are you saying he was murdered?"

Yes. But I wouldn't admit it out loud. "I can only say we found something that looks suspicious. When was the last time you spoke to him, and are you aware of his daily life?"

She sighed, and then twisted her hands together. It was the first bit of emotion she'd shown.

"I wasn't in touch with him. We hadn't spoken in nearly a year."

"Why was that?"

She bristled. "I do not see how it is any of your business."

I ignored her tone. "Did you have a falling out?"

"You could say that," she said. Then she headed for the front door. "Whatever happened between me and Donald has nothing to do with your investigation."

From her tone and anger, I wasn't so sure about that.

Chapter Nine

"Wait," I called out to Kaitlyn Jacks as she opened the front door of my practice. "I have a few more questions about your brother, Donald."

Her shoulders stiffened. "I have no answers," she said. "I need to sort my brother's affairs."

"I understand that, but his home is considered a crime scene at the moment. You most likely won't be able to go through his things for a couple of days."

She shut the door. "I do not have time for that," she said. "Why would it be a crime scene?"

Well, you stepped in that one, Em.

"Your brother's death was suspicious. Even if you weren't in contact, you might be able to help us with the investigation. Please, sit down. I promise it will only take a few minutes. Then we can find you a place to stay until your brother's death is sorted."

She sighed and shut the door. Then she took a seat in the waiting room. I grabbed my notebook out of my purse and a pen. Then I sat across from her.

"Is it normal for a doctor to be doing these interviews?"

"We do things differently here in Sea Isle, and I help the police directly with investigations into deaths."

"OK. What is it you want to know?" she asked.

"Has your brother always had an interest in trains?" I thought starting out with something a bit more mundane might help.

"That's an odd question."

"Well, he was part of our new Storyteller's Train, and I noticed he had an elaborate set up in his home."

"I've never been to his home, but that doesn't surprise me," she said.

She'd never been to her brother's home? That seemed odd.

"Yes, since he was a young boy. He always had train sets and could be quite a bother about wanting to take train rides. Our father encouraged it and would buy him anything he wanted when it came to trains."

"You didn't approve?"

Her eyebrows rose. "They say parents are not supposed to have favorites, but my father clearly did. When my mother and he divorced, he spoiled my brother. I on the other hand, didn't exist."

I frowned. "That must have been difficult." She didn't seem the type to share something so personal, which probably meant she still held a grudge. I couldn't blame her.

I'd had a difficult relationship with my mother after my father had died. She was more or less absent until much later in my life. Luckily, I had a loving grandmother. And in the end, my mother made amends before she died.

"Aye, it was. I became quite fond of books as an escape."

I wasn't sure what to do with that information. "Books can be a comfort."

"Agreed, it's one of the reasons I became an editor," she said.

I'd never met anyone in publishing. "What kind of editor?"

"I edit mainstream fiction and business books for a publishing company in England."

"Oh, so you really did turn your passion for books into an occupation."

She nodded.

"You mentioned before that you hadn't spoken to your brother in a year. May I ask what type of falling out you had?"

"I did not kill him," she said. It was the first time she sounded the least bit Scottish. Her accent was more posh English. I'd learned to tell the difference.

"Of course, you didn't. You weren't even here. I was just curious for background purposes."

She frowned and seemed to ponder this for a few seconds.

"For a time, he was my accountant and helped with my investments. That is until he lost the bulk of my retirement savings in some scheme. One that I think affected most of his clients."

"That's awful. What happened?"

"Other than I'll have to work another thirty years before I can retire?" She didn't bother to hide the bitterness in her voice.

"That must have been difficult."

"Aye. I moved everything to a different company after that. They always say never mix family and business. I learned that lesson the hard way. Never again. Not that I have any family left. Still, that didn't keep him from asking me for more money."

"He wanted you to invest again?"

"Yes. A year ago, only a few months after I lost everything. Can you imagine the gall of him?"

I shook my head.

"He said that every investment came with risks, as if that excused his bad business sense."

"Did you ever meet his business partner? Or anyone from the office?"

She shook her head. "No. Most of the time if we met it was for the holidays, which we did at mine in Glasgow. But after he asked me for more money last year, that was it. I never had any further contact with him. So if you want me to tell you about his personal life, I haven't a clue."

She still sounded quite bitter about the financial fall out. I didn't blame her. Losing her retirement had to have been rough.

"Do you have any other siblings?"

"No. He was the last bit of family I had left. I will say I'm sorry he is dead. He was my family. But I have had a difficult time forgiving his actions. He didn't seem to care about the trouble he'd caused me. He was like that. He never had an ounce of empathy. That is something I struggle with as well, but I have enough to know that he should have, at the very least, apologized."

"I couldn't agree more."

"Do you think he was murdered by one of his clients? I could see that happening," she said. "It is one thing to lose a family's money, and quite another to lose a stranger's."

"I'm sure the ACC will be investigating the clients, and everyone else connected with your brother. And no one has said murdered, yet."

"Yet? So, you do think that is what happened? It wasn't just a bee sting?"

"I wish I had more information for you. Perhaps, the ACC will be able to shine a light on the situation."

"I'd like to go see the ACC now."

As much as I wanted to help Abigail with further testing, I had an idea.

"I'll take you to the station," I said. "I'm headed that way."

"Do you really think it will be a few days before they allow me in his house?"

I nodded.

"Perhaps, you can give me a referral for a hotel or B&B if they have any here."

"It is the busy time of year for tourists, but I'm sure we can find somewhere for you to stay." I tore out a piece of paper from my notebook and wrote down the number for a B&B that was just a few blocks from the station.

"You might want to try here first. It's quite charming. Mrs. Beatty is also known for her breakfast at the B&B."

"Thank you," she said as she took the paper. "I can walk to the police station. My brother told me nothing was very far away in Sea Isle."

"He was right about that, but it is a trek up the mountain to where you need to go. And you have a suitcase. I'm headed that way. Give me a few minutes to let my assistant know that I'm leaving. I'll be right back."

I stuck my notebook into my purse and headed to the autopsy room to find Abigail. I let her know I was leaving and reminded her to go home and take some time off. Whatever tests she needed to run could wait until the next day.

"Tommy is still working in the garden. I might as well stay," she said.

There was no talking her out of it if she had her mind set on something.

"OK. Let me know if you find anything else."

"I will."

After dropping off Kaitlyn, I headed over to the train station. The police tape was gone. I'd texted Mara, and she said the train had taken two of its three trips. The last of which was due in any minute.

I wanted to speak with some of the other storytellers to see if they could give me insight into our victim.

Inside, the office area was still taped off with crime scene tape. But I wasn't concerned with that. We'd been all over the small space the day before.

"Hi Doc, last train has already gone out," Mr. Garfield, the ticket taker said. He was one of my patients at the clinic. "It should be back any minute. I'm settling the books for the day."

"I don't want to bother you, but I have a few questions about Mr. Jacks, who died last night."

"Aye? Can't say I knew him well. Still, a sad business."

"Did you two ever speak?"

He nodded. "A few times about the train. He was quite keen on the restoration. He wanted to know where we found our period paints. Had them mixed special, we did. The preservation society, who helped cover the costs, demanded it be identical to the original."

"You all did an amazing job inside and out. I've never seen a more beautiful train."

"Thank you," he said.

"Did Mr. Jacks ask about anything other than the train?"

He scrunched up his face as if he were thinking.

"No. He helped with the interiors, you know. Had a deft hand with the painting of some of the intricate woodwork. Hard to find that sort of craftsmanship these days.

"Told him he should quit the day job and go into restoring things. He told me how he'd recreated the town and the train in his home. Even invited me to stop by some time. Dinnae suppose that will be happening now."

"He did, and it was quite remarkable. I saw it earlier today. I was curious if you had seen him last night and if anything seemed different about him."

"You were here. So you know we had quite the crowd. I do remember him coming in a bit early with the other story tellers. He seemed fine. Said he was excited about the first trip. That's why I was so surprised he never made it on the train."

I shouldn't have been surprised that he'd known that fact. The more secrets one tried to keep in this town, the faster they spread.

Abigail had even made a sign for our office because patients would say they'd seen certain people in the waiting room.

The sign read: *What happens in the Doc's waiting room, stays in the Doc's waiting room. Everyone deserves their privacy.*

Not that it helped but at least we'd tried to protect the right to privacy.

"Did you notice anyone last night who maybe should not have been here?"

He shook his head. "I never saw the invite list. Our lass, Mara, kept up with that. She would know better than I would."

"I don't remember seeing you on the train; did you stay here while it went out?"

"No, I was on there. I was helping in the engine room. One of our lads was sick. I got on right before we left."

"As far as you know, no one stayed behind?"

"No. I locked up the station before getting on the train. And before you ask, I thought I'd locked the office where they found the poor lad. But I was rushing, and I may have missed it."

The door had been unlocked when I'd tried it. But I didn't want to make him feel bad, so I kept that bit of news to myself.

"Do you remember seeing him get on the train at any time?"

"No. From what I've heard, he died before we took off. Though, you would know more about that than me." He was digging for information, and I wasn't about to give him any. Ewan would have my neck.

"Right. Before yesterday, did he have any arguments with anyone associated with the train?"

He crossed his arms. "Let me have a think. He was at all the committee meetings. He stayed quiet unless there was something he didn't agree with, I suppose."

"Like what?"

"The uniforms for the staff. They wanted to wear costumes from the time period or their own clothes. He insisted, more than once, that they should wear the proper uniforms."

"The ones with the jackets and pants."

"Aye, he won out in the end. The story tellers can wear anything, but the train staff had time-period uniforms. I can tell you he liked things a certain away and believed we should be proper."

"You sound like you agreed with him."

"Aye, I did. If we are going to do something, it should be proper."

"I understand that I asked this already, but I'm wondering if you noticed him acting any differently last night?"

"I only saw him from afar, and he seemed fine."

"Was he talking to anyone in particular?"

"I cannae say I took notice. He was here at the start when everyone arrived. I did see his costume, though. He looked like something out of a Philip Marlowe novel. Trench coat and fedora, I believe. He spoke with some of the other storytellers as they arrived. I could not hear what they were saying." Mr. Garfield continued, "As you saw, even though we weren't selling tickets, I was at my station, until it was time to help out the engineers. When I got on the train, no one was in the building."

Except for a very dead Mr. Jacks stuffed into a cupboard.

Chapter Ten

A half-hour later the train arrived from its last run. I waited for the passengers—there were quite a few who exited. That was good news for the town. It was important they recoup the costs of this latest venture. That was one of Mara's main concerns. After the last passenger disembarked, the storytellers and staff climbed down the steps.

I knew quite a few, as that was one of the pluses as the town doctor. Many of them were patients or their family members were.

But I decided to home in on Sarah Billingsley. She was head of the train committee and a bit of a busybody. She always seemed to know what was happening in town, and didn't mind sharing every bit of gossip she heard when she was in the office.

Today, the fifty-year-old was dressed in a vintage sequined dress, with buckled heels and a small hat with a feather. She appeared as if she'd stepped out of a 1930s fashion magazine.

I waved at her, and she walked over to me.

"Doctor, is everything OK? Please tell me no one else became ill on the train." Her expression seemed strained.

"Nothing like that. Please don't worry yourself."

She blew out a breath. "After last night, I take nothing for granted. Mr. Jacks's death put quite the damper on our festivities."

As if realizing what she said, her eyes widened. "Oh. My. You know what I mean. We had all been so excited about opening night and none of us could have imagined such a tragedy."

"It was sad," I said.

"So, why are you here, Doctor?"

"I'm trying to get some background on Mr. Jacks. I understand he was quite a vocal member of the committee."

"Aye, he was. In many ways, he was quite insistent about perfection. I tried to explain to him that many of our staff are volunteers. We really couldn't make demands upon them or force them into any sort of training. And the uniforms. My goodness. That ended up being a great deal of expense fitting everyone. I, among some others, was not happy about that expenditure. It took a great deal of our budget, which was limited."

"So, he made some enemies?" I asked.

"Oh, that is a bit harsh. I would say some of us were not his biggest fans. Though, I must admit everyone does look quite smart and professional. In the end, his suggestions were warranted, and he was right. I told him as much when we arrived yesterday. I still cannae believe he's gone." She put a hand to her chest and shook her head. Her words appeared to be sincere.

"How did he seem last night before the train ride?"

"Excited," she said. "We all were. We've been working quite hard on this and praying that it would turn a profit for our volunteer efforts. It is also such a bonus for the town. We've been trying for years to make it happen. It was surreal when we all were on the train, and it started moving. And then equally surreal when we heard about his death. Just awful."

Mara had told me all about the history of the train and bringing it back to life. It had taken them years to acquire the donations needed.

"I wonder if you noticed any sort of swelling on his face?"

"So, it was a bee sting? I'd heard rumors around town. I was curious."

"During an active investigation . . ."

"You cannae say. I know the rules. Ewan is always telling us. But to answer your question, I don't believe so. He seemed more animated than usual. Maybe even a bit nervous.

"We'd all practiced our stories with mock audiences, but he considered himself a shy man and not a performer. Though I sat in on one of his early sessions, and he was quite good. We loved that he used literature from the 1930s, which was having quite a renaissance here in Scotland during that time."

"So, other than he was a bit nervous, you didn't notice anything different about his behavior?"

"No. I put his nerves up to performer's anxiety. We were all very excited that it was actually happening."

"I know I asked this before, but it is important. Do you remember him speaking to anyone else that night? Or did anything happen that made you curious before you boarded the train?"

"I'll be honest, I was quite busy with our guests." She closed her eyes. "I do remember him speaking with a man over in the corner near the champagne. They seemed to have quite an intense conversation, but I was across the room. I could not tell you what it was about. Why are you curious about who he was talking to? I thought it was a bee sting."

I cleared my throat. I kept stepping into these situations where I gave too much away with my questions. I needed to stop doing that.

"I'm trying to set a timeline," I said. "From the time he was, uh, stung, until his death."

"Oh. Well, I remember seeing him with the man."

"Do you know what he looked like?"

She frowned. "I'm sorry. We were so busy, and other than he was male, I do not remember anything about him. But he had to be one of the guests. Mara has the list, and she might be able to tell you. And that was it. We were helping the guests get on the train and none of us noticed Mr. Jacks didn't make it. Poor man."

Poor man, indeed. One question bugged me more than any other I had. If he'd seemed fine before everyone had boarded that train, how had he ended up in that cupboard?

Chapter Eleven

By the time I finished speaking with some of the other storytellers, it was early evening. No one had much to say about Mr. Jacks, other than he was a meticulous man, who felt strongly about the train rides being authentic.

While some of them didn't seem to be his biggest fans, none of them were angry enough to kill him.

Or if they did, none of them admitted it. That would have made things much easier.

As I was leaving the station, my phone buzzed. I'd forgotten about a meeting with Mara and the festival committee. The end-of-summer festival was a week-long celebration with different events.

I'd been coerced by my best friend to be a part of the committee, though most of the time I was there only in an advisory capacity. If they gave me a job to do, it was usually fairly simple and flexible.

As the town doctor, I had to be around for any mishaps that might have happened to the visitors or locals.

When I arrived back at the practice, I texted Mara that I would be a bit late and to start without me. Abigail and Tommy were gone, but she had left reports stacked on my desk.

All of the lip balms we'd collected, along with his shaving cream, had been contaminated with the bee serum. Someone had gone to great lengths to make certain he used the tainted concoctions on his skin and that there was enough toxin to be deadly. But that also meant the person who killed him might not have known that he would react that night.

So, perhaps, the killer hadn't thought the death would be so public. Once the reaction reached deadly levels, his throat and tongue would have been too swollen for him to speak.

But surely someone would have noticed his misshapen face and the fact he couldn't breathe. Someone had followed or shoved him into that office and later into the cabinet where I found him.

Ugh. I was no closer to finding the killer, but it had to be someone who was there that night. Mara had sent the complete list to Ewan, but I was going to ask her for a copy as well.

After freshening up, I headed down to the pub. It was Saturday night, so it was more crowded than usual. It was unusual for the committee to have a meeting on a Saturday night, but Sunday was the kick-off to the festival week.

It started with fairy boat rides on Sunday afternoon for visitors. I was scheduled to go on the five o'clock boat, which promised views of fairies on one of the nearby islands.

I had had no idea what a fairy boat was. At first, I thought they were saying "ferry" in that delightful Scottish accent. But they had meant the kind that fly around and are magical. They spoke about fairies as if they were real. Like many things in Sea Isle, it sounded charming. I was also curious how the boat captains could guarantee fairy sightings.

When I arrived at the pub, Mr. Wilson, who was behind the bar, motioned me to head out back to the patio area. A private party sign was above the door leading out to the area.

Since it was cool at night, Mara had turned on some of the courtyard heaters that stood like soldiers around the place. The ten committee members were there at a long table. Many of them had served on the train board, as well.

They had drinks, and plates of hors d'oeuvres placed down the table. Mara's love language was food, and that was one of the many things I adored about her. Mine was eating said food.

She had a black and tan waiting for me in a space next to her. Next to me was the Assistant Chief Constable, who was also the mayor. He didn't always sit in on the meetings, but my guess was he wanted to make certain we had adequate security for the various events. No one would ever say Ewan wasn't conscientious.

I sat down next to him. He always smelled of fresh pine, and tonight he wore one of his cable-knit sweaters with jeans.

He was incredibly handsome, but he wasn't one of those guys who acted like he knew it. He was self-assured, but never boastful. And even though we'd butted heads more than once over various cases, I knew him to be kind and caring—especially where his townspeople were concerned. He looked out for everyone.

"Evening," he said, as I sat down.

"Hi," I whispered. "Did I miss anything?"

He shook his head. "We're just getting started."

Sarah Billingsley, who was also head of the train committee, called the meeting to order. She had her fingers in everything and could be a bit heavy-handed with opinions, but she was one of those people who made sure things were done. The world needed women like her to keep us all going.

Part of that was her forceful nature. The other part was her type-A personality. In her mind, there was no room for failure, which was why her blood pressure sometimes ran a bit high.

"Thank you for giving up your Saturday evening to help us," she said. "I called this meeting to make certain we have everything set for our week of fun."

She handed out small, collated binders. "Thanks to Mara, we have a comprehensive list of each event, with the volunteers and times of everything."

With the exception of Abigail, I'd never met anyone more organized than Mara.

They went through the larger scheduled events. Everyone agreed to take on their part of the bigger plan. This was a team of efficient organizers. I was just along to help out however I could.

"First night, we have our fairy boat rides starting at four and going until nine," Sarah said. "The volunteer boats have been decorated, and we have designees to be the lore tellers. Everyone will be following the same script, so visitors do not feel they are missing out if they are on a different boat from their friends."

When I'd done my research, I discovered Scotland has as much fairy lore as Ireland. Though, I noticed many of the tales I'd read that were set in Scotland happened to be much darker in nature.

Sarah went on for several minutes about the various days of the festival. "Does anyone have any questions?"

I did, but I was too embarrassed to ask. I would wait until they were all gone and ask Mara.

"While I have you here, I have a few questions about the night Mr. Jacks died," Ewan said.

Most of the people around the table grimaced, and a few of them shivered.

"ACC, this isn't the place. Besides, we've spoken to your men," Sarah said.

"Aye, you have," Ewan said. "I was wondering if perhaps something had jogged your memory. Maybe you saw Mr. Jacks going into the office at the train station. We are still trying to find witnesses who may have seen if someone entered the room with him."

"Are the rumors true?" Sarah asked.

"I'm not sure what you mean," Ewan said.

"That he was possibly murdered," she said. "There wouldn't be such an intense inquiry if he had died of natural causes. And Anne Marie's husband, Jed, says he saw Mr. Jacks's face, which looked like someone had beat him up. I hate to think of that sort of crime happening in our town."

"Tis best if we do not listen to rumor, as it can distort the actual facts," Ewan said. He was much better than I was at keeping things close to the vest.

"Did any of you see him go into the office the night of the event?" I asked, trying help Ewan bring the inquiry back to his original question.

Everyone shook their heads.

Mara pursed her lips. "I've already told you that I remember checking him off the list. At the time, he seemed fine. But I do remember his lips appearing plumper than usual. Almost in a way that I thought he'd gotten lip filler or something. I remember now, because I thought it was strange for him to do that. I mean, plenty of women do it, but maybe I'm being sexist."

"So, when he checked in, you noticed swelling?"

She nodded.

I glanced at Ewan. We both understood what that meant. The reaction had already begun before he'd even arrived.

"I can't believe I didn't think of this earlier, but did he have a plus one?" I asked.

"He didn't arrive with anyone else," Mara said. "I can go check the paperwork to see if someone else was his plus one, though. It's possible they arrived later since the storytellers had to be there early."

"I can't imagine he would have had a date," Sarah said.

All heads swung her way.

"I said that out loud, didn't I?" She laughed nervously. "I only meant he didn't seem the type to date. He cared more about trains than people. That much was obvious from the meetings he attended. His whole life seemed to be focused on trains. Apart from his job. At least, that was how he appeared in our discussions," she said. "I know I told you he was a perfectionist about the uniforms for the staff, and he'd dressed quite creatively as a detective. I'm sure I mentioned that earlier."

"Did you notice the swelling on his face? Any of you?" Ewan asked.

Jasper had been unusually quiet throughout the meeting. He was usually up at the crack of dawn to get things ready at his bakery. I assumed he was tired this evening.

He raised his hand tentatively.

"You do not have to raise your hand," Ewan said.

"I've been thinking all day that I may have seen him when I was washing my hands in the loo. Before I set everything up in the train, I was in there. I remember because he was coughing and wheezing a bit. I thought he shouldn't be at a party spreading germs if he was ill. Now, I feel terrible for thinking such mean things about him."

Jasper could do sarcasm with the best of them, but he had one of the kindest hearts. "I remember thinking I wanted to get away from him. Getting sick was not on my agenda. I can't afford to be ill with my business." He shook his head. "What if he needed help and I just left him there?"

"I doubt he knew what was happening," I said. "He probably did not think to ask for help until it was too late."

"Are you going to tell us what killed him?" Sarah asked.

"I know it isn't what you want to hear, but we really are still running tests," I said. I looked at Ewan and cocked my head.

He nodded at me again.

"I can say he had an allergic reaction of sorts. What we can't figure out is why he went into the office rather than seeking medical help."

"Maybe, he was searching for the first aid kit that is kept in there," Sarah said. "Per the laws, we had to make sure we had a set up on the train and in the station. He and our station master set up the office while we were all volunteering to refurbish everything. He would have known. He had a checklist for that area."

The Scots in Sea Isle were very fond of their lists.

Maybe, he had gone in looking for an EpiPen. Most people with severe allergies kept the pens on their person or nearby in a backpack or bag. But we hadn't found one on him or at the scene.

At least, we had part of our answer as to why he was in the office in the first place. Maybe, he'd been searching for an EpiPen.

But it didn't tell us who had stuck him in the cupboard.

* * *

Not long after, the meeting was dismissed. It had been a busy couple of days, and I was ready for bed. But as I went through the pub, I noticed the victim's sister sitting in the corner alone.

She stared out the window.

"Who are you looking at?" Ewan said from behind me.

I hadn't heard him come up.

"The sister," I said.

"I have some follow up questions for her, do you want to come along?"

I stared up at him with surprise. "I don't think I'm ever going to be used to you asking me to be involved."

"Like I said before, better to just allow you to be a part of it so you dinnae get hurt."

He makes a good point. I snorted as I followed him across the pub.

"Ms. Jacks, do you mind if the Doctor and I join you? I have a few follow-up questions about your brother."

She frowned, but then motioned for us to sit down.

The noise in the pub died down, as people became curious about the ACC and me sitting with someone they probably didn't know. As I had said many times, we lived in a nosey village where gossip was currency. The whole town would know soon enough about this little encounter.

"I'm not sure what I can tell you," she said. "Nothing has changed from earlier. My brother and I didn't talk much."

"Right," Ewan said. "Your estrangement was over money?"

"Aye, and the fact that he liked his trains and numbers more than people. We had never been that close for those reasons, but when he lost my savings on a bad investment, I was angry."

Her eyes went wide as if she realized what she'd said. "Though, not enough to kill him, mind you."

"When was the last time you saw him in person?" I asked.

She blew out a breath. "About six months ago. We attended the funeral of our great aunt Minerva. I'd forgotten about that. I don't think we said a single word to one another. He steered clear of me."

"Was he embarrassed about the financial losses?" I asked.

Ewan nodded as if that was a good question.

"No. If he had been, maybe I could have forgiven him more easily. He said that investments were always a risk and that I should have been prepared to lose it all." She bristled.

"That wasn't at all what he said when he'd asked for my money," she added. "Back then, it had all been a sure thing. He had said there was no way to lose my retirement."

"That would have made me angry, as well," I said.

"If he had not been so nonchalant about it or had even apologized, things would have been better between us. If you think his death was suspicious, I would look at his clients. If he acted that way with them, they would have been furious. But he was my brother. I might have been angry, but I couldn't have killed him or anyone."

She made a good point about the clients. I'd been thinking along those lines, as well.

"Were you aware of his allergy to bees?"

She nodded. "He had to be careful all of his life. When he was about twelve, he ended up in the hospital after he was stung twice by some bees in our grandmother's garden. In fact, after that, he didn't play outside much. He fell in love with trains and was always adding to his collection."

"So, the last time you spoke with him was at your aunt's funeral?"

"Aye. Well, I saw him. We didn't really speak. But we were aware of one another."

"And there were no phone calls or any other communication since then?" For some reason Ewan didn't seem to believe her.

"Not that I can recall," she said. "We had no reason to speak. As I said, I'd been waiting for him to apologize. Though, I have to admit, I'd given up on that ever happening. I'm curious—why all the questions? Are you saying someone killed him? I'd heard that he had an allergic reaction. You mentioned the bees. He'd had a problem his entire life."

"It is an ongoing investigation, and we are still waiting for a complete autopsy from the doctor," Ewan said.

"We are nearly done," I promised.

"Right. But I don't understand what is so suspicious if it was a bee sting? You know he was allergic."

Ewan and I glanced at one another.

"What are you not telling me?" she asked.

"We will have more information for you soon," I said. "As soon as we complete our tests. It takes a few days."

She sighed. "When will I be able to get into his place? His lawyer has already contacted me. I'm his sole beneficiary, which surprised me."

"Oh?" That was news.

"Aye. I had no idea. Though, now everything falls to me, I suppose I should put together a wake, and then there is the packing up of his belongings. I would like to get started with that soon. I need to get back to my job."

"We are almost finished with the investigation at the house," Ewan said. "I'll call you when we are done." They had been checking the house for additional stores of cash. I was curious if they found more. I'd be checking the files on the computer when I went home.

She nodded. "I am confused. I asked before but I would like a straight answer. Do you think someone killed him over money?"

"Hopefully, we will have answers soon," Ewan said. "I have your information. I will call when we are finished with his home. And if you would like, there is a volunteer women's group in town who sometimes help pack the belongings of deceased family." He handed her a card. "They'll also help you find places to donate items to those in need."

She took the card from him. "Small towns are so different," she said. "In Edinburgh, I barely know any of my neighbors. Here, everyone seems to know me, even though we've never met."

Ewan and I smiled.

"Word does travel fast," I said. "And I will alert you to our findings as soon as we finish, and Ewan gives the OK." I'd said that already, but I wanted her to understand that we did care and would not leave her hanging indefinitely.

"I can't help but think you are hiding the fact that someone may have killed my brother." She held up a hand. "I realize you can't tell me now. But if someone did hurt him, please catch them and bring them to justice. We may have been arguing, but he was the last of my family."

Ewan nodded.

We were already on the hunt for a killer and had more than one suspect.

The hard part was finding which one of them did it.

Chapter Twelve

The next afternoon, I bundled up for the fairy cruise. The weather had taken a turn. It was overcast and drizzly, which wasn't unusual for the summer months in Scotland. I'd moved here from Seattle and the amount it rained here in Sea Isle was on par with my former town. It was just much colder, even in the summer.

But nothing would stop these tours or the kick-off of the ten-day end-of-summer festival. I had hired one of the private boats so that Tommy and Abigail could come with me, Mara, Jasper, and our friend Angie. Tommy didn't do well with crowds, but he had been curious about the fairy stories. I'd overheard him talking to Abigail about the trips.

I wasn't much for crowds either, so I'd decided to hire one of the smaller boats for us to take out.

"We're here," Abigail bustled into the front of the clinic. "I hope we aren't too late."

"You are right on time," I said. "I was just putting on my mac and looking for my rain hat."

"It's in the small closet by the pharmacy room," she said. "I'll grab it for you."

Leave it to Abigail to know how everything in my home and office was organized. Before I could say I would do it, she was gone.

Tommy stood just inside the door staring at the floor.

"Are you excited for the fairy boat tour?" I asked.

"Dinnae know if they are real," he said in his stilted and careful way.

"The fairies? Me either," I admitted. "I saw that sightings are guaranteed. I don't understand how they can do that."

"Thought I saw one once in the garden but could have been a trick of the light. I like the stories."

He didn't usually carry on conversations like this. A few words and then he was gone. I loved that he felt comfortable enough with me to speak.

"Me, too," I said. "I don't know many of the tales, but I've read a few. I'm hoping to learn more today."

Abigail came back in with my hat, and we made our way to the docks where our friends waited for us at the pier. By the time we'd made it down, the drizzle had stopped, though it was still cool and cloudy.

I was surprised to see Ewan and Henry there.

Mara smiled at me. "The guys were in the pub grabbing a late lunch, and I asked if they wanted to join us," she said. "I hope that's OK."

"I—of course," I said. "The more the merrier. I'm just surprised you have the time."

Ewan nodded. "We are waiting on some specific warrants for the files. We have a bit of time before those come in."

I cleared my throat. "That's great."

Abigail blushed as Henry waved hello to her and Tommy.

"Hi Henry," Tommy said. "Abi bought me a new game. Will you come play it with me?"

"Aye, maybe even tonight if we dinnae get back too late," the officer said.

Tommy nodded.

Henry was so good with him, as was Ewan. Growing up, Tommy hadn't had the best male role model, but he did now. And luckily for him, he'd always had Abigail in his corner. She cherished her younger brother.

"Doc, do you mind if we come with you? This is the first time we've made these excursions a part of the end-of-summer festivities." Ewan asked. "I wanted to check out the format." As the laird, mayor, and ACC, he had his hands in everything.

"Of course, I don't mind," I said. "We are happy to have you."

"Hello, all. I'm Captain Gillispie," said an older gentleman with white hair and Santa Clause worthy beard. He wore a blue and white captain's hat. "My vessel is the Galbraith, and we are heading into fairy territory. This is my daughter, Isobel, she is a master storyteller and knows all of the folklore for our islands where many a fairy and wee folk live. Welcome aboard!"

Isobel motioned for us to step onto the craft. She was dressed in jeans and a cable-knit sweater but had a pair of fairy wings attached to her back.

The boat was bigger than I'd imagined, for which I was grateful. There were benches facing out to sea, and a small cabin with more seats in case the weather turned rough.

As the Captain headed up top, we sat down on the benches. I was surprised when Ewan took the seat next to me.

"Any news?" I whispered.

He shook his head. "We're waiting for a warrant so we can go through the business files. His partner is acting suspiciously, and I'm curious what we will find."

"I thought you already had a court order."

"Only for the deceased," he said. "I want to see if there are improprieties with the business as a whole."

"I was thinking about that. He lost the sister's money, but I'm sure that at least some of his other clients had to be involved. I know we spoke about it before, but money is a good motive."

"Aye, it is," he said. "But this murder seems personal, and the killer, or unsub, as you American's say, would have had to have access to the lip balms. That would take someone who was a part of his everyday routine or had access to him."

"Does that mean only the people he worked with? That narrows down your suspect list."

"Unfortunately, no. Several of those he volunteered with remembered that he was addicted to his lip balm. When asked, they all said he'd used it in their presence. And he'd invited some of the volunteers to his house to show off his trains. One of those people could be involved."

"Oh, bummer."

"Yes, it leaves us with a fair number of suspects, all of whom were at the event that night."

I scrunched up my face. "Of those who were there, did he lose their money, as well?"

"We are cross-checking, and that is why we asked for the warrant for the business, rather than just his papers. I think I mentioned I'm bringing in a forensic accountant to help us go through everything."

"That's smart."

Jasper and Angie stopped to hug me as they came on the boat. The newly married Angie was so busy with all of her stores, and her husband, but she was determined to make time for her friends.

"Thank you for inviting me," she said as she squeezed me tight. She was a few decades too late for the punk era, but her wild outfits never disappointed. Today, she wore a sequined sailor shirt, with white leather pants and a rhinestone studded cap.

"I'm glad you could make it. Where is your husband?"

She rolled her eyes. "In London again," she said. "Though things are finally settling down. And he was able convince the shareholders not to jump ship. He promised another few weeks, and we should be back to normal."

They had their fair share of family trouble. Some of which had nearly ended with us both dead.

Jasper carried a basket. "I brought treats," he said. "I know how you are about your snacks." He pointed at me.

Everyone laughed. I loved our group of friends, who had become like family to me. Even though I'd been in Sea Isle for only a year, I didn't know how I would do life without them. I prayed I never had to find out.

"Open your mind and pay attention," Isobel said. She waved her hands in the air. "You never know when a fairy might be peeking into our world. We'll be circling the islands where you might catch a glimpse of them flying around. And if you see a seal, it may be a selkie or a mermaid or merman in disguise. While they cannot stay on land for long, we sometimes see them shed their seal masks and dance by the firelight."

Her voice was rich and bold, and I couldn't help but smile. I sometimes wondered if everyone in Scotland was a great storyteller.

As soon as the boat moved forward, Tommy cupped his hand over his eyes as he peered out to sea. I had a feeling he was already looking for the mysterious creatures.

While I wasn't the type to believe in fairies, it was fun to watch Tommy and the others as they pointed out various sea life.

"Seals," he whispered to his sister as he pointed toward the bow of the boat.

"It tis." She grinned at him.

The creatures swam along with the boat as if guiding us along the way.

"Some of our fair isles are the home of witches as well," Isobel said. "Kind-hearted souls, who would only wish you the best life has to offer—unless you try to double-cross them. The last person you want to anger is a Scottish witch. They are powerful and always get their way." Her charming brogue made her stories come alive.

She went on to tell the tale of "The Witch of Fife," about a man with a witch for a wife. He wanted to find out what she did when she was away for many days. He followed her one night and discovered that perhaps he didn't want to know the truth when he was nearly burned by magic. After that, he left his wife to her own devices.

The stories continued as we neared an island, the overcast skies made it seem much darker than usual. On the island, there were flicks of light, like fireflies dancing through the trees.

"Speak softly, lest we scare the wee folk away as they work to bring fruits and berries home to their kin," Isobel whispered.

Tommy leaned over the boat trying his best to see the lights on the island. Abigail put a hand on his belt to keep him from tumbling over.

The lights flickered and seemed to move quickly. It was a trick of the eyes, but it was easy to imagine they might be fairies flitting in and out of the forests on the islands. I had some research to do when I arrived home, as I was curious if they were really fireflies. I didn't know if Scotland even had them. But there were definitely lights zooming in and out of the trees.

I didn't want to break the spell everyone seemed to be under by asking such a rudimentary question. A few minutes later we circled another island, where seals had settled in for the evening on the beach.

"It takes a trained eye to see fairy folk in their true forms," Isobel said. "If you squint just right, you might be treated to a glimpse, though they are smart and know we are looking. So dinnae feel bad if you only see the seals."

Isobel's stories were wonderful and fun, she had a couple for each island we circled in the boat. On the way back she offered us warm cups of apple cider. While I considered it a drink for fall, I didn't complain. Out on the water it was colder than it had been on shore.

"Made by mum for these chilly nights," she said. "It will warm you from the inside out. It's said the apples will bring the people you need into your life."

She wasn't wrong about it warming me from the inside out, and the beverage was just the right amount of tart and sweet. I could have had a gallon of it without blinking an eye.

While we traveled back, Isobel continued to share folk tales about the islands we passed. She was a gifted storyteller. Then something that had been niggling at my brain came to the forefront. The name, Gillispie. I'd seen it on one of the files when we'd been in Donald Jacks's home.

I climbed the steps up to where the captain stood at the helm.

"This has been a wonderful experience," I said.

He smiled and nodded. "My Isobel is talented with the stories. I think she should be an actress, but she loves the sea like her Da."

I grinned. "Well, your passion for it shows. You two have made this really fun."

"Glad you are enjoying it."

"I have a strange question for you, and I hope you don't think I'm being too forward."

"I'm happily married, Doc. You've met my wife, Cecile."

We laughed.

"I have. She's lovely. This has more to do with my job of investigating deaths."

He frowned. "That sounds serious. Tell me how I can help?"

There was a noise, and I glanced back to see Ewan on the steps leading up to where we stood. I was certain he stopped to listen.

"Right. When we were searching Donald Jacks's home, I remember seeing your name on one of the files."

He frowned and shook his head. "Aye, he was our accountant. Emphasis on was."

"You don't seem to have liked him very much."

"Shifty fellow," he said. "He was always trying to get me to invest in different projects. The only investment I'm interested in is me and this boat. I do what I must to keep things going, and I'm careful with my money. Besides, if you listen to anyone in town, you'll hear stories about him."

"What kind of stories?"

"Losing people's money," he said. "Some said he was a trickster. I was looking for someone else to keep the books because I'd lost trust in him a while ago."

"How long had he kept your books?"

"Oh, about four years. But it has only been in the last year and a half that I had trouble with him. Always bugging me to invest in one thing or another. After hearing some of the stories, I'm glad I held onto my money."

This wasn't the first time I'd heard about the bad investments. Even though I was certain the killer had to be someone close to him, it could have been one of his clients. They would have to know his habits and his addiction to lip balm. We lived in a small town and the victim seemed to be ruled by his daily habits.

* * *

By the time we made it back to the docks, some of the other boats were coming in from their tours. As we disembarked, I heard someone arguing. I turned to see Kiara, from the Lotions and Potions shop, having words with Sarah Billingsley. The conversation appeared quite animated, but as if they realized at the same time that we were all staring at them, they closed their mouths tightly.

Kiara ushered Max down the main pier doing her best to ignore Sarah, who stomped along behind her. I was more worried about Max, Kiara's son. He was sensitive and the arguing might have caused one of his rashes. He was prone to hives when he encountered any sort of stress.

I glanced up at Ewan, who frowned.

"I wonder what that was about?" I asked.

"No telling with Sarah," he said. "She likes to poke her nose into places it doesn't belong." He seldom said things like that about people in town, but Sarah seemed to push his buttons.

"Do you think it has something to do with the case?"

He shook his head. "Knowing Sarah, she was trying to convince poor Kiara into working on one of the many committees she heads."

I'd been at the other end of Sarah's pushiness, though I knew she meant well.

"Probably," I said.

A phone dinged behind us, and Henry glanced down at a message. "ACC, the warrant has come in," he said. "Should I head over now, or in the morning?"

"We'll go tomorrow," Ewan said. "It's late and I'd rather surprise them first thing."

"Yes, sir."

"Can I go with you?" I asked.

Ewan's eyebrows went up. "Do you know accounting?"

I shook my head. "No, I thought I might look to see if he kept more toiletries at the office and if those had been loaded with the venom."

"Henry gathered them up for you and Abigail to test," he said, and his brows drew together as if he were confused.

"I wasn't thinking of looking for those things in his office," I said. "I thought I might check the partner and executive assistant's desk. The killer was in close proximity to be able to dose those balms. Who better than someone who worked with him? Maybe, we'll get lucky and find the actual venom."

"But his partner and assistant weren't at the train station when he was put into that cupboard."

"That doesn't mean they didn't have an accomplice," I said. "You've known we've run all the tests we can. Though, we're still waiting on DNA from his clothing, which takes a minimum of forty-eight-hours."

"I'll have that report in the morning," Abigail said as she came up behind us. "I had to send some of the fibers to Edinburgh, so that will be another couple of days."

She'd become quite the forensic specialist and knew how to run all of our machines in the lab. I'd done a fair amount of studying, as well, when it came to forensics.

I hadn't read the fine print of my contract when I moved to Sea Isle. The wording that had said I would be the town doctor, as well as the person who investigated death. They didn't really have coroners in Scotland, but that was what I called myself.

Since Ewan was the mayor and laird, he could appoint any political position he wanted in town. And when he'd sent the contract, I hadn't read the part about signing and investigating death certificates.

But I took my job seriously and had learned a great deal about solving crimes over the past year. Even though my real job was to determine cause of death and if there had been any sort of foul play. I'm me, so of course I took the investigating a step further.

In the beginning, most of my knowledge had come from the UK mysteries I watched. But like Abigail, I'd done a fair amount of research into forensics and crime solving. I found it all quite fascinating.

In many ways, I related it to my working in the ER for more than a decade. Back then, I never knew what kind of case might present itself next, and I had to do a fair amount of medical deducing rather quickly.

Though, when it came to solving crimes, I still had a great deal to learn. Not the least of which was never making assumptions, something I was prone to do, even though Ewan demanded we have evidence to indicate someone was guilty.

He wasn't wrong. It was just annoying.

* * *

After I left with Ewan, Jasper caught up with us.

"Hey, before you go, there is something I need to tell you," Jasper said. "I didn't want to ruin your time on the boat with local gossip."

We moved up the pier a little bit away from the crowds getting off the various fairy boats.

"What is it?" I asked.

"I didn't realize where she works, but Catherine Allan was in the bakery earlier. She ordered several dozen petits fours for the office. It seems they have some important people coming in tomorrow. While she was in the bakery, she was speaking quite loudly on her cell phone."

I bit my lip to keep from laughing. Jasper didn't approve of people talking on cell phones in his bakery. He even had a sign that stated as much.

"If she hadn't made such a large order, I might have kicked her out. She told me she was talking to her boss, who wanted to make certain that the baked goods were fancy. That the clients they had coming in were very important."

Ewan and I glanced at one another. If the search was to take place the next morning, Catherine and her boss, Jeremy Burns, were in for a big surprise.

Chapter Thirteen

Bright and early the next morning, I met Ewan at the pub. Abigail had rearranged my appointments at the clinic for later in the day, so I could join the investigators when they went to Donald Jacks's office.

Ewan and Henry were finishing up what looked like a full Scottish breakfast.

"Ewan said you were coming," Mara said as she handed me a bag. "I made you one of those egg and bagel sandwiches you like so much." Then she handed over a paper cup. "And of course some coffee."

I'd already had two cups, but I wasn't about to turn down a third.

"You are a lifesaver," I said.

"Can't have our Doc going hungry," she said.

"We have time if you want to eat here," Ewan said.

Their plates were nearly clean. "I can eat in the car on the way up the mountain," I said. "If it's OK with you."

"Aye, it tis," Ewan said. He put several bills on the bar for Mara.

Henry laughed.

"What's so funny?"

"You're the only person he would allow to eat in his car," Henry whispered.

I was certain that wasn't true.

On the way up the mountain, Ewan and Henry told me what they'd learned so far.

"The forensic accountant is going through the files we found in Mr. Jacks's home," Henry said. "She dinnae have much to say yet, but she did mention that she would be comparing the files with what was found in the office."

Ewan nodded. "She also mentioned that many of the investments appeared to be bad from the get-go. Almost like he'd planned to lose his clients' money."

"That doesn't make any sense," I said. "He had to know if he continued to lose their money, he wouldn't have any clients left. Why would anyone in his business make such dumb mistakes?"

Even as I said the word, something clicked in my brain. "Unless—he was trying to find ways to launder funds."

"Did you see that on one of your detective series? This isn't the sort of place that happens." Ewan replied. He didn't say it in a derisive way, more like he was curious how I came up with the idea.

"I mean, it's not exactly a place where murder happens either, but it does sometimes. It's possible. Bad people live everywhere. I don't know much about laundering money, though. Seems like even then you'd need to be successful, or your clients would be less than happy with you."

In truth, most of what I knew about laundering money came from that Ben Affleck movie *The Accountant*. But I was having a problem with the idea that the victim lost money on purpose, especially when his sister was involved.

"True," Ewan said. "And you would be talking more about organized crime, and we haven't seen any sort of link to that in our town. Maybe in one of the bigger cities, but not Sea Isle."

"The ACC is right. That is something we keep a close eye on here."

I took a bite of my sandwich. Mara had used thick Scottish bacon, which was so good. The over-medium egg was perfectly done, though it dripped down my chin a bit. I used the paper napkin in the bag to blot the mess. The last thing I wanted to do was lose my eating privileges because I'd dropped egg in Ewan's pristine vehicle.

"Do you have any solid suspects yet?" I asked. "I mean, anyone we should keep an eye out for while we're going through Jacks's files?"

"Other than the people he worked with, and those who were involved with the train event, no." Ewan shifted the gears as we went up the mountain.

"What about his clients?" I repeated what the boat captain had told me the night before. "I don't know if you heard everything he told me. We've said this before, but if he lost their money—and a lot of it—people have killed for less."

"True. What isn't clear at present was did he lose the money of just his clients, or was the whole firm involved?" Ewan said. "That would open up the suspect pool quite a bit. And would give us a reason why they are already under suspicion."

I finished my sandwich as we pulled up in front of the accounting firm. Some of Ewan's officers stood by the door leading into the offices.

After tossing my empty bag into the trashcan by the light pole, I followed Ewan and the others into the office.

The shock on Catherine's face said it all. Her desk was piled high with boxes from Jasper's bakery. Her eyes were wide, and she appeared terrified.

"You can't be here," she said. "We have important clients coming in this morning."

"We have a warrant that says otherwise," Ewan said as he held up a piece of paper. "We're going to have to ask you to vacate the offices while we conduct a search."

"What the blazes is all this commotion, I can't hear myself think," Jeremy Burns bustled out of his office. "What is all this? Why are you here, ACC? We've already answered your questions."

"They have a warrant to search everything," Catherine said, as she pointed to the paper in Ewan's hand.

"Let me see that," the other man said angrily.

He read it over, his frown deepening. "I'm calling my solicitor."

"I'd highly suggest that," Ewan said. "But the warrant means we can investigate all of your files without delay."

"What does this have to do with Donald's death? You can't possibly believe one of us would harm him," he said. "He was a trusted colleague and brought in a fair amount of business."

"Then he lost some of his clients' money," Ewan said. "Well, not some—a great deal of money."

"Markets go up and down," Burns said. But his eyes had gone wide when Ewan had mentioned losing money. "That is the nature of the beast. When one is in the business, we understand that investing is for the long haul."

He was doing that sort of double-speak people used to confuse others.

Burns glanced furtively at the door. "I have important clients coming in any minute," he said. "This will have to wait."

"I suggest you take your clients somewhere else or use your conference room across the hall. We will be here awhile." Ewan pushed past the man and waved a hand for us to follow. Several of his officers held file boxes.

"Catherine, set up quickly across the hall." Burns sounded exasperated but there was nothing he could do. Ewan wasn't the sort to back down, no matter how he'd been challenged.

And if Burns fought too hard, he would look even guiltier.

I noticed that Ewan's team were putting very little into the boxes in the way of files in Burns's office, but they were taking several photos of the contents.

I sat down in Burns's chair and went through his desk drawers with a pair of gloves on. There wasn't much to find. A bottle of good Scotch in the bottom right drawer, and the assorted office supplies one might expect.

The bottom left drawer held several files, but the inside appeared shorter than the right side. Once again, my skills from watching too many mystery shows made me curious.

"That's strange," I said as I pulled out the files and set them on the desk.

"What's that?" Ewan, who had been going through one of the file cabinets, walked over to me.

"There is something weird about this drawer. There was a small piece of fabric near the front of the drawer, and I pulled up on it. The false bottom lifted and there was a small laptop hidden underneath. Just as there was in Jacks's desk.

I assumed it would be password protected, but I opened the lid just the same. *Property of Donald Jacks* flashed across the screen.

"Why would Burns be hiding his partner's laptop?" I asked. "And how many laptops did our victim have? This is weird, right?"

Ewan's eyebrows went up. "Definitely strange, and a very good question about the multiple computers."

"It is password protected, but I have an idea," I said.

"We have a specialist who can come in from Edinburgh." Ewan frowned. "I dinnae want to chance getting locked out."

"I'll just try twice and then I'll stop. I was able to open the other one, right? Let me give it a try."

Ewan didn't look happy, but he nodded.

I typed in, locomotive, but it didn't work. It beeped loudly, which was annoying.

I glanced up to find Ewan smirking.

"One more and then I'll stop." I typed in trainspotting1, and it worked. I couldn't believe my luck. I'd read in one of my investigative books that most people weren't very clever when it came to their passwords. Of course, Jacks had chosen a different version of the same one.

"I'm in," I said. I clicked on some of the files. They were spreadsheets with loads of numbers and what looked like accounts. But none of it made any sense to me.

I went to his email and, luckily, he was still signed in and had several unopened ones.

"Do you mind if I look through his email?"

"Flag any you think might be interesting."

"Will do."

I was surprised by how many unopened emails he had in the last week. Some were ads, but many of them appeared to be from clients who wanted to know about their investments. His clients sounded worried. If things in Scotland were like home, people usually received monthly or quarterly statements for their investments. Some of the ones he'd already opened showed his clients were quite worried, and he hadn't bothered responding.

One email had me raising my eyebrows. The note was from BlueBird320, and the client was not happy about a recent turn of events where they had lost more than a hundred thousand pounds in one of Jacks's schemes.

One phrase stuck out. *You will pay for what you've done.* The problem was, there wasn't any sort of name on it. Still, it would be easy for Ewan and his team to figure out.

Ewan had walked out of the office, so I flagged it as he mentioned. But I also took a picture of it with my phone.

A few emails down, I found another threatening one. This one from HighlandFarmer26. Again, no name, but threats about losing some of their retirement funds.

While I understood the ups and downs of the market, as I kept track of my own retirement investments, it seemed as though the dead man was more prone to losing his clients' money than making it.

"He wasn't very good at his job," I said under my breath.

"What's that?" Ewan asked as he came back into the room.

"It's like before with the papers we found at his place. For someone in charge of his clients' money, he seemed to lose money in excessive amounts. It looks like one bad investment after another. Most of these emails are from angry people who were ready to kill him. I'm afraid as we go through these, your suspect list will grow. I'm flagging some of them for you."

"Thanks," he said. "We have to think which customers might have been close enough to know about his lip balm habit, and how they would have had the proximity to use the venom."

"Right. But I think it is worth taking a look. The problem is—none of them have actual names."

"Our expert can trace the emails, so that won't be an issue."

I had figured as much. Ewan was right about the proximity, but from what others had said, he used the balm all the time.

One thing dawned on me, and I made a mental note to check. While Scottish weather was harsh on the skin, why was Jacks always using the balms?

I needed to know if he had a medical condition that may have caused the dryness.

My phone dinged with an alarm. I only had an hour before I had to start seeing patients. "I need to go," I said. "I have a full schedule this afternoon."

"I'll have Henry run you down," Ewan said. He took the laptop from me and put it one of the file boxes. "Thank you for your help. Oh, can you write down the password?"

I found a sticky note in the desk and wrote it down. Then I handed it to him.

"Thanks." He smiled.

"You're welcome. Will you let me know if you find out anything else?"

"Yes," he said.

We'd come a long way when it came to trust. I used to have to pry information out of him, but now, more or less, he considered me a colleague. I didn't get the automatic response everyone else did about it being an ongoing case.

As I was walking out of the building with Henry, Angie and her grandfather were going into the accountants' office.

Her eyes went wide when she saw me. "What are you doing here? Do you use this firm?" She asked.

I shook my head. "They are part of the investigation of the murder I was telling you about yesterday on the boat."

"Oh. Ohhhh. I dinnae make the connection." She turned to look at her grandfather. "One of the partners is the fellow who died at the station."

Her grandfather shook his head. "Poor fellow."

"What are you two doing here?" I asked. It came out a bit harsher than I meant. "Are you clients?"

She shook her head. "Not yet. Now that Damian's business matters are more or less settled, we were thinking about making a move to Sea Isle. Well, at least buy a weekend place so I'm not always having to bunk with grandad."

"I told you I don't mind," her grandfather said. They owned a tartan shop that sold all kinds of tartans, kilts, macs, and other outerwear. They had shops all over Scotland, and Angie was in charge of the business. She might have pink hair, but there was a wicked clever brain in that head of hers.

She crooked her arm in his. "I know. Anyway, I thought I might check out an accounting firm here to help keep an eye on the business."

Something must have flashed over my face, because she frowned. "Why? Is there something wrong with the firm?"

"Uh." I was at a loss for words. "I really need to get down the mountain. I have patients to see."

She let go of her grandfather. "You go on inside. I'll be there in a minute."

He seemed confused but she opened the door for him.

Angie grabbed me by the arm and pulled me down the block a bit. "I need you to tell me what is going on. Is there something I should know?"

"I will get in trouble if I say anything," I said. "You know how Ewan is. But as you can see the firm is under investigation."

She pursed her lips. "But that's just because he was murdered, right? You don't think it was someone here at the firm?"

I shrugged. "We honestly don't know. I shouldn't say anything. I'm fairly certain it is against the law. But you are one of my best friends. Just be careful with these people."

"Are they crooked? That's the last thing I need."

"That I can't say. I've looked over some of the paperwork in Jacks's files. I can say several of his clients were not happy with him. I couldn't tell you about the other partner though. Ewan is still taking a look at things. They have brought in an expert."

She frowned. "OK, good to know. I wasn't crazy about moving the accounting to Sea Isle. It's just that grandad likes to feel like he's a part of it all, and he doesn't like going to Edinburgh for the financial side of things."

"I honestly can't say whether you should trust these people or not."

She pursed her lips. "Answer me honestly."

"I will if I can."

"Would you put your money in their hands?"

I cleared my throat. "Uh. No."

"That's good enough for me. I will sit through the meeting, but I won't use them."

"At least, they have some of Jasper's baked goods."

She smiled. "Well, that is a plus."

"Please, don't tell anyone I said anything."

"Mums the word."

* * *

After Henry dropped me off at the clinic, I headed back to the kitchen for some coffee. Then I grabbed my tablet to see who we had coming in.

It was funny how much my life and medical practice had changed over the last year. In the ER, I often saw patients every five to ten minutes.

In Sea Isle, some appointments took more than half an hour and were scheduled accordingly. Nothing was rushed in this town, and I loved getting to know my patients.

And it was a small town, so I'd often see them out and about in Sea Isle.

When I'd first arrived, everything had been a little too different from the weather to the people, but I'd grown to love every bit of it. I had a beautiful old church that was my home and practice. And I had a lovely circle of friends for life, and a town that counted on me. I took that responsibility seriously.

I sat down at my desk with my tablet and coffee, when the front door opened and closed.

"We're here," Abigail called out. "I heard you were at the accounting office this morning. Did you find the killer?"

I smiled. Henry must have been chatting with her.

"Not yet in regard to the killer. I did have an idea for some additional tests I'd like to run," I said as she came into the office.

"I'm curious about his lips. He wasn't dehydrated, but perhaps he had some sort of infection like angular cheilitis or eczema. From what those close to him have said, he used the balm constantly, as in several times an hour. I'm curious as to why."

She nodded. "I'll grab some cells and run the labs."

"Thank you," I said. Abigail really could do anything. "Is Tommy in the garden?"

"Aye, and I need to speak to you about something."

She ducked her head, which meant she was nervous.

"You can tell me anything. Is he OK?"

She waved a hand. "Oh, he's fine. But he wanted to speak to you about growing a vegetable garden in the greenhouse. He says he will use his own money, but he wants to give it a try."

"He will not," I said.

Her head snapped back like I'd slapped her.

"Use his own money," I said quickly. "I'd love to have fresh veggies. I think it is a great idea. But I'll only agree if I can pay for it."

She laughed as she put a hand on her chest. "Oh, that is a relief. Not about the money, just that he can do it. He will not stop talking about this book we checked out at the library about growing organic fruit and vegetables. He wants to ask you himself, but I thought I would give you a heads up, as you like to say."

"I'm happy to talk to him about it." They were family as far as I was concerned. Whatever made them happy was fine with me.

It wasn't long before my first patient arrived.

Almost every conversation started with, "That poor man you found at the train station . . ." or "I know Ewan won't let you say anything . . ."

I'd smile and nod. "Ongoing investigation," I'd add. Of course, that didn't stop the questions or the various summations of what might have happened. Nobody had any real information to add.

That was until my last patient of the day.

Todd was an Englishman, who had moved to Sea Isle a decade ago to raise Highland cows. He often said it was his calling. He'd been a dentist before that.

"This is Horace, our wee addition to the family," he said as he showed me a picture on the phone. The baby cow was furry and adorable. He shared the photos like a proud father. I didn't mind because the fuzzy cows were gorgeous.

"He's so cute," I said.

"Aye. His mum is the one who gave me this." He pointed to his foot, which was still in a cast. "She's a good girl, though. She didn't mean it. My foot was in the wrong place at the wrong time."

I smiled. He spoke about his cows like most people did about their dogs.

"Well, we'll take another X-ray to check, but hopefully we can get that cast off today. Though, I have a boot for you to wear for a few more weeks. It will help your foot to further heal. Promise me you'll wear it. We want those bones to continue to mend. Is your son Angus still helping you?"

"He's a good lad. He's been working hard on the farm since he graduated university. He's helping with the books, and he even set up social media for the herd. I never thought strangers would be so interested in a bunch of cows, but they are. He tells me they are up to seventy-five thousand followers."

I chuckled. "Well, they are very cute cows," I said.

"They are. He's working on merchandise now. Says we need stuffed animal replicas. If it helps support the business, like he says, I'm all for it."

"He sounds brilliant."

"Aye, we are proud of him."

"Heard you were investigating Donald Jacks's death. Terrible business. Do you know how he died?"

"Oh, did he keep your books for the farm?" I asked avoiding his question.

"For a time. But he kept trying to get me to invest in various schemes. He was a pushy sort. As I said, when Angus came home from university, he offered to take over the books, and I let him."

"When was that?"

"Beginning of summer," he said. "Jacks was furious and wasn't particularly kind when we made the change. He was a disagreeable sort. Did someone try to kill him? I only ask because I heard some rumors in the pub that he was murdered." He held up his hands. "Aye, I know it's an ongoing case, but I'm just curious. If he acted like he did with us to his other clients, I could see someone wanting to cause him harm."

"Oh?"

"He wasn't happy about us pulling our business. Said some unkind things to me and Angus. Made me angry, and I told him I'd be telling everyone I knew to pull their accounts from him."

"What did he say to that?" I asked.

"Threatened to take us to court," he said. "And he was serious. Said he'd sue if we besmirched his name. Those were the words he used."

"Before all that happened, what was he like?"

The farmer shrugged. "Bit of a cold fish," he said. "I thought it was because he was an accountant, and he didn't like to talk. But now I know, he was an unfriendly sort."

I nodded. "You and Angus were at the train celebration the night he died. Do you remember seeing anything?"

"The police asked us the same. We didn't even remember seeing him there. It was crowded, though."

"Maybe, you did see him but didn't realize it. He wore a fedora and a trench coat, with black-rimmed glasses."

He frowned.

"What is it?"

"I do remember seeing a man in a trench coat. I thought it was a bit warm for a coat like that indoors."

"Do you remember when or what he was doing?"

Todd's eyebrows went up. "Well, come to think of it, I did see a fellow going into one of the rooms off the main part of the station. There was someone with him. I only saw the backside of them, though. I couldn't tell you if it was a man or a woman. Jacks blocked my view."

"Do you remember what the other person might have worn?"

He sighed. "They wore one of those Scottish caps like the other servers on the train. And a black jacket, but that's all I can remember."

"You didn't see their face?"

"No. I remember wondering if that was the loo, but then I was distracted when the conductor called, 'All aboard.' We hustled onto the train after that. I'd been standing a fair amount of time and was needing to have a good sit."

"And the other person was dressed like the food servers on the train?"

"Yes. Wore a tam, one of those Scottish caps that they all wore. That much I remember."

Had the killer blended in because he'd worn a uniform?

I texted Ewan: *I have news.*

Chapter Fourteen

While it had been a long day, I had promised to go with my friends to the Summer Arts Festival, which was up the mountain. None of us were volunteering tonight, but we wanted to show our support for the carnival and the artists and crafts people who had booths on the site.

I had a longtime love of arts and crafts. I looked forward to picking up some new purchases. Even though it had been almost a year that I had been living and working in the old church, I was still trying to make it my home.

While I didn't like a lot of stuff around, I did have a love of being surrounded by beauty in both the clinic and the house. Making things pretty for patients helped to put them at ease and gave them things to look at while they waited.

Every few months, Abigail helped me switch things around in the patient rooms, so there were always pieces of interest. Those things could open up conversations with patients, who might be curious about the items. Once they were relaxed, they could more easily tell me what was really going on.

I met my friends behind the pub, where the shuttles were stationed to take people up and down the mountain. It was a way to control traffic, and to keep the downtown part of Sea Isle free of too many cars.

With Abigail, Tommy, Mara, Jasper, and Angie with me, we scored a private van.

"I'm sad we're missing a new episode of *Professor T*," Mara said.

"We can watch it tomorrow," I promised.

"No," she said. "Tomorrow is s'mores on the beach. Remember? You contributed to that one. And the big bonfire by the pier."

"I forgot," I said. "Maybe, when this week is over, we can catch up with the good professor." We actually watched several different UK mysteries together. We called them wine and chill evenings, and we usually did them a couple nights a week.

Even though I didn't believe in gossip, it was one of the best ways to keep in touch with what was going on in the town.

"Any news about the murder?" Angie whispered so the driver didn't hear.

I shook my head. "Nothing definitive. One thing I wanted to run by you all is did any of you see the victim with a server at the train party? The person wore one of those Scottish hats that has the pom-pom on top."

They shook their heads.

"Why? Do you think one of the volunteers killed him?" Mara asked. "That's terrible. I have the list of servers if you need it. Well, I already gave it to Ewan."

"I spoke with him, and he and his team are following up," I said. "I only wondered if one of you might have seen the face. The person who told me about the food server outfit only saw them from the back. And if it was our killer, there is a chance they borrowed the outfit for the night."

"The ones who wore those outfits came from the catering company," Mara said. "I'll be honest, I wasn't responsible for checking them in, as they were part of the vendors. I only checked in volunteers and guests."

"So, someone could have snuck in without you knowing?"

She nodded. "And if that person never made it on the train, I wouldn't know," she said. "They could have gone onto the platform but taken one of the paths into the forest behind the station."

I hadn't thought of that. I'd been thinking the killer would have to go back through the front entrance. But the platform behind the station had steps on each side with paths going in different directions. That way people exiting the train didn't necessarily have go back through the building.

That was how the murderer could have escaped. I wondered if Ewan had considered the same thing. Most likely he had. When I texted him earlier, he said he would meet us at the art fair.

And yes, he'd been joining our crime television nights. He sometimes made fun of the procedural elements on a few of the shows, and I'd learned a great deal from him when he explained what was proper.

"I'm surprised you don't have a booth for your pâtisserie," I said to Jasper.

He laughed. "I needed my nights off. I've been baking twenty-four/seven the last few days to keep up with the demand of the festival. Even with help, we've been exhausted."

Jasper's business had grown so much in the past year, I wasn't surprised. Everything he made was delicious.

"I hear you," Mara said. "I'm ready for summer to be over. Though, our summer help will be headed off to university. We have such a strong crew, and they are like family. I mean, who works for free at that age? They all volunteered to help out on the train that night as different characters."

I snapped my fingers. "Maybe, we could ask them if they noticed anything strange that night."

Mara laughed. "I kind of did already, and they didn't remember anything out of the ordinary. But now that we know the person might have been dressed in one of the server uniforms, we can ask. Come by tomorrow before dinner service."

"I'll do that."

The van pulled up to the huge stone library on the edge of town. The fair was in a large field behind the building where several booths had been set up.

"It's loud," Tommy said softly.

Abigail reached into her bag and pulled out his noise-cancelling headphones. He was sensitive to sounds and too many people. They would be sticking to the outskirts, except for the small Ferris wheel in the center of a small carnival. I'd drawn the straw for riding it with him as his sister was not a fan of heights. It was her brother's favorite thing at the carnival.

"Come find me when he's ready," I said. "I'm going to look at some of the art."

"He'll want to play games for a minute and throw all my money away." She laughed.

"You love those games just as much as he does," I said, smiling.

"Aye."

"I'll come with you," Jasper said to Abigail. "Can we start with the ring toss?"

Tommy made a thumbs up.

I laughed.

"I need to find some new art for the pub," Mara said.

"Let's hit that first row," I said looking out over the colorful booths.

The first one featured the glass blowing artists. The fragile pieces from vases to glasses to spears and statues were gorgeous. I recognized the man behind the counter.

"Evening, Doc," Mr. Agnew said. "And Mara, they let you out of the pub tonight."

We laughed. "They occasionally let me have some free time." The joke was she enjoyed every minute she worked at the pub, and she had taken it over so her grandparents could travel more. After working in the corporate world for a while, she loved having her own business.

"Your work is beautiful," I said. We'd talked about his studio when he'd come in a few months ago. I'd meant to get up the mountain to it but hadn't had the time.

"Dinnae be saying that, it'll go to his head," his wife said. Mrs. Agnew was a hoot. While he was the artist, she ran the business side of things and was quite practical.

They laughed as if that was the best joke ever. It was hard not to smile around them. In truth, many times she had told me how proud she was of her husband.

"I love these spheres," I said. The sparkling lights hung from booth to booth, caught some sapphire ones that were mesmerizing.

"They are witches' balls," Mrs. Agnew said. "Long ago they were used to help float sea nets. Nowadays, people put them in baskets or on a stand like this." She held up a brass one.

"I love these," I said. "And I like the idea of having different colors in a basket."

"Lara, five booths down, makes the most beautiful baskets," Mrs. Agnew said. One of the things I so admired about this town was how people looked out for one another.

"I'm thinking this ship needs to go on the back of the bar," Mara said. "I have no idea how you did that with glass."

"Lass, you have great taste," he said. "And 'twas a tricky one."

"I have a glass box on one of the shelves with the liquor," Mara said.

"I know the one," he said. "It will fit."

We made our purchases and Mrs. Agnew promised to deliver them the next day.

We visited several more booths before Jasper came up. "It's your turn with Tommy and the Ferris wheel." He laughed. "I offered, but he wants you."

I nodded. "We've been talking about it for weeks. He thinks it is funny that his sister is afraid of heights. He calls her the bravest woman he knows, except when it comes to Ferris wheels."

"She is," Mara said. "Who else do we know who has been through more, and is as kind and smart as she is?"

"You make a good point."

I headed toward the Ferris wheel where Abigail and Tommy stood waiting. He had an enormous stick of cotton candy but handed it to his sister when he saw me.

I'd loved roller coasters and Ferris wheels when I was a kid. While I'd never considered myself an adrenaline junkie, working in the ER all those years had the same sort of thrill.

But I'd mellowed with age and my new practice as a country doctor was just fine with me. The pace was slower and hours shorter most days.

Helping to solve suspicious deaths in Sea Isle had helped that old adrenaline junkie though. Even if the subject was sad, it was fascinating to be learning new skills at my age. That said, on the investigating side, I still had a way to go.

When we reached the top of the ride, it paused for longer than normal. My guess was Abigail had asked the operator to do that for Tommy. It was one of his favorite things to be up high and have a view of the town's two parts. One part down the mountain by the ocean, the other laid out in front of us.

The scene was like a painting, it was so beautiful everywhere I looked.

Tommy pointed toward the sea, where the full moon was reflected over it.

"Gorgeous," I said softly. I smiled. He saw beauty in so many places, especially in the garden. And many times, he'd share it with me and Abigail. I took my phone out of my pocket and snapped a few pictures. One of which, I would have framed for him.

The ride jolted again and began to roll down. That's when I saw them.

Jeremy, the dead man's partner, seemed to be arguing with Catherine, their assistant. He was shoving a finger in her face, and she slapped it away.

I wonder what that is about?

A movement caught my eye, and to the left of the arguing couple, Ewan stood with his back to them. But I had a feeling he was listening to every word.

On the next round we made on the carnival ride, the couple had moved off, and so had Ewan. I tried to find him but wondered if maybe he had followed them. I was curious to know what they had been arguing about.

When we got off the ride, Tommy asked if I would go on the Gravitron, where we would be sucked to the side of a whirling dervish as the bottom dropped out beneath. It wasn't my favorite ride, but I couldn't disappoint him.

Once the ride took off, I had to remind myself to breathe. While it wasn't easy, I turned my head to the right to see Tommy laughing harder than I'd ever seen him laughing before. I couldn't help but smile at the pure unadulterated joy on his face.

I lived for moments like this where my friends gave me so much happiness just by being themselves and with me. When the ride was over, we were both laughing. We stumbled out of the gate, trying to stay upright and laughing even harder.

Abigail laughed with us as she handed him his headphones back. "You're very brave, Doc."

"I'm not sure brave is the word I'd use."

"Hungry," he said.

We laughed. She'd told me that earlier, in addition to the cotton candy, he'd had two sausages and some Scotch eggs.

"I have to feed the beast again," she joked. She'd been doing that more lately as she'd grown more comfortable around me.

"I saw something earlier, and I need to find Ewan."

She nodded.

I went through the crowds and ran into Jasper near a booth that sold jewelry. Many of the pendants were on leather and were quite beautiful.

"Hey, have you seen Ewan?"

"Not lately. I was about to come and find you, though."

"Oh?"

"This is Malcolm. He used to have his taxes done by your dead man. And he has some interesting thoughts," he whispered the last bit.

Malcolm was helping another customer, so I waited. While I did, I picked out some early Christmas presents for my friends. OK, and maybe a couple of necklaces and bracelets for myself.

Malcolm was young, and totally Jasper's type, which was probably why he hung around.

"This is my friend, Dr. Em. I was telling you about her," Jasper said by way of introduction. "She's one of the ones investigating your accountant's death."

I shook Malcolm's hand.

"Was he killed?" he asked me.

"Why do you ask?"

"That's the rumor going around town," he said. "And the police do not usually investigate natural deaths. I've seen our good ACC speaking with several people tonight. And I may have heard a snippet or two."

"Everyone in this town thinks they are an investigator," Jasper said.

We laughed.

"So, he did your taxes?"

"Aye, for the last few years."

"What can you tell me about him?"

He shook his head. "Not too much. He was very professional, but a bit of an odd duck."

"In what way?"

"When we were going over my taxes last year, I made a joke. I said, well, that leaves me just enough to buy my nephew a new train set for his birthday."

"For the next hour he went off about trains, and what I should buy him. It was the longest conversation, though one-sided, that we'd ever had. He wasn't what you would call a conversationalist, until we started talking about trains."

That didn't surprise me since trains had been his passion.

"Did he ever try to get you involved in one of his financial schemes?"

Again, he shook his head. "I barely keep my head above water with my jewelry business. By the time I pay travel expenses to various fetes, I break even but that works for me. I dinnae need much, and I get to do what I love. So, he probably wouldn't have asked. I never have much extra, and what I do have I put into a very safe retirement account."

His face seemed familiar to me. "Were you at the opening of the Storyteller's train?"

"Aye, I was. That's where I met Jasper. I was gobbling up his macarons. They were heavenly."

I glanced at my friend, who blushed.

"Right? I've gained a good five pounds since I met him." That wasn't a joke, but we laughed.

"Do you remember seeing Mr. Jacks that night? Maybe, before we boarded?"

His face scrunched up as if he were thinking. "Was he dressed in an old-timey detective outfit in a trench and fedora?"

I nodded.

"Then yes, I saw him across the room. I think he was talking to one of the waitstaff handing out champagne. I can't recall the other person's face, though."

That was the second time someone had mentioned someone in the servers' uniforms.

"Did you notice anything else?"

"When he turned, his face was very red. I remember that. I couldn't imagine what had made him so angry. He always seemed a bit drab and unemotional when we spoke. He dinnae get excited about anything besides trains."

So, he had been arguing with whoever had been in that uniform.

There had been a photographer there that night. I wondered if he had perhaps taken pictures that might help us identify who had been wearing that outfit.

It seemed unlikely the normally even-tempered accountant would get angry at a waiter over a glass of champagne.

I made my purchases and thanked Malcolm.

"Thank you so much." He handed me a card and then smiled as he gave one to Jasper. "Feel free to call if you need anything."

I grinned at Jasper, who had turned red again. It was sweet that he had a new crush.

Like me, he'd had his heart broken. He had come to Sea Isle to heal and open his pâtisserie. I didn't know the guy who broke his heart, but I was grateful that Jasper had chosen to come back to the town where he grew up. He'd become one of my dearest friends.

As we walked away, he had a silly grin on his face.

"Are you going to call him?"

His eyes went wide. He waved a hand. "No. I'm not ready for anything like that."

I didn't push. I couldn't blame him. I was still nursing a broken heart myself. My husband had been living a double life, which was something I only discovered the day he died.

Trusting again had been difficult. Though, my friends here had helped. As had Ewan. But I would never tell him that. He was a good man and looked out for his town.

We'd been spending more time together. Well, as a group. When he came over to watch our shows with us, though, I'd never been the one to invite him. Mara had. She also always included him if we went out together.

While he and I often argued, we'd grown closer. He too had a past, which had made it difficult for him to trust anyone, as well. That, and his job didn't help.

Not that there was much crime in Sea Isle, but he had seen the worst of it.

"There's Ewan." Jasper pointed to a booth where it looked like he was buying Tommy a hot pretzel.

"Tommy is going to have a stomachache before the night is done."

"I doubt it," Jasper said. "He is a bottomless pit and never gains an ounce. It isn't fair."

"True," I said.

We laughed, and then walked over to the booth.

"You know, you don't have to date him. You could just call him to be friends."

He sighed. "Maybe."

"There she is," Abigail said. "Ewan was wondering where you were."

I held up the bag of jewelry. "I was doing a bit of early holiday shopping. I was looking for you," I said.

"To go shopping with you?" Ewan joked.

I rolled my eyes.

"I saw you from the Ferris wheel and wondered if you'd overheard anything."

"Let's talk over there," he said. He motioned to a spot behind the booths that was free of nosy listeners.

I waved goodbye to my friends and followed him over.

Without asking, he tore his pretzel in half and handed it to me.

I smiled. "Thanks. But this is not going to shut me up. I saw they were arguing. Did you learn anything interesting? And how about the search of their offices? Did you find anything yet?"

"They were arguing about our visit, though it seemed like she was more worried about what we might find than he was."

"What did they say?"

"She is ready to quit. She doesn't want to get arrested for playing any part in schemes that might have led to Jacks's death."

"So, are they involved in some sort of illegal game?"

He shrugged. "Other than that some of the numbers don't match up, it is hard to say. I'm still waiting for the forensic accountant to take a look at what we've found. She should know more tomorrow."

He nodded. "Luckily, she's great at her job. They've expanded the department in Edinburgh because there is so much white-collar crime these days. She said late tomorrow she should know more. Maybe then, we'll get some answers."

"It does seem odd that Jacks would have two different sets of numbers. We can at least agree on that."

"Aye. But I need solid evidence. You know how it works."

I was learning. Pesky evidence.

"Do you think one of them killed him?"

"Hard to say. They seemed surprised, truly so, that he might have been murdered when we made the initial calls. Though, they may just be good liars."

"That reminds me, we haven't released anything about how he died. Maybe, you can catch them up that way. If they know more about how he died than they should, it might show on their faces."

Ewan chuckled. "Thank you, Agatha Christie, we'll keep that in mind when we're speaking with them."

"You joke, but I'm taking that as a compliment. She was a brilliant writer and criminologist in her own right. No one gave her enough credit."

"She used poison for most of her deaths."

I rolled my eyes again. "Not always. Sometimes people were shoved down the stairs. Besides, poison makes sense. It's easily found and used. And as you pointed out on a previous case, poison being used mostly by women is a misconception."

"True," he said.

"So, do you have any other suspects?"

"We're looking into some of his clients. Especially, the ones where he lost a large amount of funds with his schemes."

"That makes sense. I spoke with one of his other clients."

I told him about Malcolm.

"What else did he say?"

"Basically, the same thing as everyone we've talked to about the case. That he was quiet, until the subject of trains came up."

Ewan nodded.

"Malcolm didn't have enough to invest, so he wasn't upset with him. While we haven't found any evidence that he had a girlfriend or boyfriend, have you discounted that? I mean, he seemed to keep to himself. But maybe there was someone who shared his interest."

"Why do you ask that?"

"I don't know. It seems odd that he was arguing with one of the waiters from the other night. More than one person saw them arguing. Maybe, it wasn't over money."

He sighed. "It is possible. Though I feel certain money was the motivation here."

"You're probably right. I remember what you said about assuming. I have a habit of deciding early on why someone was killed, and I learn later that it had nothing to do with my early assumptions. I want to keep an open mind."

He grinned.

"What?"

"You're learning. Until we have evidence pointing us one way or another, it is a good idea to keep an open mind."

"And here's you thinking I never listen."

He chuckled. Then just as quickly, he frowned.

I turned to see what he was looking at.

The victim's sister was arguing with Jeremy, the partner, and she didn't look happy.

What was that about?

Chapter Fifteen

Ewan had to take a call and walked away. I was curious about what was going on between the sister and Jacks's partner. I headed that way. They were close to some of the food booths, so I stood there listening, but acted as though I was trying to decide what I wanted.

"You cannae tell me there is no money to be had," she said. "You were partners."

"I am not sure how many times you need me to say that he lost a great deal of our clients' money," he said. "We are still climbing out of the hole left by his bad investments. And he never invested his own funds. There is no money."

She huffed. "Says you. But you were partners, and I know that he went over everything with you. He wasn't the only one investing."

"How would you know anything? You haven't spoken to him in a year," the partner sneered. "We were more his family than you. All you want is money. You dinnae care a wit for your brother."

She pointed at him. "You are a thief. How will your clients react when they find out you refused to give me what money is owed. I know he used some of his own funds for investments, and they were not all bad. The last time we talked he was telling me about some development happening outside of Edinburgh. He asked if I might be interested, to which I said no, given what happened the last time I invested my money with you."

"You have no idea what you are talking about," he said.

"Yes, and there is a difference between short term and long, where your money is supposed to accrue," Kaitlyn Jacks said. "You wouldn't have used the firm's funds in your schemes. I know that because he told me. I want what rightfully belongs to our family. And I'll sue to get it if I have to."

Burns sneered again. "He always said the only thing you cared about was money. When that investment went bad, he knew you would never let him forget it. But that doesn't mean he owed you anything."

"We'll see what my lawyer has to say about that."

He laughed but it wasn't a happy sound. "Waste your money, go ahead. He signed a contract when he joined the firm. You'll find you aren't owed a cent." His tone was vicious and unnecessary.

He stormed away. He'd been smarmy when I'd seen him at his office. I didn't trust him. But was he a killer? And what would be his motive?

Money. Maybe the forensic accountant would find something that would help us nail down the suspects.

Kaitlyn bent down and put her hands on her knees. It appeared she was having trouble breathing.

I went to her. "Are you OK?"

"I'm having trouble catching my breath," she said between wheezes.

"Come sit down." I guided her to one of the tables set up for people to eat.

Had Burns done something to her?

"Do you have any allergies, like your brother?" I asked. As I helped her to the chair.

She shook her head.

"My chest is tight," she said between trying to take great gulps of air.

"Are you prone to panic attacks?"

"I dinnae know," she said. "Never had one."

"Lean onto the table and put your forehead on your hands. Count to four as your breath in, and I'll do it with you. One. Two. Three. Four. Now breathe out. And again."

It didn't take long to regulate her breathing. She sat up, and the color returned to her face.

"Thank you," she said. "That's never happened to me before."

"Do you suffer from anxiety? I only ask because if you do, it can make you prone to panic attacks, which is what you just experienced."

She shrugged. "Not any more than the next person. We all have anxiety, right?"

I nodded. "True, but sometimes it can affect us emotionally and physically. I saw that you were arguing with Mr. Burns. That kind of stress could bring it on. Do you want to talk about it?"

"Not really. He's a slimy—I have no idea why my brother went into business with him. From what I understood, he never liked the bloke. But he wanted to live here in Sea Isle and couldn't see opening an accounting firm to compete. So, they joined forces."

"That makes sense. We are a small town."

"But now, he's saying the family is owed nothing. That cannot be true. Yes, my brother made some bad investments, including with my retirement fund, but he also helped the firm to make money."

"I'll be honest," I said. "I have no idea how any of that works. I'm lucky to have a great guy who handles all of my investments in the states."

I pursed my lips. "I shouldn't tell you this," I whispered. "But the police have a forensic accountant who will be going through everything. I'm sure if you're owed money, they will be able to figure that out. You should speak to the ACC, though, and let him know how you feel. That way he can make certain you receive what you're owed, if the evidence proves your allegations. I have no idea about the financial side of things. I'm only thinking about your brother."

She gave me a watery smile. "Thank you, Doctor—on all accounts. I thought I might have had a heart attack earlier."

I nodded. "It can feel that way when your chest tightens. Anxiety can often come out of nowhere. It has been a very stressful few days with the death of your brother and trying to deal with everything. Even if you had been on the outs, it is obvious you cared about him."

She sighed, and then shoved a hand through her hair. "I know we weren't that close, but he was the only family I had left in the world.

"And yes, we'd been estranged because of what happened with my money. But I couldn't quite write him out of my life. I liked at least knowing he was there."

"That makes sense."

"Do you know if they have any idea yet if someone tried to kill him?"

"Even if I knew, I wouldn't be able to say, as I'm a part of the team investigating his death."

"Yes, but that says it all, right?"

"What do you mean?"

"If his death hadn't been suspicious, why investigate? And why keep me out of his home?"

"Those are good questions, and I wish I could answer. I understand you didn't speak much, but do you know if he had someone else in his life?"

"Like a girlfriend?"

"Or boyfriend."

She chuckled. "I wouldn't know, but I doubt it. He never dated even when he was younger. Numbers and trains are all he's ever cared about. Why do you ask?"

I shrugged. "When we were in his home, he seemed to be a bachelor, but one never knows."

"Even if he were seeing someone, he wouldn't have told me."

"I had to ask," I said. "Are you feeling better?"

She took a deep breath. "Yes, thank you."

"Why don't you come by and see me at the office tomorrow."

"Oh, I'm not interested in taking medicine. I'm sure this is all temporary."

"I am, as well. But I thought we might go over some breathing exercises in case it does happen again."

"Oh. Uh. Thanks, that is kind of you."

I handed her a card from my bag. "You can make an appointment online or call. It is up to you."

"Any idea when I'll be able to take my brother back to Edinburgh?"

"Once the investigation wraps up, and we've finished with the testing. I'd say by the end of the week at the earliest."

She nodded. "It's weird."

"What's that?"

"I've been so angry at him for so long, but now I'm sad. I wasted so much time being mad at him. I loved him, and I will miss him."

"I can imagine. I felt that way when I lost my mom and grandmother. They were the last of my family, and I felt so alone."

"Is that why you moved across the pond? I mean, it's obvious you are American."

"Moving here was one of the best things I've ever done for myself."

"I've been so stuck in Edinburgh. Maybe I should make a move."

"You're the only one who can make that decision. I will say, it isn't such a bad thing to shake up your life every once in a while."

"You might be right about that. Thank you again for your help. I'm exhausted. I think I'll head back to the B&B."

I nodded, and then went in search of my friends.

They were all coming off the merry-go-round.

I smiled when they came through the gate onto the fairway.

"Did you have fun?"

They were all laughing.

"We did. Tommy tried to tell us that the ride was only for small children," Mara said. "He thought it was too much of a kiddie thing for adults to do. We showed him how wrong he was."

"I still like the Graviton better and the Ferris Wheel," Tommy said before putting his headphones back on.

We laughed again.

Everyone was tired, so we headed to the shuttle to take us back down the mountain.

After speaking with Donald Jacks's sister, I didn't think she had anything to do with his murder. It was more a feeling than anything to do with evidence.

But someone had wanted him dead. And it could have been his business partner, the executive assistant or one of their angry clients.

The problem was, which one was responsible for his death?

Chapter Sixteen

While I'd come up with the idea for s'mores at the bonfire the next night, I hadn't volunteered to help out. But I was curious about what they called The Burning Ritual. The event had been around for more than 800 years in Sea Isle.

I had read a book from the library about how it was believed to have been started by the pagans, who used fire to bring on the new harvest.

In Sea Isle, they liked to keep their traditions, no matter what religious background they might have. But The Burning Ritual had turned into a way for people to write down their regrets or things they wanted to remove from their lives. Then they tossed them into a fire. They used a special flash paper that burned cleanly, so it wasn't harmful for the environment.

I headed down to the pier that evening to see how it all worked.

There were several smaller fires on the beaches where people were making s'mores and doing their own form of the ritual.

At the pier, well, beside it, a huge bonfire had been built below. I took the stairs down to the sandy beach where everyone had gathered.

There were several writing stations set up around the huge fire. People with baskets would gather the folded notes they were given, and then toss them into the fire.

The crowd would say, "hurrah," every time a basket full of paper was tossed.

While I'd let go of most of my regrets long ago, there was one part of my life I was ready to say goodbye to. I'd dealt with the betrayal of my former husband through therapy, but I didn't think it would hurt to say one last goodbye.

I wrote down: *I forgive you and myself.* For so long, I'd felt dumb for being fooled by him. But we all make mistakes, and often trusted without question those we loved. But I was finished with that feeling. I folded my note and tossed it in the basket when it came around.

Not long after, the papers were tossed in the fire, and I joined in on the hurrah. Strangely, I did feel lighter. Maybe, there was something to this burning ritual.

A text beeped on my phone, and I pulled it out.

On the beach in front of the pub. Come get s'mores. Mara had texted. *I have news.*

She didn't mention what the news was about, but I assumed it was the case. Abigail and I spent the short amount of downtime we had at the office to go back over the tests. We were still waiting on DNA evidence, which took longer than the rest.

We were able to prove conclusively he was killed by bee venom. We'd also found venom in a few more of his products. All of which, had come from Kiara's shop.

I liked Kiara a great deal, and I couldn't imagine her killing anyone. I was certain the venom had been added after the products had been bought from her store.

What I didn't know was why? Did the murderer mean to implicate the store owner to take the focus off themselves? And why target Kiara? Was it just a matter of convenience?

I found Mara and the rest of our gang, minus Angie, who had gone to Glasgow for business, near a large fire exactly where she said.

"Did you lose all your regrets?" Jasper asked. "That's what I use the burning for, at least."

"I try not to have regrets, as I prefer to see every mistake as a lesson. But yes. I let go of the last piece of my past."

"That is why you are so wise, and I make pastries," he joked. "I always have regrets. Sometimes it's having one pint too many. Other times it is falling in love with the wrong person."

"You are not alone with any of that. I did let go of some of the things I'd been holding onto from my past. We will see how that goes. Sometimes the past likes to hold on tight."

"So true," Abigail said. She and Tommy sat on a couple of beach chairs. "I'm still working on that."

She had a difficult upbringing and had become Tommy's caregiver at an early age. While she didn't see it in herself, she was one of the strongest women I knew.

One of the things I loved about my friends was that I could talk to them about anything. They did the same with me. Mara jokingly called it friend therapy, and she wasn't wrong.

I often spoke to my patients about the importance of having a good support system, and I had one of the best since I'd moved here. I wasn't sure I'd been closer to a group of people in all my life, and I was beyond grateful for them.

"We waited for you to make the s'mores," Mara said.

"Well let's get to it." I took one of the sticks she'd gathered.

"I want you to know I've developed a new skill," Jasper said. "Mara made me whittle the ends so the marshmallows would stick."

We laughed.

"Soon you'll be making bears and lions out of wood," Mara joked. "It is a good skill to have."

"So, how long do you keep them in the fire?" Abigail asked.

"It depends. I like a bit of burnt on mine, so I wait till they catch fire and then blow it out. Some people like it to be slightly melted or golden brown. It's personal preferences. And we have graham crackers in the US, so it will be fun using your Scottish biscuits."

"Maybe, we should try all the ways," Mara suggested with a grin.

"Agreed," Jasper said. "It is chocolate and marshmallow—what can go wrong?"

"I dinnae like fire," Tommy said from his chair where he played his video game. He hadn't bothered taking off his headphones, which he wore most of the time when he was out in public.

"I'll do it," Abigail said.

After two s'mores, and a cup of coffee, I settled back in my chair. Along the beach, families had put together their own fires. Everyone was making s'mores. I felt like I had made a great contribution to my town.

"OK, I say these should be a part of our weekly get-togethers," Mara said. "We can make them in Em's fireplace."

The others nodded in agreement.

"I'm not sure how you have all survived so long without them."

"My guess is people will be stopping by tomorrow to thank you," Jasper said. "Be prepared."

We laughed again. My shoulders dropped about three inches as I breathed in the sea air, mixed with the burning embers in the fire. It was chilly but beautiful.

"So, you said you had some gossip," I said to Mara.

"Well, you mentioned last night that you'd seen the victim's sister arguing with the other partner. Today, she and the executive assistant had lunch in the pub."

"Oh? How did that go?"

"We were so busy. I couldn't catch much of what they were saying. But they seemed friendly enough. I did hear the sister thanking the assistant for looking into things. They even hugged when the lunch was over."

I raised my eyebrows. That was interesting.

"Did you get the idea they maybe already knew one another before his death?"

"I couldn't say," Mara continued. "But they did seem friendly, which I thought was odd given what you said about the partner last night. Do you think maybe the partner really is the murderer?"

I bit my lip and shook my head. "He was out of town the night of Jacks's death. He has an alibi."

"Could be more than one person," Jasper offered. "We've seen that before. Maybe he poisoned the victim, and someone working with him shoved him into that closet."

The group went quiet as I stared at him.

"What?"

"How do you know all that?

Jasper laughed loud. "I run a pâtissier that is very popular with the police. They talk to one another without any fear of who might be around. That, and from what you've told us, I can put the puzzle pieces together. I mean, what kind of amateur detective would I be, if I couldn't at least do that?" he joked.

I snorted. "Well, just make sure if Ewan questions you, you don't bring me up in that conversation. He's not fond of the fact I include you guys in the investigations. And I promised him I wouldn't tell you everything.

"But it's not my fault you are all brilliant."

Mara held up her coffee cup. "*Slainte Mhath* to that."

"When I took my afternoon walk, I saw Ewan in Kiara's shop. She was crying," Mara said. "I may have hung around the pier across the street and waited for him to leave. But when I went in, her assistant was at the counter. I asked after Kiara, and she said her boss wasn't feeling well."

"I just saw her at the pier with her son," I said. "She seemed fine. I wonder what Ewan said to upset her?"

My friends stared at me expectantly.

"Fine." I huffed. "I'll ask him tomorrow. I hope he doesn't think she did this. I mean what kind of motive would she have?"

They shrugged.

The wind picked up, as the clouds covered the starry sky above. The temperature dropped several degrees in a few minutes.

"Looks like a storm is coming," Jasper said as he doused the fire.

The rest of us stood and helped clean up our area. The police would be patrolling the beach to make sure everyone did their part when it came to the clearing of the fires and party gear.

As we headed up the sand to the street, Ewan walked by.

He nodded at me. "Doc, I need to talk to you."

I waved goodbye to my friends and followed him up the hill.

"What about?"

He glanced around. "Let's wait until we get inside your place. Not as many ears."

I nodded.

When we arrived at my place, we paused.

The door to my clinic was open.

"Uh. I know I locked it when I left. And Abigail and Tommy were already gone."

He stuck his hand up. "Stay here," he whispered.

I nodded, but then wondered if I might be safer closer to the guy with the gun. Even though it was dark outside, I'd left a few lights on in the interior part of my home.

But the office was draped in shadows. Still, it was easy to see that someone had been searching through the paper files. What an outsider wouldn't know was those were old. Everything that was current with our patients was stored on the computers and protected with several layers of security needing authentication, to which only Abigail and I had the passwords.

"I wonder what they were looking for?" I whispered.

"Normally, I'd say drugs in a medical office, but they were searching through the files. So, information."

My office was more of the same. I didn't keep much paper in there, but it was obvious someone had gone through my documents and moved stuff around. Some of it was on the floor. Nothing was broken, it was just a lot of mess.

I followed him back to where we had all of our tech and machines for labs and such. The bookshelf that hid the secret door was still locked. There was a security code to get in now, which had been added when we'd been broken into the last time.

"Thank goodness," I said.

While paper could be replaced, we had several thousand pounds-worth of equipment back there.

Then I followed him through my house.

The pharmacy door was locked tight. There were two deadbolts, and a key card was needed to get inside. While I couldn't imagine anyone in Sea Isle breaking in for drugs, we had a lot of visitors in the summer.

Except for the extra locks, the door looked like some kind of pantry.

"OK, so not drugs," Ewan grunted.

"Or they couldn't find them," I said. "But you're right. It does look like they may have been searching for information. But why?"

"They want to know how much we've discovered so far," he said. He shook his head. I think he might have been more upset than I was over the intrusion and that was saying something.

Even though this sort of thing had happened before, it still felt like the worst kind of violation of privacy. I had cameras and locks to keep the place secured. And Sea Isle was normally so much safer than anywhere else I'd lived.

This kind of thing only seemed to happen when there was a dead body involved.

We went through the kitchen and to the freezer I called the autopsy room.

The keypad had been smashed, but the door was locked.

"You don't think they stole the body again." That had happened on my first case here in town. The killer had stolen the body and dropped it at sea. More than likely hoping that it would never be found, but he had bad luck in that regard. The ocean currents had not been in his favor.

Ewan tried to shove the door open, but it wouldn't budge. Without the keypad it was impossible to get inside.

"Well, if it's that difficult, then they probably didn't make it through the door."

"Most likely. I'm calling my team."

It had been a long day of work and a full evening. I couldn't help but yawn.

"Let me check your room upstairs and you can go to sleep," he said. "I'll take care of all this."

"I'm tired but now I have a good case of the nerves. Who would break into my office and why did they want the body?"

"Well, let's take a look at the camera video and see if we can find out."

Chapter Seventeen

We went back to the front office and Ewan handed me a pair of gloves from his pocket. "We'll need to fingerprint everything, so use these to get into Abigail's computer," he said.

I nodded.

I put on the gloves. Then I typed in the password and used my phone for the authentication code. Abigail had put in several fail-safe measures for this reason.

Once the screen popped up, I clicked on the video file.

I sighed when I saw the figure dressed in black.

"Why do they always wear hoodies and dark clothing." It had been so dark outside that it was difficult to even see the figure, who kept their head down.

"The outside light didn't come on," I said.

Ewan went through the front door. "Busted," he said. "They knew what they were doing. And you didn't set the alarm before you left, or it would have notified you and us. We've talked about that."

He wasn't wrong. I'd been in a rush and running late. "I must have forgotten."

Whoever it was had definitely been looking for something. We had one camera facing Abigail's desk. Whoever it was didn't even try to get into the computer. They went through the paper files. Tossing most of them on the floor.

"They are keeping their head down," I said. "It seems like someone who has been here before and knows I have cameras. And they didn't come through the front door. Maybe, the back?"

"We'll check. Or just a clever criminal, who would know to look out for them."

He wasn't wrong.

Ugh. This was so annoying.

"You're better at this than I am," I said. "Can you tell if the hooded figure is male or female?"

He shook his head.

"Could be female or a smaller male."

"That doesn't really narrow things down. They have to be after information concerning Jacks's murder, right?"

He shrugged.

I sighed. "I know, we should never assume."

"Exactly."

"Did this ever happen with the former doctor? Why do people keep breaking into my office and home?"

"It did a few times but most of them were teens or someone looking for drugs."

"This is supposed to be my safe haven," I said. It was frustrating. And I wasn't easily frustrated, except for these times when someone wanted to mess with my Zen to commit a crime.

"I don't understand why they would go after the body. It is days after the murder, and we've run all of our tests. We are waiting for some of the results. It doesn't make sense."

"While I won't make an assumption, my guess is they were after information. Perhaps something they thought might be in the clothing or the body. Or it might be the labs. They want to know what you figured out so far."

I snapped my fingers.

"What is it?"

"I'm sure Abigail went through the clothing. We should check the evidence bags to see what's in there. Maybe he was carrying something in that coat he wore."

"Abigail is always thorough, if she found something suspicious, she would have told us."

"True, but we were moving quickly that night. It's possible she didn't think it was that important."

Henry was the first one through the door. "Evening, Doc. Sorry about this."

"Thanks," I said.

He carried a large kit that they used for evidence gathering. More of Ewan's officers followed not long after.

"I need you to make me a copy of the security tape, and we'll go over it again. Oh, and let's check the autopsy door cam."

I clicked on the separate file. The light was a bit better back there because I'd left the kitchen lamp on. The person was smart enough to keep their head down, though. And they wore gloves. If we could see the hands, it would have helped. It seemed like the hands were larger and perhaps male. But it was impossible to tell.

There was a moment when the burglar turned their head and a short bit of black hair shone under their cap.

"Who have we been talking to that has dark hair?" I paused the video to show Ewan.

His eyebrows rose. "The partner," he said.

I nodded. "But why? He isn't even a suspect, right? He had an alibi."

"True. The killer could have hired someone, though. If it is him, he could be trying to clean up a mess left by someone else. It is within the realm of possibility."

"True."

"But it is also a reach. There are many people with dark hair in Sea Isle. Let us get on with things," he said. "Why don't you go up to your room and get some rest."

"Ewan, someone just broke into my home and business. I will not be able to go to sleep."

He crossed his arms and stared down at me. He had that please-do-what-I-ask-just-this-once look on his face.

"But I will stay out of your team's way while you do your job."

"Thank you."

I picked up my purse off the desk and went into my living room where I dumped it on the side table.

More than anything, I wanted to make my way into the autopsy room to go through the evidence bags, but with the security panel broken and part of the crime scene, it would have to wait.

I flipped on the television and put on an episode of *Agatha Raisin* I'd seen many times. I loved the M.C. Beaton books, and the television show they had adapted from them. It was what Mara called murder-lite and comfort television. Quaint English village with a great group of friends, who solved crimes together.

Yes, it was familiar.

At some point, I must have dozed off. Funny, since my home was full of officers, but it had been a long day.

When I woke, the room was dark, and the television was off. Someone had covered me in a blanket, but I'd fallen asleep in a weird position and my shoulder was killing me.

I sat up to find Ewan asleep on the other end of the couch. He hadn't wanted to leave me alone. Even though we often disagreed, he was very protective of me. I appreciated that he cared enough to know that I was unsettled by the break-in.

I checked my watch to see that it was six, which was about an hour earlier than I usually woke up.

After a quick shower, and a change of clothes, I headed back downstairs. The sofa Ewan had been on was empty, but the scent of coffee wafted in from the kitchen.

I found him at the coffee maker waiting patiently for it to brew.

"Mornin'," he said.

"Thank you for staying over. You didn't have to do that."

"I'm going to have one of us here until we solve the case," he said.

"Do you think that's necessary? Since they were unsuccessful, they probably won't come back."

"We have no way of knowing exactly what it was they were after. And it is for your safety, as well as Abigail and Tommy."

I'd known him long enough to understand he wouldn't back down.

"OK. I need to know who to call in order to get the security system on the autopsy lab fixed."

"I've already taken care of it. They'll be here in an hour. As will Henry. He'll be working from your office today."

I smiled. "Abigail will be happy about that." After a moment, I asked, "Did they find any fingerprints or fibers from the person who broke in?"

"No. They wore gloves. We saw that in the security video."

"Is there any way we can get into the autopsy suite?"

He shook his head. "Solid steel door, and with the mechanism jammed, it's impossible. We tried a couple of times last night."

There was a click at the back door, and we both stiffened. Ewan took a step forward, just as Abigail and Tommy came into the kitchen.

It was comical the way her eyes went wide at the sight of Ewan and then me. Her eyebrows went up, and Tommy, who was staring down at his handheld game bumped into her.

"I. Uh."

"There was a break-in," Ewan said quickly.

"Again?" She asked exasperated. "Why dinnae you call me, Em? I could have come and stayed with you. What did they take?"

"It was late, and I didn't want to bother you," I said. "As far as we know, they didn't take anything."

"That may be something you can help us with," Ewan said. "Do you remember when you were going through Jacks's clothing if there was anything of interest? Something maybe other than the lip balm?"

She blew out a breath. "If I did, it would be in the evidence bags in autopsy. I'll go check."

"You can't get in," I said, and then I explained what happened.

"Oh. Bother. Why can't people mind their business? Do we think it's the killer? That means the Doctor isn't safe." She constantly worried about me. I wasn't sure the last time in my life I had someone who was so concerned with my welfare. All my new friends were like that. I was extremely lucky.

"I'm fine," I said.

Ewan explained that there would be an around-the-clock watch until the killer was caught.

Her shoulders, which had bunched up with stress, eased down a few inches at the mention of Henry coming to work from the office.

"I thought with all the precautions we took after the last time, this wouldn't happen." She stared pointedly at Ewan.

"The security team will be back today, and I'm having them put more cameras in the office area, and back door near the autopsy room."

She nodded.

"Do I get a say as to where cameras go in my home and business?" I asked.

They stared at me.

"OK, then. As long as they aren't in the bedroom or bathroom, and as long as we are the only ones with access."

"How did they get through the front door?"

"They didn't," he said.

That was news to me. The front door had been open when we'd arrived the night before.

"They exited that way. But they came in through the kitchen window, which wasn't locked."

He pointed to the large window that overlooked the cemetery in the backyard. It had been stuffy in the kitchen earlier, and I'd forgotten to close it. As for the cemetery, I'd long ago come to terms with my fellow residents, who were dead. So much so, that I often forgot they were out there.

"The window hadn't been locked?" Abigail asked.

I pursed my lips. Then I sighed.

They turned toward me.

"It was stuffy in here yesterday even though it was cool outside." The AGA stove was always on, which was great in the winter but could make it too toasty in the summer months.

"I think I shut it before I left last night, but I must have forgotten to lock it. Sorry. I'll be more careful in the future."

They both looked at me with disappointment.

I wanted to say people make mistakes, but I knew better. I should have locked the window.

"Garden," Tommy said. He'd been so quiet I'd forgotten he was standing there. He handed his headphones and game to his sister and then bolted out the back door.

I smiled. He didn't like any sort of drama or confrontation. I didn't blame him. I was about to bow out with my own exit.

"I'm starving and need a full Scottish. Do you want me to bring something back from the pub for either of you?"

He shook his head. "I'm going. I'll give you a ride down the hill. Henry is five minutes out." He turned back to Abigail. "Again, he'll be working from your office today, if that's OK."

Her cheeks turned a dark pink. "I'll make a place for him," she said and then cleared her throat. "When they open the autopsy suite, he and I can go through the evidence we collected and bundle it up for you to have at the station," she continued. "I was already going to do that today. We should also have all the DNA tests back in the next twenty-four hours.

"Ewan, you might be able to rush the ones I sent to Edinburgh along."

He nodded.

I loved this bossy side of Abigail. It didn't come out too often, but she had blossomed over the last year and was much more confident. It was a lovely thing to behold—even if she was bossing me around as well.

* * *

The ride down the hill with Ewan was a short one.

"Thanks," I said, as I went to open the door.

"Wait," he said, and then jumped out of the SUV. When he came around to my side, he opened the door. "There is something I need to ask you."

"About the case?" I couldn't imagine there was anything we hadn't already discussed.

"No. Uh." He never stammered over his words.

"What is it? Is something wrong? Are you feeling OK?"

"I'm fine. It is nothing like that."

Then he just stood there with the most uncomfortable look on his face.

"We sometimes disagree, but you know you can tell me anything," I said softly.

Something seemed to be troubling him in a big way, and he was nervous. I'd never seen him like this.

He took a deep breath. "Right. I need a date for a gala my mother is throwing on Friday night. I wondered if you might come with me."

Is he asking me out on a date? I'm sure my eyes were wide as saucers.

"Uh." I couldn't quite form a sentence as my mind traveled in so many directions at once it was impossible to answer intelligently.

Why me? That was the real question I wanted to ask. He was good-looking and wealthy and sometimes went out with beautiful Sottish celebrities.

"It's for a children's charity," he said quickly. "If I bring a date, then I don't have to worry about my mother trying to fix me up with the daughter of one of her friends."

I chuckled. "I see. That's so flattering."

He sighed again. "I'm making a mess of this. To be honest, there isn't anyone I'd rather go with." He cleared his throat. "That's what I meant to say. You're intelligent and beautiful. I'll be the luckiest man there."

He was being sweet. It was odd, but I smiled. "Is it black-tie?"

"It's my mother so very formal, yes."

"I see." Then I frowned.

"What is it?" he asked.

I glanced down at my phone. "I can't remember if I volunteered for something with the festival on Friday night."

I pulled up my calendar on my phone. I wasn't sure if I wanted to find I was already busy or not. I liked Ewan, more than I would ever admit, but he made me nervous.

Friday was enjoy-the-carnival night, which I'd already been to with the rest of the gang.

"I guess, I'm free."

"Good. I'll pick you up at six, and it will be a late night. You might want to pack an overnight bag. We'll stay at my mother's."

"OK."

"Thanks, Em. You're a good one." He shut the door and then went to the other side and hopped in the SUV.

He drove away.

I stood there like an idiot staring after him wondering if I'd just imagined the whole scenario.

A few minutes later, I headed into the pub and sat down at the bar.

"Earth to Em," Mara whispered.

I shook my head. "Sorry, were you talking to me?"

"Asked for your order. Is everything OK? I heard what happened at your place last night. You should have called. I would have stayed with you."

"Oh. It worked out. Ewan stayed and everything is being taken care of."

"Well, I'm glad you weren't there. I hate to think of what might have happened if you were."

"Well, I hadn't thought about that until now." I chuckled.

She made a funny face. "Sorry. Is that why you look like you've seen a ghost."

"Do I?"

"Aye."

"No. It's just that . . ."

I became a bit more self-aware, enough to realize most of the pub had stopped what they were doing to listen.

I glanced behind me and then smiled. "I'll tell you the specifics later. But I need you to go shopping with me. I need a dress for a special occasion."

She clapped her hands together. "Do you have a date?" she whispered.

I nodded.

"With whom?"

The pub was still unnaturally quiet. "I'll tell you when we go shopping. For now, I need a full Scottish. I have a long day ahead."

"Fine, I'll get your breakfast, but I need you to text me who your date is. I may die of anticipation if you don't."

I laughed but did as she asked.

I heard her phone ding in the kitchen.

When she came out her eyes were wide. "It's about time," she whispered.

"What do you mean?"

"You two have been circling around each other for months now. It's good you have a proper date."

"I don't know what you're saying, I think I'm helping him keep his mother at bay. That said, I still want to look nice, it is for his mother's gala."

"Oh, I'll be there as well. It's why we scheduled the time for families to enjoy the carnival on Friday night. So we could get away. I think Jasper is doing part of the catering, he'll be there as well. Oh, and Angie and her husband were invited. The whole gang will be attending."

I laughed hard.

"What is it?" She whispered again.

"He has to know that you all will be there. He probably didn't want me to feel left out."

She scrunched up her face. "I'm going to say something I shouldn't."

"What's that?"

"He isn't someone who has trouble finding a beautiful woman to be at his side, if you know what I mean. That he asked you, I'd say is significant. He wants to spend time with you."

"I hadn't thought of it that way," I said. "I mean, I know about the celebrity dates." The town loved their laird, and he was quite often the talk of the older set, all of whom thought it was time for him to settle down.

"As I said, it's about time."

"Speaking of time, when is your shift over? I have patients until three. Then I thought I'd hit up Lulu's to see if she has anything new."

"Oh, she does, vintage and contemporary. I was talking to her earlier this morning when she came in. She told me I needed to stop by and shop for a dress for the talent show and maybe the dance Sunday night."

"Oh, I forgot about the dance on Sunday. I'll need something for that as well."

"This is going to be fun." She clapped her hands together.

An hour later, I had finished my meal and was about to head to the office when I noticed Jacks's partner embracing a woman who seemed familiar to me. I'd seen her before. She was platinum blonde and wore four-inch heels with her short skirt.

I'd gone through the files on Jeremy Burns, and I thought I'd read he was married. I was quite sure this wasn't his wife. Though, they didn't seem to be worried about hiding their relationship as they kissed.

Being the creeper that I am, I took a quick snapshot with my cell. They were kissing, and didn't notice me, for which, I was grateful.

Who is the mystery woman?

Chapter Eighteen

When I returned to the office, we already had patients waiting. They were hours early, but that sometimes happened here. If they hadn't been able to book an appointment online or through Abigail, they just showed up early.

Since I loved my job, I never minded. But Abigail was always annoyed with them for breaking the rules.

"I told Mrs. Gilroy that you are fully booked and offered to make her an appointment for tomorrow," Abigail said louder than her normal very quiet speaking voice.

"And the same with Mr. Cahill. Though his is more of an emergency."

Mr. Cahill held a bag of ice to his cheek.

"That must have hurt," I said to him.

"Aye. My fault, I wasn't paying attention. My Bessie was trying to get my attention. She's a good girl."

I turned back to Abigail. "Bessie?"

"One of his highland cows," she said as if that explained everything. In this small town we had a fair number of cow-related injuries as there were more of them than humans.

"You'd better come back," I said.

"I was here first," Mrs. Gilroy said, bristling. She had her knitting needles crossed, and her eyebrows were up. She was dressed as if she might be going to church. Her ailments were real though. She was tough, and only came in when she wasn't her best.

"And you dinnae have an appointment," Abigail reminded her. "We see those patients in order of the worst trauma."

I hid my grin with a cough. Abigail had a way of putting people in their place in her matter-of-fact soft speaking voice.

The older woman huffed but sat back in her chair and went back to her knitting.

By the end of the day, I'd put casts on assorted broken bones, mostly belonging to tourists who were learning how to surf in the cold sea.

But there had also been a fair amount of summer colds, mostly children. Something was going around before school even began.

"Is it me? Or has cold and flu season started earlier than normal?" I locked the front door after the last patient had walked out that afternoon.

"Aye. We have a full schedule for tomorrow as well, many of them with the same complaints."

"I can't do much for colds, except to check and make sure they don't test for flu."

She shrugged. "I think given the viruses going around the last few years, people may be more paranoid about that sort of thing."

I nodded. "And who could blame them? You're right, it's better to be certain. I do have something to add to my schedule. I'll be gone Friday afternoon and night. I should be back sometime early Saturday."

Abigail stared up at me. "Oh?" I could tell she was curious.

"Uh. Ewan asked me to help him out by being his date at his mother's gala."

"Oh. Ohhhh." Her face lit with surprise.

"It's not a big deal. Just a friend doing another friend a favor."

"Rigggght." She absolutely didn't believe me.

My phone dinged with a message from Mara. *Saved by the bell.* She asked if I was ready to go shopping.

I was exhausted, but I did need to find a dress or two. I texted back that I'd meet her in front of the pub in fifteen minutes.

Then I remembered the photo from earlier. "Abigail, you're going to think I'm weird, but I promise this has to do with the case."

She'd been typing on the computer and stopped. "What is it?" She asked curiously.

I pulled up the photo of the couple.

"I think I remember reading that Mr. Burns, the partner of Mr. Jacks, was married. But I don't think this woman is his wife. I swear I've seen her before, but I can't remember in what context."

I showed her the picture.

She grunted, which was very unlike her. "You are right. That is not his wife, who is a patient of ours. I think that is Davina, who sang at the pub last month during open mic night. Henry left for a few minutes to check on something, but I can have him confirm when he comes back."

"Was I there? I don't remember her."

"You were there. It's the hair," she said. "Last month she was a red-head. She changes the color fairly regularly."

"But she is definitely not his wife, right?"

"No. I cannae believe he would be doing that in front of the town. His poor wife will be crushed."

"Well, we won't be the ones to tell her," I said. I gave her a look.

She held up her hands. "Not a word from me, but if they were in front of the pub, the whole town will know by now."

I laughed. "You aren't wrong. I'll send the picture to Ewan. It may not have anything to do with our case, but you never know.

"At the very least, it shows that Mr. Burns is not exactly a pillar of society. It is strange, though."

"What is?"

"I thought I caught a whiff of something between him and the executive assistant. Like maybe they'd been having an affair. But, perhaps, it is just a close working relationship.

"Well, if he's having an affair, there is a good chance he's had one in the past."

"You may be right about that. Still, it brings another suspect into the picture."

"How so?" Abigail asked.

"She was on the train, I remember now. She had on a flapper dress and headband. She wasn't one of the storytellers, but she still dressed up."

"I dinnae remember."

"I was up taking a look at the engine. She was running late, and the station master was telling her to hurry."

We stared at one another as if we realized the same thing.

"If she was running late, she may have had time to shove the body in the closet," I said.

Her eyebrows went up.

"She's thin, but tall," Abigail continued. "And he would have been in a weakened state. Maybe she was helping her boyfriend out."

I nodded.

"I definitely need to call Ewan."

Chapter Nineteen

By the time I left the clinic, the sun had run away, and a steady rain fell. Summers in Scotland were as unpredictable as the winters, and I'd learned to dress in layers for any kind of weather. I found Mara waiting outside the pub.

"What happened to summer?" I asked.

She laughed. "Are you excited about finding a dress?"

"I actually need two," I said.

"Oh?" She shared her umbrella as we walked the short way to Lulu's shop.

"One for the gala tomorrow night, and another for the dance on Saturday. You're the one who reminded me."

"Oh, right. Have I mentioned it's been a busy day? Summers are killer, as you Americans like to say. And that is a good idea. I can't wait to see what Lulu has in stock."

"I hope she is resting that wrist," I said.

"Oh, she was with her shop assistant, Mrs. Quinn, who was fussing over her."

Mrs. Quinn was another one of my patients and a lovely, caring soul. "I had no idea she was working there."

"She's helping out through the holidays to earn a bit extra," Mara said. "Her grandchildren are coming for Christmas, and she wants to spoil them." Of course, Mara knew the whole story. She was easy to talk to and there were no secrets in this town.

That didn't surprise me. While she wasn't great at keeping her blood sugar and blood pressure under control, she was as sweet as they came.

It thundered as we entered the eclectic shop. Lulu had a mix of everything from baubles, which is what they called Christmas ornaments, to art, clocks and other antiques, and assorted gifts. Those were in the front of the shop, and the back was dedicated to new and vintage clothing.

Some of the 1960s and 1970s styled outfits were made by Lulu. The shop was a treasure, and I'd never failed to find a gift in there, nor something to wear for an event. I prayed that held true today, as I had no time to shop in Edinburgh.

"Good afternoon, kids," Lulu said as we made our way to the back of the shop.

I loved that we were middle-aged, and she considered us kids. Today, Lulu's outfit was bright fuchsia and her eye shadow matched.

"How are you feeling? I hope you are resting that wrist."

"Aye, Doctor, I'm behaving." She smiled and pointed to her wrist, which rested on the counter. She was sitting, as well.

"So, miracles do happen," I told her. She wasn't the sort to follow instructions if she didn't agree and even though she was in her seventies, nothing slowed her down.

Well, except a roller blading accident.

"Oh, you." She pointed to me.

"I'm making sure she keeps that ankle up," Mrs. Quinn said as she bustled out of the backroom. Her arms were full of clothes on hangers.

"Bless you, Mrs. Quinn, for looking after our Lulu," Mara said.

"I dinnae need looking after. I'm perfectly capable," Lulu argued.

I hid my smile.

"That you are, which is why I'm grateful you're letting me help out," Mrs. Quinn said as she hung up clothing on the racks. "I didn't realize how bored I was at home. It is so fun to have people to talk to and selling them gifts they love."

"You've been a blessing to me, Minerva."

Mrs. Quinn's plump cheeks turned pink. She was quite good at managing our friend Lulu. Today Mrs. Quinn wore a simple black dress, which was her color of choice since her husband had passed away two years before. She spoke often of him and had wonderful stories she shared during her appointments.

"Is there anything specific you are wanting today?" Lulu asked.

"We are shopping for the big gala in Edinburgh for Ewan's mum's charity. And Em needs a dress for Saturday night, as well. Maybe I do too."

"You're in luck," Lulu said. "I've several new shipments come in the last few days, and Minerva has steamed and hung up most of the garments."

"We only have one more box to open, I'll do that now while you shop."

Mara and I gathered several outfits each. I picked some long gowns, one of which was an emerald color, that I prayed fit. In the dressing room, I put it on first.

The tag read Tadashi Shoji. I didn't know the designer, but as I slid on the crepe sheath, I was more than pleased with the fit. The V-neck emerald dress had long bell-shaped sleeves, and the front gathered into a flower of sorts made of the same material. The way it hung was quite flattering to my figure.

"I found a winner," I said to Mara, who was in the dressing room next to me.

"Already? Let me see."

I stepped out and she pulled her curtain to the side. She wore a bright yellow frilly dress that was definitely not her.

"Oh, that is pretty," she said. "I can't believe you found something with the first try-on."

"It was the color."

She snorted.

"What's so funny?"

"Well, I thought I could wear yellow, but not this sunshine version. It makes me look sallow and the ruffles seem like I'm playing dress up with my mum's clothes."

"I have a silver kitten heel that will look perfect with that, Doc," Lulu said. "Minerva, get her a size eight. They are to your right behind the door in the back."

Minerva nodded.

"And you, young lady, that is not your color," she said to Mara.

"Moving on," Mara said.

Finding the second dress took a bit longer, but I found a peacock blue tea-length that would be perfect for the dance on Saturday. The event was for the whole town, and jeans and a top would be fine, but sometimes it was fun to dress up.

Mara and I had been so busy trying things on, we hadn't noticed the other customers coming in. One of whom, was the possible mistress of Mr. Burns.

She was at the counter with a pile of clothes and gifts.

"I'll need your ID," Lulu said.

The woman handed it to her.

"It doesn't have the same name as the card, this is a gentleman's card," Lulu said.

The mistress pointed a finger. "Stop messing about. He gave me the card to buy myself some things."

"I've no way of knowing that do I?" Lulu held her ground. "You could have stolen it."

The woman huffed. She pulled her cell phone. "Jeremy, this old woman at the store is giving me a hard time with your card."

Lulu's eyebrows went up. No one who knew her would dare to call her old.

The woman handed her the cell phone.

"Hello?" Lulu said.

She seemed to listen for a few minutes.

"Right. Well, enough. Except, I have the right to kick out customers when they are rude, and that will be happening, Mr. Burns. You might mention to your lady friend that in the future she is not welcome in my shop."

She handed the woman the phone. "Out." She pointed a finger toward the door.

"How dare you," the mistress bristled.

"I do not know who brought you up, but manners matter in Sea Isle. We are a kindly town, and we treat others with respect. Minerva, please escort her out."

"Well, I never," the woman stuffed the card back in her purse.

"And you never will in my shop," Lulu's tone was biting.

The woman turned and bumped into another lady standing there staring at her.

"You said Jeremy," the woman said. "Would that be Jeremy Burns?"

"What does it matter to you?" the mistress said.

"Because he's my husband," Mrs. Burns said. Her face showed no emotion. "So, the reason he didn't want me shopping today was because he knew *you* would be here."

"I've no idea what you mean," she tried to push past Mrs. Burns, but the other woman grabbed her arm.

"You aren't special, and you aren't the first or the last. You are one of many." The words were said softly, almost as if she were sad, not angry. I understood that kind of betrayal. It was not an easy experience.

The mistress yanked her arm away. "Do you think I care? He likes to spend time with me and buy me presents. Maybe you should think about not being such a shrew. Then he wouldn't cheat on you."

The gasps in the shop were audible. I may have been guilty as well. I felt sorry for the wife, and I sympathized with her. I was surprised she kept her cool. I'm not sure I would have been as graceful.

As much as I wanted to go after the mistress to ask about the night of the murder, it wasn't the right time. I could imagine, though, she would be cold enough to help kill someone, as she showed no remorse to Mrs. Burns. I had a feeling if she was to benefit financially, she would do just about anything.

Once the woman left, all the color drained from Mrs. Burns' face.

"Minerva, take Mrs. Burns to the break room and make her a cuppa," Lulu suggested softly.

Mrs. Burns sniffed. "You dinnae have to do that," she said.

"We have to look out for one another," Lulu said. "That horrible woman will get what she deserves."

Mrs. Burns glanced at the door. "One can hope. I have no idea what he sees in them. Other than they are young and fit. Usually, he keeps them in Edinburgh, though. This is the first time I was forced to meet one of them. And before you judge me, he's always been like this. I enjoy doing my charity work and he leaves me alone. I join him for events and play the dutiful wife. It works for us. But this was a bit beyond belief."

"You'll find no judgment here," I said. "We just want you to be OK. That was too much for anyone to bear."

"Thank you for understanding," she said. Then she ducked her head to hide the tears rolling down her cheeks.

"Come along dear," Minerva said. "Have a cuppa with me."

Mara and I took a deep breath at the same time. The atmosphere had been tense.

"Sorry you had to witness that," Lulu said.

"Dinnae apologize," Mara said. "That was brilliant, Lulu. You put her in her place."

"Will not do any good. She's one of those women who thinks of no one but herself. I'm not one to judge about relationships, but she could have at least pretended to be ashamed."

"Agreed," I said. "Thank you for looking after Mrs. Burns. That is sweet of you."

"Minerva has a way with people. She'll get her settled. A blessing that one. I'm glad to have her helping me. Now, you two get back to shopping. Let's see what you pick out next."

After grabbing more shoes and bags to go with our outfits, we checked out. Minerva came out of the back to wrap our packages and put them in the shopping bags.

"Well, that was interesting," I said as we stepped outside.

"Do you remember her being at the train station the night of the murder? The girlfriend, not the wife."

"Aye. She wore that ridiculous red wig that came past her bum. I remember thinking she was one of the storytellers in her flapper dress, but she mentioned she was a guest when I couldn't find her on my list. She was Mr. Burn's plus one. But I explained he hadn't RSVPd. She said he had. We had room, so I let her in. She was holding up the line, and I didn't want to argue."

"That's strange. Why would she go without him? Maybe, they planned the murder together." I hadn't realized I'd said the last bit out loud until I noticed Mara's expression.

"And I was the one who let her in." She made a face.

I waved a hand. "No. No. Don't do that to yourself. We have no idea if she was there for nefarious purposes."

But she had opportunity, unlike the partner. And if the accountant had been feeling poorly, which was likely, she could have shoved him in that closet.

For the second time that day, I texted Ewan.

He replied he was hung up with something, but he would come by later that evening to talk.

My phone dinged. It was Jasper.

The text said: *Help! Please come to the shop.*

"Jasper needs us," I said. "He's in trouble."

"Oh, no," Mara said.

We hurried down the sidewalk.

Chapter Twenty

It was nearing four, and Jasper's shop usually closed at half past three. The door was locked.

I peeked in and saw him behind the counter. He glanced up, and I waved. He hurried forward. His shop was something straight out of Paris with its pink, white, and black décor and lovely glass shelves with all sorts of goodies.

When he opened the door, we were assaulted by the lovely scent of his pâtisserie, and the sound of sobbing. Mara and I turned at the same time to see the mistress sitting in a corner at one of the wrought iron tables. She was alternately sobbing and stuffing a variety of pastries in her mouth. Mascara streamed down her face, and there were bits of cream and pastry on her lips.

"Oh, my," I said.

"Exactly," he whispered. "She was like that when she came in and bought one of everything I had left. I asked if she was all right, and she cried harder. I dinnae know what to do."

"You're the doctor, Em, what do you suggest?" Mara asked.

"You're the bartender," I joked. But I knew a mental breakdown when I saw one. And that was no laughing matter. My personal opinion of the woman didn't matter. She needed help, and I'd taken an oath long ago to do exactly that.

Mara took my shopping bags, and she and Jasper went to the back where the kitchen was. But I had a feeling they would be listening. My sweet friends were just as nosey as I was.

I sat down across from her. She was busy stuffing a lemon tart into her mouth but looked up when the elegantly scrolled chair I pulled out for myself scraped against the tile floor.

"Who are you?" she sniffed.

I handed her a small package of tissues I pulled from my purse. "I'm Dr. Emilia McRoy, the town doctor," I said. "You seem distressed, and I hoped I might be able to help."

"A doctor? I'm not sick, I'm just sad. My boyfriend is furious with me because his wife found out about us. I don't think you have pills for that sort of thing."

"Right. But I can listen if it will help you. Let's start with an easy question. What's your name?"

She shook her head. "I'm Davina. You'll be no better than the rest of them. Everyone always takes the wife's side. They have no idea how awful she has been with him. I've been looking after him and making him happy for months. We were having a good time.

"But she just confronted me in a shop, and he took her side. He said we are through, and he wants his debit card back."

Oh. My. This was a level of shallow I seldom witnessed, but here we were. She must not have noticed us in the shop during the showdown with the wife.

"I could take it to him, if you don't want to see the man who broke your heart."

She waved a hand at me. "Oh. No. I'll be throwing it in his face, once I buy myself everything I want and get a good cash advance off it. He cannae just use me like that and throw me away. I'll show him."

"Right." The best thing, to avoid a tirade, was just to agree with her.

"Besides, I know things. Secrets that could cause him big trouble. He seems to have forgotten that. He'll come to his senses."

"Oh?"

"You're a doctor, right?"

"I am. Why?"

"If I tell you things, it is confidential, right? Like a barrister?"

"Well, yes, if you are a patient. But I need to remind you that you aren't. I am looking into the death of your boyfriend's partner, Donald Jacks."

"Oh, that isn't the secret. He didn't kill him, though I'm sure he wanted to," she said.

"Why is that?"

"He was costing the firm a lot of money and clients with some bad decisions. That's why Jeremy was furious with him."

"Angry enough to kill him?"

She shrugged. "I don't think so. Jeremy isn't like that. Sure, he has a temper, but I can't see him bothering to kill someone. Though he might hire someone to do it for him. Jeremy doesn't like to get his hands dirty."

She didn't seem to realize what she was saying. I glanced up to find Jasper and Mara with wide eyes. They'd heard everything she said. I had warned her that this wasn't confidential, so it wasn't my fault.

"You think he hired someone to kill his partner?"

She sighed. "No. I mean, that sort of thing only happens in the movies. I was just saying that he would never do something like that himself. He'd convince someone else to do it. He can be very persuasive when he wants to be."

"I see."

"He wasn't even there that night, though. He had to do something with the wife in Edinburgh. She sits on some charity board, and they had a do. He wasn't happy about having to cancel with me."

"Oh?"

"I told him I was going to go have fun without him. I just wanted to make him jealous, you know? And it worked. That's why he gave me his card. He wanted to make it up to me. So, even though I thought the train thing might be boring, I went without him."

"I loved your dress." I needed to keep her talking.

She smiled. "Did you? I took special care when I found out we could dress up. I did some acting you know."

"I didn't know that."

"I like changing up my look for different roles. Not that there is much going on around here. But where I live in Edinburgh, I do a lot of local stuff. I've been in several commercials. Maybe, you've seen me?"

"I'm sure I have," I said. "So, where do you stay when you're here?"

"Jeremy has a summer cottage by the beach. I've been staying there. Though, since he's angry with me, he'll probably want me to go home for a bit. But he'll get over it, he always does." She stuffed part of a chocolate croissant in her mouth.

She waved at Jasper like he was a waiter. "Can I get a box for the rest of these?" She had a platter of goodies in front of her.

"Did you see Mr. Jacks the night he died?"

She blew out a breath. "Yes. He was leering at me. I may have given him the finger."

"Leering?"

"Yes. He didn't approve of me and Jeremy. He liked the wife for some reason and threatened to tell her what was going on. I told him that night it was none of his business. And if he said anything, he'd only be making Jeremy angry."

"So, you spoke to him?"

"Aye, I did."

"Did you by chance notice anything strange about him?"

"What do you mean? I was trying to avoid him. Not only was he mean about me and Jeremy, all he ever talked about was his blasted trains. Most boring man on the planet."

"Think back," I said. "When he was leering at you, do you remember anything different about him?"

"His face was pudgier than usual. I noticed his lips were kind of puffy. If it was anyone else, I would have thought Botox. But I can't see him bothering with that sort of thing."

"So, his face appeared to be a bit swollen?"

She nodded. "Yes. I guess it was. Not that I've paid much attention to him ever."

"Do you remember seeing anyone around him that night?"

Her eyes widened. "Like a killer?"

"Yes. Or even one of the waitstaff who might have been close by?"

She shook her head. "After he yelled at me and called me some not-so-nice names, I did my best to avoid him. I dinnae remember seeing him on the train, though. I thought he was supposed to be telling detective stories from the twenties and thirties. That was in the program. But I was trying to avoid him, so I didn't check out his chat."

Jasper came over with a box, and then quickly went away.

I took one of my cards out of my purse. "If you think of anything that might help us about that night, please call. Or if you need a doctor for anything, I'm here for you."

She might be shallow, but she was young. I felt a bit sorry for her. Jeremy was much older, and while I tried not to judge others' relationships, he was cheating on his wife with a much younger woman. It was difficult not to.

And this young woman had played her part. It would be easy to blame her, but I didn't. She was young and shallow, but I couldn't see her killing the victim.

She gathered up her box of goodies, and Jasper let her out.

"Talk about throwing someone under the bus," I said.

"Sad thing is, I don't think she realized what she was doing," Jasper said.

"She's so young," Mara said. "That Jeremy Burns is a creeper, as you like to say, Em."

I did say that a lot about men who leered a bit too much.

"True. Part of me feels sorry for her," I said.

"With all that makeup and the terrible wig, I thought she was in her late twenties," Jeremy said. "But she told me she was twenty-one."

Mara and I glanced at one another.

"That's even worse," Mara said. "Just, yuck."

I agreed. Burns was taking advantage of the young woman's naiveté.

"It was interesting what she said about Jeremy, though," Mara said. "What if he did hire someone? Maybe one of the waitstaff to kill his partner?"

I blew out a breath. "Hiring a killer? Maybe, if we were in a bigger city with some organized crime syndicate. It feels like a bit of a reach for Sea Isle. As we know, poison is very personal. And this was quite specific."

I tapped a finger on the table.

"What are you thinking, Em?" Mara asked.

"I don't know. My thoughts are whirling. But someone broke into my office for a reason. That took a person with some knowledge of security and how to avoid those cameras. It's all so confusing."

Both Mara and Jeremy nodded sympathetically.

"One minute I think the killer is someone sophisticated enough to know what they were doing. The next minute, I wonder if they were just lucky. I need time to sort it out in my head, and to talk to Ewan."

"You'll have plenty of time on your date," Mara said.

Jasper clapped his hands. "Finally! You have a date with our ACC?"

I rolled my eyes. "I wouldn't call it that. More of one friend helping out another." I explained how his mother kept trying to fix him up with one of her friends' daughters.

"Really?" Mara asked. "Or was he just trying to get you on his side so you would go out with him?"

Had he done that? "Stop making more of it than it is."

"We shall see," Mara said.

"I'll be there with David," Jasper said.

"Oh?" David owned a coffee shop in Edinburgh. He'd helped cater an event where Jasper's patisserie was on display. They'd been going the friend route, attending movies and such.

He held up a hand. "Like Em, it is more of a friend's thing. He offered to help me put out the cakes. Once that's done, I'm free to enjoy the gala. It was a chance for us both to get dressed up."

"Well, while we are confessing," Mara said. "I'll be there with Teddy, the dentist I met at Angie's wedding. And before you make more of it than it is, we too are just friends."

"Oh? I didn't realize you two had kept in touch."

She cleared her throat. "We didn't. He was here surfing a few weeks ago, and we had dinner."

"You didn't tell me," I said, surprised.

"Well, it is good for women to have a bit of mystery."

* * *

"Look at us all having dates," I said. "Almost like we're grownups."

We laughed.

As we headed home, I wasn't thinking about my date with Ewan. There was time to worry about that later. No, I had a killer in mind.

But how and when did the killer strike? Those were the two biggest questions. If the victim was already showing symptoms, why hadn't he used an EpiPen? Or asked for help?

It was frustrating that I was no closer to an answer with any of my questions. I needed to speak to Ewan. Maybe, he could help me piece together what I'd just learned with the facts of the case.

I need answers and I need them now.

Chapter Twenty-One

The day of the gala, I had a bad case of nerves. I was glad we had such a busy schedule at work, so I didn't think about what was about to happen later. The last time I'd gone on a date, it hadn't worked out so well for me. Though, as Ewan had said quite clearly, this was just one friend helping out another.

Still, I was nervous. I'd showered and had on my new dress, which I loved. The sparkling shoes were fancier than anything I'd worn in years. As I waited in my office for Ewan, my hands shook as I tried to put the diamond studs my grandmother had given me into my ears.

I did feel good in my dress, though. Thank goodness for Lulu's shop. I always seemed to find the perfect outfit for an event when I shopped there.

Ewan used the buzzer to announce himself. I knew it was him because his face came up on my computer screen. He was dressed in a tux and was more handsome than any man had the right to be.

The nerves multiplied and swirled in my stomach. I took a deep breath and shoved them all down.

When I answered the door, he just stood there for a minute staring at me.

"Is everything OK?" I asked glancing down at my dress wondering if I'd managed to spill something on myself.

"You are beautiful," he said. And then the swirling nerves started all over again, but it was more like a tornado in my stomach.

"Uh. Thanks. You clean up well, too."

He grinned at that. Then he crooked his arm. I put my hand through, and he guided me to the car. After opening the door, he helped me make sure my long skirt made it into the seat. Then he grabbed my overnight bag from the doorway. He took my key to lock things up, even though I knew he had his own. After all, he owned my office and home.

When he climbed in the other side, there was a strange tension between us.

"So, I haven't had a chance to talk to you about something, but I spoke to Jeremy Burns's girlfriend the other day. And before you get mad, it was completely by accident."

I told him what had happened at Jasper's.

Discussing the case was our safe space. He listened intently, as he always did, as we made our way down the highway toward Edinburgh.

"Do you feel like she had a hand in the murder since she was there?"

"I don't think so," I said. "I mean, she could have unknowingly done something if Jeremy told her to do it. She might be right about him keeping his hands clean. But, no, I can't see her coming up with such a clever way to kill or stuffing him in a closet."

"You dinnae sound like you care for her much."

I grunted. "I didn't mean she isn't bright, but she might be more interested in hurting Jeremy than his partner at this point. I feel sorry for her in a way."

"She's dating a married man," he said. There was no judgment in his voice, but he spoke from experience. He'd found his ex-fiancé in a compromising position with another man. The two of us had that sort of betrayal in common.

"Have you and your team gone through the client list? It seems to me this all may be related to him losing their money."

"Aye, we have been. Most of them have alibis or were nowhere near the murder scene."

"That's the thing though. I don't think the killer had to be there," I said.

"What about the closet?"

"Well, I've been thinking about that," I said. And I had.

"What if he put himself in there?"

Ewan glanced at me with surprise. "Why would he do that?"

"The toxins in his blood may have meant he wasn't exactly thinking clearly. Maybe he had been looking for the restroom and mistook the office. His brain may not have been his own, and he could have been severely disoriented, as in out of his mind completely. Funny things happen when the brain isn't getting the oxygen it needs. Perhaps he saw the door and thought he was going into another room."

"Really?"

I nodded. "His face wasn't the only thing that was swollen. There was a great deal of inflammation in his brain. The killer made sure his lip balm was dosed heavily, and perhaps, never even meant for him to die at the train station. I can't imagine they would have picked such a public place to carry out the murder. In fact, they might have thought it would happen at the office or home."

"So, you believe he could have been that far out of his mind that he thought the office was the loo."

"We have no way of knowing. All I can say for certain is that he was most likely very confused between the palpitations in his heart, and what may have been going on his brain. As I said, he was likely quite disoriented."

"That puts a different spin on things."

I sighed. "I could be totally wrong. You understand that, right? Could be the killer was there. But it might have been too obvious. I feel like someone would have seen the victim being shoved into the office. Everyone I've talked to didn't see any such thing. How about you?"

He nodded. "It's the same. A few of the witnesses remember seeing him in the trench coat and fedora, but they have no recollection of anyone around him at that party. Except for one of the waiters. He argued with the waiter who served him that he wasn't holding the tray correctly."

"That sounds like Jacks. And if it didn't happen at the train station and that was all an accident, it narrows down the possible suspects," I said.

"What are you thinking?"

"It's either someone who was in his home, at work, or was part of the volunteer group helping to bring the train back whom he invited into his home. He didn't get along with a few of them because he was such a perfectionist. I remember some of the committee members telling me that. But I can't imagine him inviting someone into his home if he didn't get along with them.

"It might be a good idea to go back with those he did invite and speak with them. And then of course our most likely suspects are the people he worked with at the firm."

"We have to tread carefully with the business partner and the executive assistant," he said.

"Oh? Why is that?"

"They've called the solicitors in."

"Do they realize that makes them look even more suspicious?"

He chuckled. "I don't think they care. They were tired of us bugging them. That doesn't mean we've given up on them as suspects. The forensic accountant finally has the files. It is taking longer than expected, though. I hope to hear from her soon. If nothing else, we may be able to get them on fraud."

I scrunched up my face.

"What?" Ewan asked.

"I never like the idea of a killer getting away."

"Nor do I. But at least it's something. She is going through hundreds of files and comparing those with the records on multiple laptops."

"I'm surprised, if there is fraud, that the partner hasn't taken off for some nonextradition country."

He chuckled. "Probably thinks we won't figure it out."

"Or he may not know the extent of it," I said.

"What do you mean? He is a full partner in the firm."

"Yes, but what if Jacks was the real criminal and had been hiding things? I remember something the executive assistant said about Burns being angry at the victim for messing things up."

"Hmm. You may be right. But that gives him even more motive for murder."

"There is that."

A half hour later, he turned off the main highway and drove up the side of a mountain.

"I thought this was in Edinburgh," I said.

He grinned. "We're on the outskirts. The estate has been in my family for hundreds of years. Mum uses it for charity events."

"Estate, so not one of your castles?" His family had a few all over Scotland. Though one would never know about his wealth if they met Ewan. He was as down to earth as they came, and likely to get his hands dirty if the situation required it.

He was wealthy enough to live off his laurels for many lifetimes, but he wasn't that kind of guy. He worked hard and helped as many people as he could. There was much to admire about Ewan, even if we didn't always get along.

The road curved around and then opened up to a grand estate. It was like something out of Downton Abbey but with more gothic architecture. The mix of stone and pillars gave it a grand dame sort of appearance without being too fussy.

"Let me guess, some of this was refurbished when the Normans made their way into Scotland.

He chuckled. "You've been reading up?"

"I have. Everything is so much older here than anything we have in the States—by several hundred years. I find it fascinating how each invader sort of brought their own spin to the residents of Scotland."

"That they did," he said. "You might be interested to know that this wasn't originally our land. It once belonged to someone who betrayed the king. He then handed over several properties to my family, for taking care of that problem."

My eyes must have gone wide, as we paused in the valet line, because he laughed.

"As in off with the betrayer's head," I said.

"Things were a bit more brutal back then, but yes. I'm afraid that's true. My family could be quite barbaric when necessary. It isn't always such a pleasant thing to discover just how far they were willing to go."

"I'm slightly envious of your family's history. Especially, since I know so little about my own."

"I thought you were digging into that?"

I shrugged. "I have been. The records are spotty though. I found a great uncle, as you know. The one who used to be a minister in Sea Isle. There was also information about his father, but not much. I can't find anything that shows how they ended up in Sea Isle. But I was told many of the older records may be spread out over Scotland and that they are just now building a centralized genealogy system. I'm hoping to learn more this winter when things slow down a bit."

"You may be right about the records, though I think it also depends on the clan from which the family came when it comes to information. Some of them kept better records than others."

"Ah. That makes sense. I've been so busy, I haven't checked any of the other archives, but I will. Visiting those is on my bucket list of places to go in my new country."

He smiled. A valet opened the door for me and helped me out of the SUV.

"Our bags are in the back," Ewan said. "Can you take them to my mother's suite of rooms?"

"Yes, sir," the valet said.

"Thank you," Ewan said.

There were several stone steps leading up to the mansion, which were tricky in a long dress and heels. Ewan offered his arm, and I gratefully took it. Lifting the front of my dress with my other hand, we went up the stairs.

While Ewan's family had several homes, and even a few castles, they had opened up most of the refurbished ones to use for events such as this and weddings. Others were also open to tourists. It made good financial sense for the upkeep and gave the public a chance to see the gorgeous architecture and interiors.

At the double front doors, we were checked off a list. Inside, the stone-arched ceilings were massive and stole my breath.

"I've never seen anything like this," I whispered.

Ewan glanced up as if he'd forgotten what was up there. "Again, a bit of architecture from our French ancestors, who preferred things a bit more ornate and much larger. Originally, the structure had the entrance in a different place. Most of the stonework is also new; well, it was done within the last three-hundred years."

I laughed. "Only in Scotland could three-hundred years be new."

He grinned. "Aye. Being you are American, I can see how that would be different."

"It's beautiful, though." We followed several other well-dressed couples to another set of tall double doors made out of ornately carved wood.

Waiters with glasses of champagne stood on each side. Just inside the door was a receiving line. An elegant woman in a long-sleeved chiffon dress, held out her arms.

"There's my boy," she said. Her grayish hair, with a white streak in the front, was pulled into a chignon. She radiated both power and class. And she was gorgeous in her long flowing gown.

She pulled Ewan tight to her in a mother-bear hug. There was no mistaking who she was.

And I already liked her.

"Hi, Mum. Everything looks nice. You did a good job."

She put his face between her palms. "Are you eating? Make sure you eat tonight. You're looking too thin to me."

I grinned but said nothing. Ewan was extraordinarily fit and took very good care of himself. But then, I wasn't his mother.

"Mum, Da, may I introduce you to Dr. Emilia McRoy," he turned to me. I held out a hand to shake, but his mother pulled me in for a hug.

"We've heard so much about you, Emilia," she said as she squeezed me tight. "Our Ewan cannae stop talking about you every time we see him. He tells us how much you've done for his wee town."

I glanced up to see Ewan's cheeks turning a light pink.

He cleared his throat. "She has done extraordinary work for the community," he said. "We are lucky to have her in Sea Isle." He sounded so formal and was obviously embarrassed.

I couldn't help but smile.

"If my wife will let go, I'd like to shake your hand," his father said. "And maybe later, you can help me with this bursitis that is bothering my golf game."

The father was as tall as Ewan and just as big a presence. He had a white beard, but his hair was the same mix of brown and red as Ewan's. It was easy to see where Ewan's good looks had come from; his parents were beautiful.

"Da." Ewan shook his head. "She is here to enjoy herself."

I shook his father's hand. "I'd be happy to chat with you about it. Just find me later on."

"See, son, she doesn't mind. There's a good lass. Thank you."

"You're welcome."

"Take her and dance," his mother said. "Oh, and do not forget about the auction. It is all for a good cause."

I turned to follow Ewan, who crooked his arm again. Since I wasn't used to wearing a long dress with heels, I took it gratefully.

"Sorry about that," he said. "They can be a bit much sometimes."

I smiled. "I thought they were wonderful, and they obviously love you."

He grunted. "Sometimes a bit too much. My father and I dinnae always see eye-to-eye, but it is has been better the last few years. He seems to be mellowing with age."

"Don't we all?" It was funny when I thought back over the things that stressed me out when I was younger. None of that mattered now. With age comes wisdom was a true adage.

"I suppose you are right."

Five huge crystal chandeliers lent light to the ballroom, the arched ceilings in here had been painted beautifully, and it reminded me of the Sistine Chapel in a way.

"Your family spared no expense when it came to décor, did they?"

He glanced up to see what I'd been looking at.

Once again, he grunted. "Took seven years for them to return that ceiling to its former glory. Da wanted to just paint over it because of the cost. But Mum wouldn't have it."

"I'm glad she got her way, it is gorgeous."

"She usually does—get her way that is."

"I'm not surprised. Hard heads seem to run in the family."

He laughed at that. "You are right about that, Doc."

We hadn't gone far when I recognized a couple in the corner who appeared to arguing.

"Wait, is that who I think it is?"

Ewan turned to see who I was looking at. "What are they doing here?"

It was a very good question.

Chapter Twenty-Two

I was curious how an accountant and his wife from Sea Isle had landed an invitation among some of Scotland's most elite. Not that I was a snob about it. I only had an invite because of Ewan. It just seemed odd that after everything that happened earlier in the week with the mistress that the couple was at Ewan's mother's gala.

Someone touched my arm.

"It's me," Mara whispered.

I turned to find her on the arm of her new friend.

"Do you remember, Teddy?"

I didn't but I waved hello and smiled. "It's good to see you again. Mara, you look beautiful."

"That she does," Teddy said good heartedly. "I'm a lucky man."

She patted his tuxedoed chest. "Yes, you are."

We all laughed.

"Did you see who was in the corner?" She threw her thumb in their direction.

"I was curious about that," I said.

"The most likely scenario is this is one of her charities," Ewan said. "She mentioned that during the interviews we did that she was involved with several and her main residence is here in Edinburgh. But I can ask my mother."

"Or we could just ask Mrs. Burns," I said. "Though, isn't it odd he has his business in Sea Isle if they live here?"

"Aye, he said there was less competition in a small town. He didn't like having to compete with the bigger firms here in the city. And he'd grown up there and knew his clients."

"And it probably made it easier for him to keep a separate residence for his affairs," I added

"You may be right about that."

"Let's go chat with them."

"I told you he's called in his solicitors," he said.

"Right, but this is a social event, and we are only going to say hello." I pulled Ewan along with me.

He seemed resigned. Of course, Mara and her date joined us. But before we reached them, a bell chimed and we all turned toward the stage where Ewan's mother stood among the musicians, who had been playing.

"I'm sending a hearty welcome to our distinguished guests and thank you for supporting such a worthy cause," she said. His mother went on to talk for a good five minutes. "As you enjoy your evening, please bid wildly on our auction items, and kindly make your donations. These children need our help, and we should be there for them."

While she'd been speaking, I lost sight of the accountant and his wife.

"Do you see them?" I asked Mara and Ewan.

They shook their heads.

"I have an idea," Mara said as she looked from Ewan to me.

"What's that?"

"Why don't we take a night off from the snooping, and just enjoy ourselves for once?" She grinned.

"I'm all for that," her date said. "Though, I had no idea we were looking for someone. May I ask who we were snooping on?"

Ewan cleared his throat. The last thing he'd want was to share the case with a stranger.

"You make a good point. I wonder where Jasper is?" I said, changing the subject.

As if I'd conjured him, Jasper walked up to us. He was dressed in a tuxedo, as was the man with him.

"Whoa, you two look so handsome," Mara said.

"I agree," I added.

Jasper blushed a bit. "I know some of you have met David, but I wanted to introduce him to the rest of you."

I smiled. David owned a coffee shop and also supplied the free-trade beans that Jasper bought for his shop. They did make quite the handsome couple.

There was a chorus of hellos.

"How are you?" I asked.

David smiled. He had red hair and freckles, and he was quite handsome in his black tux. He'd been in a flannel shirt and jeans last time I saw him. He'd been at Jasper's shop making a delivery, and we'd been introduced. Jasper had said they weren't dating but they looked like a couple to me.

Everyone shook his hand.

"Ewan's mom is the one who is throwing the event," I said, "which is why we are all here."

"She has very good taste," he said. "Everything is quite elegant. I haven't been to something like this in years. I wasn't sure my tux would fit."

"But you look grand," Jasper added. And then he blushed again when he realized he'd said the words out loud.

"Um, we were heading toward the auction items," Ewan said. "Would you like to join us?"

The auction items were on the other side of the ballroom, and it took some time to make it through the crowded room. Thankfully, Ewan kept to the edges. He seemed to remember that I wasn't so fond of crowds.

There were several tables lined up against the far wall where the items for auction had been set up. Everything from artwork to trips abroad were displayed on the various tables. We all separated.

After picking up my auction number at the table where people checked in, I found several folk-art pieces from local artisans that I bid on, as well as a trip to Spain. I'd never been there, and it might be fun to warm up during the winter months if I won.

By the time we'd finished, it was time to find some nibbles as Mara called them. Off the ballroom in one of the dining areas, several tables had been set up for people to sit down. The food was served banquet style, which I appreciated. I liked being able to pick and choose.

After grabbing an assortment that we would all share, we sat down at one of the tables on the far side. But in our direct path we could keep an eye on the accountant and his wife who seemed, once again, to be deep in conversation at the table next to ours.

They weren't as angry looking as earlier, but still seemed tense.

"Isn't that the partner of the man who died?" Mara asked.

"What man?" her date questioned.

Mara's eyes went wide. "Oops, sorry, Em and Ewan. I wasn't thinking."

I nodded. "It's OK."

Ewan cleared his throat again. "We're investigating a suspicious death of someone in our town," he said. "As Mara said, that is the man's business partner."

"Is the woman his wife?" David asked.

Mara and I glanced at one another.

"Yes," I said.

"What was that look?" David asked.

"We aren't very good at keeping things under wraps are we," I said. "No wonder you get so frustrated, Ewan."

He chuckled. "If you don't mind, I'd rather they didn't think we're spying on them," he said.

"If I remember the gossip, she's a bit of a social climber," Mara said. "At least, that is what was going around the pub. She keeps a place in Edinburgh, and he prefers to stay in Sea Isle. His girlfriend has been staying in their summer cottage."

"His girlfriend?" David said with surprise. "This sounds like one of my gran's soap operas."

Mara sighed. "Super sleuth, I'm not." She turned to face Ewan and me. "Sorry."

I shrugged.

"Well, everyone in town already knows the girlfriend was having a breakdown in my shop," Jasper said. "Minerva, who has been helping

Lulu, saw her in there. And I heard she'd helped take care of the wife after she had a run-in with the mistress. By late afternoon it was all over town."

I wasn't fond of it, but that was the way things were in a small town.

"I think I've seen him in the coffee shop," David said. "I never forget a face or an order. He must have been with the other woman when he was there. I remember she wore a weird sort of wig and had an insane order with about ten different items in one coffee. Don't tell anyone, since I run a shop that serves coffee and source beans, but I'm not a fan of anyone who tries to cover up the taste of such a wonderful brew."

We laughed. "I couldn't agree more," I said. "I like black, like my heart."

Everyone chuckled again.

"I remember thinking he seemed embarrassed how she kept going on and on. I honestly, thought she was his daughter."

"Oh?"

He shrugged. "A vibe, that's an American saying, right? She was pawing him, but he seemed embarrassed or annoyed. It was hard to tell which one."

"He probably didn't appreciate the pawing out in the open," Mara said. "He dumped her when she told the wife about the affair. That was why she was in Jasper's shop eating herself into a food coma."

I'd told Ewan all of this, but he didn't seem happy we were talking about the accountant and his marriage woes.

"Is something wrong?" I whispered. "Are you mad that we're talking about them?"

He shook his head. "It isn't that. Look at her face. I'm worried she's been poisoned. She doesn't appear well."

I did as he asked, and he was right. She'd gone pale, especially around her mouth.

Suddenly, she stood.

And then she fell to the floor, her husband catching her before she hit too hard.

Ewan and I rushed over.

"Stand back," I said, as I grabbed her wrist and took her pulse. It was strong, but she had definitely passed out.

"Do you know if she took anything?" I asked the husband.

"No, she didn't," her husband said. "One minute she was fine, the next she said she felt nauseous and dizzy. When she tried to stand, she fell."

"Ewan, I need a damp cloth, and something to prop her feet above her head."

Mara handed me a napkin that had been dipped in ice water. And Ewan soon came back with some pillows. A crowd had gathered around, and I glanced up at Ewan.

"Everyone, please stand back. The Doctor needs space."

"I had mum call for an ambulance," he said. "They should be here in fifteen."

"I didn't bring my doctor's bag with me." I leaned down to listen to her breathing. Everything seemed fine.

"Did she eat today? Do you know if she's diabetic?"

Her husband shook his head. To his credit, he appeared genuinely worried about her. "She's had a lot of stress the last twenty-four hours," he said. "Could that do it?"

"Yes," I said. "But she appeared ill just before she fainted. Did she say anything to you?"

"No. Only what I mentioned to you. It's my fault. We've been arguing most of the night. It was just too much for her. I blame myself."

Her eyes fluttered open but she appeared dazed. "What happened?" she asked me.

"You fainted," I said. "I need to know if you've taken anything."

"Like drugs? No. Of course not. I can't."

This time it was me who frowned. "Are you diabetic?"

"No. It's—uh—" she glanced at her husband.

"Please, tell me," I said. "I want to help you, but I can't if you don't explain what is going on."

"I'm pregnant," she whispered.

There was a gasp behind me. I turned to find her husband wide-eyed and as pale as she had been.

"You're what?" he asked.

"Pregnant," she sniffed. "It was what I'd come to tell you in Sea Isle. I went in to find a gift that might help me explain the news. We've been trying so long that we'd both given up. But then that harpy of yours told me what you'd been doing . . ."

I wanted to ask why she had come to the gala with him tonight, but it wasn't the time.

"I'm so sorry, luv. So sorry." He seemed genuine, as he sat on the floor next to her and took her hand. "I will do whatever you want. Tell me how to make it up to you."

"That's why I was so excited, but then all of this happened, and I heard that you might have killed Donald, and I didn't know what to think."

"You what? How could you think I would hurt Donald?"

They seemed to have forgotten they had an audience. I glanced up at Ewan, who shook his head.

I didn't say a word.

"You were so angry with him about work. You never told me why. And I didn't want the father of my child to be a murderer."

"Of course, I didn't kill him," he said. "Yes, I was furious with him, but I couldn't have hurt him. It's because of him our accounts are being pawed over by the government. You know me better than anyone, how could you think such a thing?"

"Do I? I knew about the other affairs. But this one seemed much more serious."

He shoved a hand through his hair. "Yes, I've been an idiot. But I'm not a murderer, and she meant nothing to me. I swear to you, luv. I've been a complete idiot."

She sighed, and a tear fell down her cheek. "Yes, you have."

"I'll spend the rest of my life making it up to you. Where is that ambulance? She needs the hospital."

As he spoke, the EMTs arrived. I explained what was going on and suggested they test her for dehydration, and gestational diabetes. My guess it was the former. Morning sickness quickly dehydrated pregnant mothers without them realizing how important it was to put those electrolytes back in.

I considered going with them, but the bus, as they called ambulances here, was already crowded with the husband and EMTs who had arrived. That, and her doctor had already agreed to meet them at the hospital.

"Wow," David said as they carried her out through the kitchen. "You are amazing."

I could feel the heat on my cheeks. "It's what I do."

"Do you believe what he said about Jacks?" Mara asked.

I shrugged. "That's for Ewan to decide. He did seem sincere, though."

"Well, one thing was clear," Jasper said.

"What's that?" Ewan asked.

"He had no idea he was about to be a father. Did you see the shock on his face? This was like our own *Coronation Street* or something. Affairs, pregnancies, murders."

He wasn't wrong.

I straightened my dress, which had twisted around my waist when I'd been on the floor.

"I say it's time to dance," Teddy said to Mara. "I've been waiting all night to get you in my arms."

Mara ducked her head, but I was certain she probably had pink cheeks. He dragged her through the double doors and out to the main ballroom.

Ewan held out his hand. "How about it, Doc?"

"You know I have two left feet when it comes to dancing."

"I'm willing to chance it." He grinned. No way I'd be able to say no to him. He was so charming when he wasn't angry with me.

The orchestra played "Someone to Watch Over Me," and Ewan expertly guided me across the marble floor. I only stumbled once when turning a corner. But he held me up from slipping. To the outside world it only looked like a slight bobble.

Still, I was embarrassed. "I did warn you."

"Everything is fine," he said softly. He pulled me tighter against his chest and twirled me around the floor. I tried desperately not to think about how good he smelled or the fact that his chest and stomach were like iron against me.

As the music ended, his mother came up. "You two make a beautiful couple," she said. She was beaming.

"Oh. Uh." I didn't know what to say.

"Son, how about taking your mother across the floor. It has been a while."

He nodded and held out his arms to her.

Mara and her date had moved to the side of the room to watch the dancers. I walked over to them.

"You looked so happy," she said.

I frowned. "What do you mean?"

"You were smiling when you danced with Ewan. I haven't seen you grin like that in ages. You two are perfect for one another."

Embarrassed, I cleared my throat. "You know better than anyone, it isn't like that between us."

"Isn't it, though? Did you see his face? He was smiling like a big goofball. He cares for you, Em."

"You romanticize everything," I said. "We were just dancing. He was probably laughing because I had a bit of a wobble."

She laughed. "Deny it all you want, Doc, but I know what I saw. I think it might be time for you to open your heart and mind to the possibility that you like one another."

"Of course, we do. Professionally," I said. "But that is all it is."

She sighed. "Em, he could have asked any woman he wanted here tonight. But he chose you."

"Yes, to keep his mom from trying to push her friend's daughters on him. He said as much."

"He made an excuse to get you to go with him," she said. "But what you aren't realizing is that he could have asked anyone else. He picked you."

Her words reverberated in my brain, as I watched him dance with his mother. She was chatting the whole time, and he would nod or shake his head indulgently.

Did he pick me for a reason?

And how did I feel about that?

I was so confused and not at all certain how I felt. I decided to pack it all away, and just focus on having a good time.

But that didn't keep me from blushing every time he asked me to dance.

Chapter Twenty-Three

It was well after two a.m. when the last of the party-goers finally left. My friends had departed much earlier. I had hugged Mara and the others goodbye, but I felt since I was with a family member, I needed to stay up and finish out the party.

But I was dead on my feet. As soon as the last guest slipped out the double doors, I took off my heels. I didn't care what anyone thought, my feet couldn't take one second more.

I had danced with my friends, and with Ewan, all night.

And yes, I was the first to admit it had been fun.

"You must be exhausted," he said, as he left his mother to talk to the orchestra leader. The musicians were packing up their instruments.

"It was fun," I said. "Thank you for the invite. Are you sure we aren't over-staying our welcome by sleeping here tonight?"

"Not at all. Mom just told me she expects us at breakfast tomorrow morning at ten. I hope that's OK. It means we'll be getting back to town a bit later than expected."

"It's the weekend, and I don't have any patients scheduled," I said. "Sleeping in sounds good to me."

"I'll show you to your room."

We climbed the center staircase up a floor and turned down a long hallway.

There was what had to be a fifteen-foot tapestry with scenes of war, partying, and unicorns on it. "Does your family have a thing for unicorns?" I remembered unicorns on a tapestry in the castle where our friend Angie had been married.

He chuckled. "Unicorns have long been the national animal of Scotland," he said. He held up a hand. "I know, it may seem silly to an outsider. But we are known for our folklore and myths. Unicorns are a part of all of that."

I smiled. "I think it's fun. When I was a kid, I wanted a unicorn for a pet. For some reason, that never worked out."

We laughed.

"It must be incredible knowing your family's history and having these homes that express that."

He sighed. "Aye, but I'll be honest, sometimes it can feel a burden."

"Why is that?"

"It is a great deal of responsibility keeping the homes up, and making certain the legacy continues. It has only been in the last decade I was able to talk the family into using the castles and estates for nights like we just experienced. It helps to cover the costs of the upkeep."

I remembered him telling me that before.

"Does it all fall on your shoulders? What about your father?" While he often spoke of his mother, and I'd met her earlier, he never spoke of his dad. "Did he retire?"

He cleared his throat. "A long time ago, he passed over the family business and accounts. Dad loves nature and his books. He is a writer and avoids crowds at all costs. I was surprised he was here tonight."

"I can relate to the problem with crowds."

He chuckled.

"You said he didn't usually come to the events your mother holds, but he was here tonight."

"That's because his family was the one who funded the children's charity that was the recipient of tonight's donations. Mum likes to joke that the secret to a happy marriage is they live apart most of the year. She has charities and boards she sits on. Dad has his nature preserves and books to write. We usually get together for the odd holiday or birthday, but otherwise they live apart."

I shrugged. "I'm the last person to judge a relationship. If it works for them, that's a good thing."

"It does and has for years. Like I said, Da handed over everything to do with the businesses and the properties when I was twenty-one, including the lairdship."

"That is very young to take on that kind of responsibility."

"Aye, it was. And he left it a mess. He'd been ignoring things for years, which was one of the many arguments we had back then."

"Have you always been so responsible? You have taken on the running of Sea Isle, and even the job of ACC. It seems to me, you could have at least passed those duties on?"

He stopped in the hallway, and I paused with him.

"What did I say? Did I offend you?"

He shook his head. "No one has ever asked me that question. Everyone just assumed I would do whatever was necessary to keep the town running."

"And you do. I'm not trying to get rid of you, but I'm curious why, when you have estates all over Scotland, you chose Sea Isle as your home base."

"My grans," he said. "I've told you about my parents, and because they lived separately, I spent a great deal of time with my grandparents. They lived in the estate in Sea Isle, and as a young boy it felt like a magical place. Being right on the sea, and I had the run of the town.

"For me, Sea Isle was home. My grandfather taught me how to run the farm, and care for the animals. And how to fish. My grandmother was a nurse and would often help the former Doc look after the townspeople. I suppose I grew up feeling the same sort of responsibility they did."

"Everyone in town adores you," I said. "I don't know what they would do without you."

He laughed, and then started walking again. "Everyone who lives there is like family to me," he said. "And many of the older folk see me as a nephew or grandson. That can be a good and a bad thing."

I smiled. "I can see that."

"And aren't you feeling that pull as well? I've seen you interacting with the town. You aren't just the doctor. You've quickly become an important part of the community. For which, we are all grateful."

"Aw. Thanks for that. I'm amazed how quickly this past year has flown, and I can't imagine living anywhere else. I mean, during February when the wind never quit, and I felt like I was a popsicle most days, I may have thought about a warmer climate. But I've come to love the town and the people. I like that people genuinely need me. I think there is a part of all of us that appreciates that sort of thing."

"Aye. As usual, you're right. Here we are," he stopped outside what I assumed was my bedroom door.

"Thank you for tonight," I said. "I had fun. Goodnight, Ewan." I don't know why, but I rose up on my toes and kissed his cheek.

His eyes went wide, but he just nodded. Then he quickly turned away. "See you in the morning, Doc," he said as he walked away.

We'd seemed so close there for a moment in time, but we always fell back into that awkwardness that came between us. That said, I'd had fun. Even with everything that had happened with the accountant and his wife.

I couldn't remember the last time I'd danced so much or relaxed into the arms of a handsome man.

It was a great night. One I would not soon forget.

I shut the door behind me and took in the room where they'd put my things. There was an enormous canopy bed dressed in blue and gold brocade. The wooden furniture was ornate and fancier than anything I'd ever own, but it fit the overly large room that was big enough for a sofa and chairs in front of a fireplace that was taller than me.

It was hard to believe that Ewan came from such opulence. He was so down to earth, but this was his world.

I wasn't sure I'd ever fit into it.

* * *

The next morning, after packing my overnight bag, I headed downstairs. Ewan and his mother were in the dining room right off the stairs.

"Good morning," she said as I walked into the room. "Did you rest well?"

"I did. How are you?"

She laughed. "I'll need a day to recover. These old bones need more and more time after these parties."

"You aren't alone, my feet may never be the same. I'm glad I brought my sneakers for today. Hi, Ewan."

He put down his phone, which he'd been looking at, and nodded my way. "Doc."

"Son, I would hope I've taught you better manners than to be on your phone at the table."

"Catching up on a case," he said. "I wasn't trying to be rude."

"Did something happen?" I asked. "And have you heard about Mrs. Burns? Is she OK?"

"Aye, she was released from the hospital this morning. She's doing well," his mother said. "I had my assistant contact the husband. Thank you again for looking after her. We are lucky you were here."

"It was no problem," I said. "I was curious how you knew them."

I glanced at Ewan, and his eyebrows went up.

"Oh, she's lovely and sits on several of my committees. She's a hard worker. I dinnae know much about the husband. I think that may have been the first time I'd met him. I'm so glad she's doing much better."

"That's good news," I said. She had most likely been dehydrated. After some fluids, she and the baby should be fine.

"That was quick work, Doctor. You're lucky to have her in Sea Isle, son."

"Aye. We are," he said. His cheeks were pink again. His mother had a way of embarrassing him that was nothing short of delightful.

Ewan's phone buzzed and he glanced it.

"Ewan, really."

"Sorry, mum. I need to get back to town. Doc, can you be ready to go in fifteen?"

"So soon? I thought I'd get the day with you and the good doctor."

"I explained about the Highland Games. The crowds are much bigger than we expected. My team is already stretched thin. We need everyone there."

Once we were in the car, I turned to him.

"What is really happening?"

"There's been an incident at the fairgrounds."

"Oh?"

"Several of the stalls were burgled overnight."

"Why not just tell your mother that?"

He sighed. "She looks for any excuse for me to move back to Edinburgh or even Glasgow. She thinks I'm wasting my time with Sea Isle. We've had a murder, and now this. She'll think I'm not very good at my job."

I shook my head. What was it about men and their mothers? "I don't think you could be more wrong. She thinks you hung the moon and is quite proud of you."

His phone rang, interrupting the conversation. He pushed the button on the dash to answer.

"Sir," Henry's voice came over the speaker. "We've caught one of them. It's John Hamburg. We're thinking he and his friends were having a bit of a contest last night."

"How did you know it was him?"

"Caught him trying to return the goods, as that was a part of the contest."

Ewan shook his head. "I'm on my way back. Put him in a cell and round up the rest of them."

"Aye, sir."

He hung up.

"I know John. He seemed like such a nice young man," I said. He'd sprained his wrist during a rugby game, and I taped him up.

"He is a good lad. His dad took off a few months ago and hasn't come back, leaving his mum and him to run the farm and store."

"That's a lot of responsibility for a kid who is going to be a sophomore in high school."

"Aye, which is why he is most likely acting out. And this is the last thing his poor mum needs. But we have to teach him, and the others, a lesson. Some time in a jail might do them a bit of good."

"We call that scaring them straight in America, and you might be right."

"Kids get bored and do stupid things. But I'll not allow this sort of thing in my town."

He had such a sense of pride about Sea Isle, and it was one of the many things I admired about him.

"I don't blame you. One of the big draws when I came here was that there was so little crime. Though, that was before I found out you'd appointed a special role for me to investigate deaths."

"It was in the fine print." He said that every time I complained, and I could finally laugh about it.

"Why did you let me believe you had coroners in Scotland for so long?"

"It is a position I've always believed we've needed. It's one of the things the English do right. And thanks to our town laws that give me the right to appoint people to necessary positions, I decided it was time. And let's not forget, you are good at it."

Heat spread across my cheeks. "Thanks," I said. "I swore I would never admit this, but I do enjoy the investigative side of things and not just because I'm a fan of all the mystery series. I've always liked puzzles. And the one we're trying to figure out now is a doozy."

He chuckled. "I'm not sure I've ever heard that word."

I shrugged. "I don't use it much, but it is appropriate. I'm certain the murderer is someone close to Jacks. And I understand that most of those people have alibis. But those can be faked. My gut says it is someone who saw him every day."

"You maybe be right, but . . ."

"We need evidence to prove it. I know. You always want proof."

He laughed. "It is how we work in law enforcement."

"Right, but it's also annoying. Oh, did your accountant figure out where the stash of cash came from that we found? And did you find any more? I meant to ask that a few days ago. I need to write everything down in my notebook so I can keep track."

"Aye, we found more in a box in his closet. It was about forty thousand pounds."

"Wow. I still wonder if he was getting ready to make a run for it."

"We may never know. His passport is current, though."

"So, we focus on those who were closest to him. The business partner who was out of town. The assistant who was at a hen party. And maybe the sister who swears she hasn't seen him in a year, but we have no proof of that."

"Yes, and those he worked with closely on the train and invited to his home. There are three men who were on his team working to refurbish the interior of the station and the train."

"I talked to a couple of them the other day," I said.

Ewan took his eyes of the road for a second and gave me a look.

"Don't get mad. Mara gave me the list, and I knew they were working as volunteer storytellers as well. I just asked a few questions. You and Henry probably did the same. None of the three, though, remembered seeing him that night. I mean, they could be lying. But that was what they told me. They were honest about how Jacks could be annoying at times, but he was usually right. They seemed to appreciate his attention to detail."

"Aye, we came to the same conclusions. And while they did have access to his home, they never went to his office, where we found the majority of the tainted lip balms."

"Hmmm. I hope we catch a break soon."

"Agreed," he said.

* * *

After dropping me off at the clinic, Ewan said he was heading out to the station to deal with the troubled youth. I'd no more walked through the door and put my bag in the living room, when the doorbell buzzed. I glanced at my phone, to see two large men with a third hanging on their shoulders. Abigail walked up behind them.

I quickly opened the door. "What happened?"

"I'm working the med tent at the games," Abigail said. "I'm fairly certain Carson has fractured his clavicle."

"Dinnae what that is," the injured man said. Around his lips had turned white, and it was obvious by the bone poking out that he had to be in terrible pain. "But I'll be fine after a pint or two."

Abigail shook her head. "Alcohol is not going to help your injury."

"Says you."

* * *

"Right, let's get him back to the lab for an X-ray and we'll take it from there."

Abigail motioned for them to follow her.

"Don't you need to get back to the med tent?" I asked. "I can handle this." While I wasn't as fast or as knowledgeable as Abigail, I knew how to run the X-ray machine.

"I put a note out to bring anyone in need down here. And Henry is there to direct people or set up a ride until I get back."

"OK." I was grateful for the help.

Once we had him on the table in the back, I sent his friends away. Abigail helped him out of his shirt, which wasn't easy given his injury.

"What were you doing when you hurt yourself?" I asked. I gently touched the area, and he winced.

"Caber toss," he said.

I had no idea what that was. I glanced up at Abigail.

"They throw a full-sized log to see how far it will go."

"It is my best event," he said proudly. "But I lost my grip, din'I? Slipped, and fell back with the full weight of the log on my shoulder and neck."

From the contusions already forming in the area, that was easy to see.

"Abigail was right to bring you here. With bruising like this already forming there could be some serious damage."

"No, I've done worse to myself. I'll be fine."

"Well, you're here. I need you to lie still for a bit while Abigail takes some pictures."

Twenty minutes later, we had our answer. It was a serious break and needed treatment.

"Sling?" she asked.

"It's centralized, so let's do a figure-eight splint. I think we have a few in storage. Hopefully, one of them will be large enough to fit him."

By the time we finished working him into the sling and explaining that he needed to wear it all the time, it was early afternoon. His friends agreed to keep an eye on him, as he wanted to watch the rest of the games.

"You do not participate, agreed?" I asked.

He nodded.

I prayed he'd do the smart thing and sit out the rest of the day. If nothing else, the pain should keep him at bay. He didn't want a prescription and promised it didn't hurt that bad. I had a feeling he was just being a tough guy in front of his friends.

"I need to get back to the tent," Abigail said.

"It's nearly time for my shift, I'll go."

"It's OK. Tommy is watching the games with Henry. I've got this."

"Then you can join them. Besides, I've seen them practicing and treated a few injuries, but I never had a chance to see the real thing."

I grabbed my medical bag just in case, and we took one of the shuttles that had been provided up the mountain. The games were taking place behind the old church in the center of town.

After dumping my bag inside the tent that had been set up for medical at the end of the field, I walked back outside to watch the games. They were in the middle of the hammer throw. I only knew that because I enjoyed watching the summer Olympics and that had been one of the events.

The men were huge, and it was amazing to see such feats of power and strength. I couldn't imagine even picking up the tool they used, and they tossed it so far.

While the patient we treated waited on the sidelines, his friends were warming up for the event. Just behind them I noticed Catherine Allan, the dead man's executive assistant, sitting with Davina.

They were flirting with the men who were warming up.

"Well, that didn't take long."

"What's that?" Ewan asked from beside me.

I may have laughed nervously.

"Do you have ninja powers? How do you always sneak up on me like that?"

"I wasn't sneaking," he said gruffly. "You were the one who wasn't paying attention to your surroundings. We've talked about this: when you're on a case, you always need to stay aware of everything going on around you."

He wasn't wrong, but I wasn't about to tell him that.

"You could also announce yourself," I said, bristling slightly. But I couldn't help but smile. "Is there something you needed?"

"No. I was curious who you were looking at," he said. Then he followed my line of vision.

"Were we aware they knew one another?" I asked.

"No," he said suspiciously.

They were laughing and, as broken-hearted as Davina had seemed at Jasper's shop, she was definitely over it.

"Neither of them seems particularly sad given what they've been through in the last week. I mean, I'm all about finding joy where you can, but something about this doesn't fit right. Do you think they murdered Jacks together?"

He chuckled. "You are more suspicious than I am, which is saying something. They are single lasses who are having fun at the games. Where is an inkling of proof?"

"Oh, come now. You are just as suspicious of them as I am."

"Only that they seem to know one another and that hasn't come up in any of the conversations we've had with them. But that doesn't make either of them guilty. Also, which one is the criminal mastermind who thought to put bee venom in a lip balm? And what would be the motive?"

"I feel like you just made a jab at their intelligence, but you make some good points. When you think about it, though, no one in his inner circle seems to be the type who would do something like that. Far be it from me to say they aren't intelligent enough, but the killer had done their research. Which reminds me of something."

"What's that?"

"Well we know that the lip balm was clean when Kiara sold it. And we know it had to be someone in close proximity."

"Right."

"But who is to say it is just one person? It could be that a couple of his disgruntled clients could have banded together."

"We had this convo in the car," he said.

"I know. I'm just working things out in my head, and I need to say it out loud. It is part of my process."

"OK. We've gone over those lists, though," he said. "All of the clients either had an alibi or hadn't seen him in months. And again, access is the biggest part of this puzzle."

"I agree. We keep coming back to those he worked with, and it always seems to be them. But they have alibis. All of them, except the mistress. She was actually at the train station, but she most likely wouldn't have had access to his lip balms."

He was quiet, and I glanced up at him. He stared at the flirting women, but then nodded.

"You're right," I said. "I know we need proof, but I've been thinking about scenarios. What if he bought his supply of lip balms and then went to work on the train. And maybe they were just sitting out."

"And someone was ready and waiting with bee venom?" he asked.

"Well, when you say it like that, it seems dumb. But maybe. They were waiting for the right time to present itself. Maybe, they weren't even thinking the lip balms. Maybe, they were just going to inject it directly into him, but went with plan B."

"Your imagination is in overdrive."

I shrugged. "He lost people's money. To me, that is the number one motive. What if one of his clients paid the executive assistant, or the lover of the partner to put that bee venom into the lip balm?"

"That's a bit of a reach. I dinnae think that is the way it happened, but I will have Henry grab their bank statements to look for any large deposits."

"What are you two talking about?" Mara asked as she walked up. She glanced over her shoulder to see who we were looking at. "Oh. They had breakfast together in the pub this morning," she said.

"They did?" Ewan and I said at the same time.

"Aye. Seemed to be quite friendly and cheerful. I thought it was strange since the girlfriend was so upset the other day at Jasper's."

"Did it seem like they'd known each other a long time?"

She pursed her lips. "That I couldn't say. But they had definitely planned to meet up at the pub. I'd just come down to help out with the morning rush, when the girlfriend walked in, and then Catherine waved her over."

"That's interesting," Ewan said.

"Maybe even more so the guest who joined the both of them."

"And who was that?"

"The victim's sister, Kaitlyn Jacks. I overheard her talking about her brother. And she's been into the pub more than once."

Ewan and I glanced at one another.

That was very interesting.

Chapter Twenty-Four

Later that night, I dressed in my new dress from Lulu's. The midnight blue chiffon came down to mid-calf. It was quite chilly outside, and I'd almost decided on jeans and a sweater, but I really loved the dress. My feet still hurt from the night before, so I wore the sparkly flats I'd bought as well.

It had been an extremely long day, and it wasn't over yet. Thankfully, I'd managed a power nap between the Highland Games and the talent show that was to be performed in an hour.

I was glad we only had a few more days of events before this was all over. Not that it wasn't fun. It had been. But I was ready to get back to a normal schedule where I spent most of my nights curled up on my sofa watching mystery series.

As we'd planned, I met Mara down the hill behind the pub. The shuttle would take us up the mountain to the church where the event was being held.

Abigail and Tommy were already there. She was playing piano for her brother, who had surprised everyone by saying he wanted to sing at the talent show.

He had a beautiful voice, which we all knew. But he was not a fan of crowds. For that reason, Abigail had tried more than once to talk him out of it over the last two weeks. But her brother was insistent.

She'd come to me upset, and I'd calmed her down with a bit of advice. "The worst that can happen is he gets cold feet or freezes on stage. You'll just carefully guide him off and take him home."

She'd been nervous about it all week, and I didn't blame her. We were all so protective of Tommy and his wanting to perform in public was very unlike him. But he loved to sing, especially show tunes.

"Are you as nervous as I am?" Mara asked.

"Yes," I said, as we boarded the shuttle. Jasper was right behind us. We'd all come to show our support. Even Angie and her husband, Damian, planned to be there.

"Do we have a plan B, if things go south?" Jasper asked. "I feel like I want to throw up, I'm so nervous for him."

"Yes. Abigail will guide him off the stage, and Henry will whisk them home. She even bought him a new video game to distract him in case it all goes wrong."

"I dinnae understand why he would put himself through this," Jasper said. "I feel like a protective uncle who doesn't want his nephew hurt."

"You are a protective uncle, and we are the aunties," I said.

"How did he even know about the talent show?"

"He heard about it from his group therapy on the farm." His counselor suggested his patients try to step out of their comfort zones and try things that scared them. I understood he wanted to teach them that it isn't bad to fail. Instead, it's worse not to try and to then regret missing out.

"He's been attending the group for the last several months. It gives him a chance to interact with the animals, which he loves, as well as other people, who were challenged in one way or another. And it was the counselor's suggestion for them to attempt things that made them feel uncomfortable."

"Abigail was still trying to talk him out of it when I left them at the games this afternoon. But he was insistent. We will see what happens."

The shuttle dropped us off near the library, and it was a quick jaunt up a block to the church. One of the halls there had a temporary stage where the performances would take place.

By the time we arrived, the hall was filling up, but Abigail had saved us seats a few rows back from the front of the stage. She waved us over.

"I need to get backstage," she said. "I left him in a corner with his headphones and one of his games." She was paler than normal, which was saying something.

"Are you OK?" It was all I could do not to reach out with my hand to gauge her temperature. "I'm fine. Just nervous for Tommy and myself. It dawned on me that I too would be in front of the town playing the piano. What if I mess up?"

Jasper clasped her hands in his. "You just keep going. No one in this crowd will be the wiser."

She took a shaky breath and nodded.

Right after she left, Ewan walked up. "Abigail texted that she'd saved me a seat," he said. "I wanted to be near the stage in case Tommy needed me."

There it was. That innate caring and sweetness that hid behind the cranky exterior he normally wore. Warmth spread in my chest. He really was an incredible man.

"You can sit on the end by Em," Mara said casually. But I saw the glint in her eye. She was always trying to push Ewan and me together.

We sat through a Scottish jig, several singing groups, a few dramatic monologues, and then it was time for Tommy. He walked out onto the stage with his headphones on and a hush fell over the audience. His sister was right behind him. A piano was rolled out.

Then Tommy glanced Abigail's way. He didn't make eye contact, but she nodded just the same. He took off his headphones, and she began to play "Johanna," from *Sweeny Todd*. It was an odd choice of tune, but Tommy's sweet voice rang out as clear as a bell. He had the audience holding their breath.

Each note was perfect. And after singing the last bit. Tommy put his headphones on and walked off the stage. I couldn't help but smile and yes, tears streamed down my cheeks. The young man was so talented, and I knew he had no idea.

There was a slight pause before thunderous applause and whistles filled the church.

Abigail stood and curtsied, and as she left the stage, she wiped some tears from her cheeks. I had no idea if she was relieved or happy that her brother had sung so beautifully. Ewan handed me a handkerchief, and I thanked him. I wasn't the only one—all of our friends and other audience members were wiping their cheeks.

After the show, we went to find them.

Tommy sat in a chair facing a wall. His noise cancelling headphones were on, and he played a game on his hand-held system.

"That was amazing," I said to Abigail. "I've heard him sing around the house and in the gardens, and he has such a lovely voice. You both did an amazing job."

"It's all a blur," she said. "I was so focused on what he might do if he realized how many people were watching him that I forgot to be nervous for myself. That was until it was over. Now, my hands won't stop shaking."

I took her hands in mine and held them. "Everyone in the audience loved it. Did you hear the applause?"

"Aye, I did." She smiled. "I'm just glad it is over."

* * *

"Em is right, it was perfection," Mara said. Jasper and Ewan nodded. "Did he ever explain why he wanted to do it?"

Abigail laughed. "Right before we went on. I told him, we didn't have to do it. But he said he read that music could help people's souls feel better. I have no idea where he read it. He said he wanted to do his part for the community. It is one of the things they teach in his therapy group, doing for others."

"Well, he succeeded," Ewan said. "Though, an interesting choice, a song from *Sweeney Todd* to soothe a soul, but it worked."

We all laughed. It was one of the more beautiful songs from the murderous show.

"Did he know about all the applause?" Mara asked. "He was by far the favorite act. You both were. You played beautifully."

"He didn't care about all that. The clapping was just noise to be avoided for him. As for me, I've never in my life played in front of anyone but my brother. But like I said, I was so worried about him, I didn't think about myself. Probably for the best."

We hugged her goodbye, and Henry came up and offered to take Tommy and Abigail home.

Ewan glanced down at his phone, which had just buzzed. "I need to head back to the station," he said and left abruptly without saying goodbye. That was sort of his norm, though.

"That was more amazing than anything I could have imagined," Mara said as we walked toward the exit. "I'm still weepy over the beauty of it all."

"So am I," Jasper said.

"You two are not alone," I said.

Outside, a chill had whipped up the wind. I should have known to take a jacket. I had to hold my skirt down to keep it from doing a Marilyn Monroe. We headed toward the shuttle, but something caught my eye.

I stopped.

"What is it?" Mara asked as she tried to peer where I was looking.

"I swear I just saw the girlfriend and the assistant going into the office," I said. "Why would they be doing that on a Saturday night?"

"Maybe, we should snoop," Jasper suggested.

I almost said no. I knew that would be the smart thing, but my curiosity won out.

"You don't have to come with me."

"Oh, but we do," Mara said. "What if they are the murderers?"

"All the more reason to keep you safe."

"Nope. We're coming with," Jasper said.

"I have the pepper spray you bought me," Mara said.

"Hopefully, we'll have no use for that." But I had mine in my purse as well. I never went anywhere without it.

The front door to the office building was left open, and we slipped inside.

We quietly made our way up the stairs. The lights were off, but the moon coming through the windows let in just enough light that we didn't trip.

My stomach churned with nerves. We had no business being here, and Ewan wouldn't be happy with us. But my curiosity was peaked. Why were the women here and with the lights off?

The office door stood open, but we paused outside of it. As Mara moved to the other side, a board creaked. We all went wide-eyed.

"Did you hear that?" Catherine asked.

"What?" Davina replied. "I didn't hear anything. It's your imagination. Come on. We need to find the account Katilyn told you about."

I pushed record on my phone, as this was an interesting conversation.

"And you don't get it," Catherine responded. "I told you I've been going over all of his accounts since he died. I haven't found a clue as to where he'd hidden the money his sister mentioned."

"She wouldn't lie about something like that," Davina said. "In one of their last conversations, he'd said he was putting aside money for her. That money has to be somewhere. You said you could transfer the funds to one of your accounts without anyone knowing. But it does us no good if you can't find it."

"Stop nagging," Catherine complained. "You're worse than my mother. Trust me, no one wants to find that money more than I do. And the sister doesn't need it as much as we do."

Funny how people could justify stealing.

I texted Ewan. He'd be furious with us for snooping, but he needed to catch these women in the act. They could be the murderers.

There was a strange noise down the stairs.

Mara frowned and pointed to herself and Jasper. She motioned they were going to check it out.

I nodded. I tried to get a bit closer to the door, to record their conversations. It probably wasn't admissible in court since I was eavesdropping but it might help the police make their case.

There was a scream from downstairs. And then two thumps.

"I told you I heard something," Catherine said. "Come on, let's go out the back." There was a quick slamming of drawers, and then the door. I had no idea where the back exit was or I would have followed them.

Besides, after that scream I needed to check on my friends.

I ran down the steps.

"Mara? Jasper?" I called out. They didn't answer. Maybe, they'd been frightened by the scream and run out.

But as I neared the bottom step, two bodies came into view.

Mara and Jasper lay on the floor, and neither was moving.

Chapter Twenty-Five

I knelt on the floor feeling for Mara's pulse. She had one, and it was strong. Jasper was the same. What had happened to them? They were both still unconscious when the door burst open, and I put up my fists ready for a fight.

"It's me, Em. Everything's OK," Ewan said. Then he took in the scene. "What happened?"

"I don't know. I was upstairs. I heard a scream. The assistant and the girlfriend ran out the back. And I came back this way to see what had happened. This is all my fault. I wanted to snoop, and they came to help."

"Are they OK?"

"They're breathing, but I can't figure out why they both passed out. And it looks like Jasper hit his head on the banister on the way down."

I'd noticed the blood pooling on the floor, even in the dark.

Mara stirred, and then moaned.

Ewan must have found the switch and turned on the lights.

Mara put a hand over her eyes. "What happened?" she asked groggily.

"You need to tell us," Ewan said.

"Look at the front of her sweater," I said. There were two strange burn marks.

"She's been tasered." Ewan nodded.

"My chest hurts," Mara said at the same time.

"I need something to put pressure on Jasper's head."

Ewan pulled off his sweater and handed it to me. "Use this. I'm calling for a bus so we can get him to your place.

Mara sat up. Then she held her head and moaned again.

"Don't move until I can check you out," I said. "You may have hurt something when you fell."

"I'm all right." She blinked. "Someone was waiting for us when we came down. Jasper was a few steps ahead, and I heard him trip and tumble down. Next thing I knew I thought I was having a heart attack from running down the stairs, and then I passed out."

"We think you were tasered," I said. "Do you remember seeing the person's face?"

She shook her head and then flinched.

"Again, try not to move too much. I need to get Jasper sorted. He's bleeding."

Mara turned pale when she saw the blood.

"Is he alive?"

"Yes."

Ewan's team and the EMTs bustled into the room. Once I'd staunched the flow of blood on Jasper's head, we loaded them both into the ambulance.

It wasn't long until we reached my office.

Abigail met us there. I didn't bother to ask how she'd known. I felt it was a safe assumption that Henry had told her what happened.

"Tell me what you need," she said.

"Let's clean the wound and do an MRI. He whacked his head pretty hard when he went down," I said. "I think he may have hit the banister."

"What about Mara?"

"I'm fine," Mara squeaked. "Except it feels like I've been punched in the chest."

Abigail glanced at her worriedly.

"From the burn marks on their chests, we think they were both tasered," I said.

We wheeled them both to the back room. The MRI was in a room just off of the main labs. It had its own space, since it couldn't be around metal objects.

I took off Jasper's piercings in his ears and eyebrow, while she set everything up.

"Can I go home?" Mara asked. "I'm so tired."

"You need to stay with me overnight," I said. "Ewan, can you put her in one of the surgical suites?" We had some hospital rooms where we kept patients overnight if necessary.

He nodded.

"I don't need that," Mara complained. "I need something for my headache and my chest, and I'll be good to go."

"No," Ewan said. "You'll be doing what the doctor said."

"What about the scene?" I asked. "Don't you need to get back to that? What if the attacker left some DNA?"

"Doubtful, but Henry is there running the scene. No need to worry. Focus on our friends."

He sounded frustrated, and I didn't blame him. My snooping could have killed all of us.

"What's going on?" Jasper said from his bed. "Why am I bleeding?"

His being conscious was a good sign. I explained what was going on.

"I'm OK," Jasper said. "Why do my chest and head hurt, though?

More explanations.

"Just to be safe, I'm running an MRI," I said. "We can't be too careful when it comes to head wounds."

* * *

A few hours later, the patients were resting on my couch. It wasn't the first time we'd all sacked out on the huge U-shaped sofa.

They had both refused to stay in the patient suites in the back of the office, and I wasn't about to let them go home alone, as they had concussions from the head injuries.

Since I had to keep an eye on both of them, I'd agreed we could all watch a television show to help them relax.

Meanwhile, I'd set my alarm to wake them up every few hours. And I'd sent Abigail home.

Ewan insisted on staying and settled down on the big cushy chair next to the sofa and put his feet on the ottoman.

His anger was palpable.

"Yell at me. Just get it over with," I said.

"You could have been killed. The people closest to you could have died, as well. How many times do I have to tell you not to snoop on your own?"

"You also say there is power in numbers. I didn't go alone like I have in the past. And my snooping, as you like to call it, did pay off. There is something going on with the assistant and the ex-girlfriend. So, you can bring them in for questioning."

"Right. And we will. Henry already has them in separate cells. I thought a night in jail might loosen their tongues tomorrow."

"Technically, they weren't breaking and entering since the assistant has a key."

"Right, but she had no business being there on a Saturday night, and she knows it. Also, the offices are considered a crime scene. There was tape up before they broke in."

"Ah, there is that."

"Stop deflecting," he said.

"No idea what you're talking about," I countered.

"The part about where you could have all been killed."

I sighed. The last thing I wanted to do was put my friends in danger.

"I dinnae like it when Mum and Da fight," Mara complained.

"I'm with her," Jasper said sleepily.

I may have laughed, which meant Ewan stared daggers at me while I pretended to watch the show.

What tonight had shown me was that yes, Davina and Catherine were in on something together.

But what we hadn't counted on was a third party, who didn't care who they hurt.

That might have been the scariest bit of information yet because we had no idea who that might be.

* * *

Sunday was the last day of the festival. While it had been a fun week, we were all exhausted. Mara and Jasper left early that morning, promising to let me know if they had any adverse effects from being zapped the night before.

The winners from the Highland Games would be announced around noon, and I planned to be there. I hadn't slept much, since I'd been keeping an eye on my friends. I dosed up on some espresso, promising myself a nap before the dance later that night.

Ewan always threw a huge party on his estate, and the whole town would be there, along with the end of summer tourists who had come to the events.

* * *

Hungry, I headed down to the pub for a quick breakfast.

I was surprised to see Davina and Catherine in a corner booth, whispering to one another. I thought they would still be in jail. But what was even more surprising was the way the victim's sister, Kaitlyn, gave them a narrow-eyed look from a table a few feet away.

Did she know they were trying to find her brother's special accounts that he'd set aside for her? Had she been the one who attacked my friends? From the look in her eyes, I had a feeling she could taser the two women she stared at without pause.

Mr. Wilson, Mara's grandad, came out of the kitchen with a full Scottish breakfast and a cup of coffee. He set it all down before me.

"How did you know this is exactly what I wanted?"

"You saved our poor Mara last night. We're grateful, Doc. We need to keep you well fed."

"I didn't do much. She is tougher than she looks, and she's one of my dearest friends, so of course I looked after her." I didn't bother to mention that the reason she'd been hurt was my fault. I still felt so guilty about that.

"Aye, and now we are looking after you."

I grinned. "How did you even know I was here? You've been in the kitchen since I arrived."

He laughed. "Magic, and the new security cameras Mara put in the pub. I think you've made her paranoid. Dinnae know what someone might steal from the pub, but we handed over the reins so she can do what she wants."

I laughed. In addition to the security updates, which Ewan suggested when they started hosting larger events, she'd repainted the place and repaired all the booths, which had been showing some wear. That happened when something was more than three hundred years old.

"Where is she?"

"Upstairs," Mrs. Wilson said as she came out of the kitchen with a huge tray of food and drinks. "She has no business working today. I sent her to bed."

Mara was lucky to have grandparents who loved and cared for her so much.

"Did she tell you what happened last night?"

"No," Mr. Wilson said. "Only that it was police business, and she couldn't talk about it."

Well, that was surprising.

"I dinnae suppose you could give us more information?" he asked. I made the universal sign of zipping my lips together.

He laughed. "Half the town knows Jasper and Mara were attacked. There are all sorts of rumors floating around, including they saved your life."

I smiled. "Let the town think what they want," I said. "Even if I told you the truth, they would still be making up stories."

"Can you tell us if our Mara is still in danger?"

I blew out a breath. I wanted to say as long as she stayed away from me, she'd probably be safe. "I don't know for sure," I said. "But I think last night was just a case of being in the wrong place at the wrong time. I don't think the attacker wanted to hurt them."

I had no proof, but why would anyone want to hurt them? They weren't really involved in the case. I meant what I said about them being in the wrong place at the wrong time.

"You'll look after her, though." He gave me the grandpa glare he was famous for when it came to his family.

"Yes, sir. With my life."

"Enjoy your breakfast."

I hadn't realized the rest of the pub had been paying attention to our conversation. I should have known better. When I turned to look at the other customers, I found Kaitlyn's glare had turned on me. And Catherine and Davina stared at me suspiciously.

Something was up with the three women, but were they capable of murder? It felt like I'd asked myself that a hundred times, and I still didn't have an answer.

* * *

I'd finished my breakfast when Kiara and her son came into the pub. "Oh, Doctor, I'm glad we found you," she said. She glanced around the pub.

"Is something wrong?"

She frowned. "Can I talk to you outside?" She glanced around again. "There are too many ears, here," she whispered.

I nodded. After running my dishes back to the kitchen, which Mara's friends did whenever we ate here, I headed outside with Kiara.

"It's a beautiful day, why don't we go down to the beach."

"That'll be good for Max. He loves picking up shells."

While we settled on a couple of large rocks to the side of the beach, she watched her son walk along picking up shells and putting them in his pocket.

"What's going on?" I asked.

She sighed. "I need your help."

"Are you sick? Is it Max?"

"Nothing like that." She sniffed as if she were trying not to cry. "I know none of you said anything about my products being involved in the case, but this town . . ."

"What is it?"

"Word has gone around that my lip balm killed that poor man. I've had maybe three customers the last four days or so. People are afraid to buy my things. We are barely getting by as it is, if my business goes under, I dinnae know what might happen to Max and me."

"I'm sorry about that," I said. "I can assure you it wasn't me."

She nodded. "Nor the ACC, but there are a lot of people involved with the case. And some of Ewan's officers aren't always great at keeping secrets. Things are often overheard, especially after a few pints."

She wasn't wrong, but I wondered how she knew that.

"What is it you think I can do to help? I'm willing, I just don't know where you're going with this."

"I was hoping you and Abigail could test all my products. And then I could put a sign up showing that all ingredients had been tested by medical professionals."

She held up her hands. "I know it's a lot to ask. If I could afford to go out and have some independent lab do it, I would. But I can't. And since the bad news came from the case you are working on, I thought . . ."

"Oh," I said. As much as I felt sorry for her, I couldn't ask Abigail to do that. She worked hard enough.

"I already asked Abigail, and she agreed to do it," she said. "But she said I had to ask your permission since she would be using your resources."

Technically, it was the town's resources. Everything in my office, from the equipment to the personnel, was paid for by Sea Isle.

"And it isn't everything. Just more of the balms and some of the lotions. I read an article that perception is everything. If people think you two have tested my products and deemed them safe, then they will be. I know it is a crazy thing to ask, and it is over the top, but I dinnae know what else to do."

She was so sweet, and I adored her son. "Abigail said yes?"

She nodded. "Aye, I asked her last night after hearing Tommy sing. That boy has an amazing voice."

"He does."

"I dinnae like being pushy or asking for help, but I need you. Will you do it?"

It was highly unusual, but helping the community was a part of my job. Besides, poor Abigail would be running the labs, and if she said yes, I wasn't going to be the bad guy.

"We'll help you out," I said. "Why don't you drop some products off tomorrow morning? Today we'll be a bit too busy with the ending of the festival, but we will get it done in the next few days."

She grabbed my hands and held them tight. "Thank you. Thank you so much. You are a lifesaver."

* * *

As I was walking home, I felt like someone was watching me. But there was no one around. I'd been through enough to know I should trust my gut. I hurried to the practice and let myself in quickly. Then I locked the door and stared down at the camera focused outside.

No one was there.

Now who is paranoid?

But that feeling stayed with me the rest of the day. Someone had been watching me.

Why? Did the killer think I knew something? Or had the killer been the one to attack my friends? Both might be true.

I sat down at my desk and started going back through the case files and the autopsy. I pulled out my journal where I usually wrote down notes for a case. I had been so busy last week, I hadn't taken the time to review them. It helped seeing it all on paper.

As I wrote, something niggled at my brain. The answer had to be in the files.

"Let's do this," I said as I opened the files on my computer.

But I kept checking the cameras at the front and back doors. I couldn't shake the feeling someone was watching me, and I wasn't sure what to do about it.

Chapter Twenty-Six

The weather had whipped up a summer storm, but Ewan and the summer fair committee had covered all contingencies. The party was under a huge white tent, and the shuttles dropped us off at the canopied entry.

While I'd planned on wearing another of the dresses I'd bought at Lulu's, the weather changed my mind for me. It was freezing outside. This was a casual dance, so I donned my black boots, jeans, and a green sweater with bell sleeves. It would be chilly in the tent, even with so many bodies inside and the heaters that would stand tall throughout.

By the time I made it to the bottom of the hill to the shuttle, I was grateful I wore jeans and my jacket. I pulled the hood of my jacket up as cold rain spilled down from the sky.

"Evening, Doc," Mara's grandfather said from behind the wheel.

"Does your granddaughter volunteer you for everything?" I smiled to take the edge from my words.

"Aye, but I volunteered on my own for the first shift tonight. I like getting to see all the residents on their way to the fete. It's fun."

Her grandparents were some of the kindest people I'd ever met. They had been my points of contact before I arrived in Sea Isle. And they, and the town, had been so much more wonderful than I could have ever imagined.

I sat behind him and waved at each of the partygoers as they entered. When the shuttle was full, we headed up the mountain to Ewan's estate, which was just outside of town.

The enormous rectangle tent was dressed in white lights, and we went inside.

The food had been set up at the back of the tent where I found Mara and Jasper talking. She'd piled her curls on top of her head in a messy bun. But she wore a cute, sparkly, emerald dress with boots.

Jasper was in his normal jeans and rugby shirt. It was kind of a uniform for the pâtissier. He still had a bandage on his head, but other than that, he appeared fine.

"I feel underdressed," I said to Mara. "You're so sparkly."

She waved a hand. "You always look gorgeous."

"How are you two feeling?"

Jasper shrugged. "A bit stiff from the fall, but not too bad thanks to you."

Mara only had a small plaster on her temple where she'd hit the floor. "I'm good," Mara said. "I took multiple naps today."

"Me, too," Jasper added. "I only had to make macarons for tonight's event. And then I crashed. Any news on the case? I'm curious who tried to kill us."

The crowd around us all turned at once and quieted down.

* * *

"That would be a no," I said louder than necessary.

"But I still feel so guilty about you two being hurt," I whispered. "I'm so sorry."

"Hey, we're the idiots who followed you into danger," Jasper said. "And Mara had the pepper spray—I should have let her go down first."

"Since you were tasered, I'm not sure that would have helped," I said. "I don't think I'm ever going to get over this guilt."

Jasper made the sign of the cross over me.

"What are you doing?" Mara asked. "Only priests can do that."

"Well, I'm absolving her guilt," Jasper said. "Dinnae worry about us, Doc. Except for dating two men at once, it's the most exciting thing that's happened to me in a year."

"Two?" Mara and I said at the same time.

"Well, Malcolm, the guy you bought the jewelry from, called me earlier today. We're going to have lunch tomorrow before he leaves town."

"What about David?" Mara asked.

"Like I said, dating two men at once." Jasper smiled.

"Just be careful with that softy heart of yours," I said. He'd been betrayed before by someone he loved, and I didn't want him to get hurt again.

"It's just lunch, and he's leaving town. It's not like anything can really happen. And besides, I deserve a little fun."

"That you do," I said.

I grabbed a couple of macarons. Jasper's were as good as any I'd had in France. And I'd eaten more than my share there.

"This all feels very familiar," I said. We'd been at the same party a year ago. I'd been new to town then. So much had happened since those early days.

"I cannae believe you've been here for a year," Mara said. "Though, I felt like I've known you all my life."

"I feel the same way," Jasper added. "I love our little family of friends."

"I'm grateful for all of you. My life is so different than when I lived in Seattle. I wouldn't change a thing."

"Group hug," Mara said.

We laughed but hugged.

"Where is Abigail?" Jasper asked.

"Tommy didn't feel like facing the crowd tonight. He's become quite popular after singing at the talent show. When they were going to get fish and chips, people kept stopping them to tell him how good he was. He started to feel uncomfortable with all the attention. Abigail decided he needed a break."

"That voice could win him one of those popstars shows," Jasper said. "But I can understand the need for some quiet time. It has been a busy week. I'm used to people, but working night and day is getting old."

"It has been a fun week," Mara said. "And business has been great, but I'm ready for the tourists to leave and for our town to return to normal."

I nodded in agreement. I never minded being busy, but my goal for the next few months was to use my free time to do more genealogy research into my family history. My ancestors had originally come from this area in Scotland, however as I'd told Ewan, there still wasn't much known about them.

Though, it honestly didn't matter. I'd never felt so connected to a place or the people than I did in Sea Isle. It was home and always would be.

"Would you care to dance, Doc?" Ewan asked.

I turned to face him. "Have your toes recovered from the charity gala?"

He chuckled and then held out his hand. "I can take it."

He was dressed in a cable-knit sweater and jeans, and as always, was more handsome than any man should be.

"OK. But don't say I didn't warn you." I took his hand. He guided me to the dance floor.

I did my best to ignore the curious glances from the locals. Though, I was certain gossip would be flying around town before the song finished.

"You look beautiful," he said. "That color of green suits you."

"You too." I stumbled a bit. "I mean handsome. You look handsome."

He grinned.

That was graceful.

"Everything looks great tonight. It's a shame the weather didn't cooperate." I steered the conversation to something easier to talk about.

He shrugged. "That's why we always use a tent. Our Sea Isle weather is unpredictable at best."

"True. Any news from your forensic accountant?"

He cleared his throat. "Can we just dance and not think about work for a bit?"

"We can," I said.

Luckily, it was a slow song so there was more swaying than actual dancing. Still, every time I glanced around, people were watching us.

That is, except for two women in the corner. Catherine, and Davina had their heads together and seemed to be discussing something intensely.

"I wonder what that was about?"

"What?" Ewan turned us so he could see what I could see.

"Those two have become so friendly with one another. Did you listen to the recording I emailed you? It was the whole reason we were there. I was curious what they were up to."

"So much for not discussing the case."

"Well, I just remembered. You were angry with me for investigating without you last night, and it's weird that you didn't say anything."

"Mara told me," he said. "As I was helping her into the surgical suite to wait for you to be done with Jasper. I questioned Mara, and she said Catherine had been looking for an earring she'd lost. But when they heard the noise, they thought there was an intruder, and they ran out the back door."

"Right, an earring. You heard the recording, though."

"Aye, I did. But I wasn't going to play that card quite yet. I want our forensic accountant to finish her report first."

"Evidence, right?"

"Aye. We have no way of knowing if what the two women were suggesting actually exists."

"You need proof."

"Exactly," he said.

"And it would make sense if it was one of them who had tasered Jasper and Mara, but it wasn't. There is a third person involved in all of this."

"Why do you say that?"

"They were still in the office when I heard the thumps downstairs, which turned out to be my friends being hurt."

"None of you should have been there," he said. "You're all lucky it wasn't worse. You seem to have forgotten we are dealing with a killer, a smart one."

"I never forget that fact," I said. "But those two are up to something. How do they even know each other? Every time I see them together, they're whispering, as if sharing secrets. Did you ask them how they knew one another?"

"We've interviewed both of them," he said as if that answered everything.

"And?"

"They met at an event where Burns brought his mistress rather than his wife. They've been friends since then. I think it was a couple of months ago."

"Do you find their scheming suspicious?"

"Aye, but it is all supposition at the moment."

I didn't agree. They had been snooping in the office, and they had not been looking for any kind of jewelry. And why do it at night with the lights out, since Catherine had access to the office during the day?

The song ended and we joined Mara and Jasper, who had been dancing together.

"Do you not have dates tonight?" I asked.

They laughed. "I didn't want to seem too pushy since we'd already been out this week," Mara said.

"David had to do inventory tonight, and Malcom had to pack so he can leave after our lunch tomorrow. So for tonight, we are plus ones for each other."

I grinned.

Henry came up and whispered something to Ewan. He frowned.

I wonder what that is about?

"Do me a favor and keep her out of trouble tonight," Ewan said before I could ask. "I need to check on something."

And then he was off.

The tent was too crowded, and I quickly lost sight of him.

"Excuse me," Kaitlyn Jacks said.

"Hello, Ms. Jacks, how are you?"

"Please, call me Kaitlyn. I'd be better if you'd release my brother's body," she said. "I need to move on with my life. You've had plenty of time to run all the tests." She was bitter and angry. I didn't blame her, but I was curious if this was about her brother or the money she'd expected from him.

"Right. And we have. I'm waiting for the ACC's permission before I can release the body. I'm sure his investigation will wrap up soon. Don't you want to know what happened to your brother?"

Her lips were a hard line. She shrugged. "Of course, I'm not a monster. But I do have a life, and I need to get on with it. If you and the ACC are so serious about my brother's case, why are you at this party? Shouldn't you be investigating?"

"The ACC is the host of the party, and I've honestly done my part of the investigation. I can assure you, though, we are doing everything in our power to solve the case."

She harumphed, and then walked away.

"Rude," Jasper said.

I sighed. "She's lost her brother, and we've kept her here a week. She probably does need to get back to her job."

"If I were looking at suspects, she would be high on my list," Mara said.

I frowned. "Why would you say that? Do you recognize her from last night? Is she the one who tasered you?"

"I couldn't say," she said. "I never saw the person. They were in the shadows."

"Same for me," Jasper said.

"She isn't really mourning his death, is she?" Mara questioned "It is more that all of this is an inconvenience for her. She just wants it over with so she can probably cash in on the insurance. She can't do that without a death certificate."

Insurance. I hadn't thought about that. If he had any, his sister was most likely the beneficiary.

"I need to find Ewan. I'll be back in five."

"Don't go investigating without us," Jasper said.

I laughed. I had no plans to leave the tent. Last time I'd done that, I'd ended up with a bonk on the head and a stay in the hospital.

Again, it was hard to believe that was a year ago.

I couldn't find Ewan, which probably meant he had to leave the party. I texted him, but he didn't answer.

After borrowing one of the umbrellas the valets were using to help people off the shuttles, I walked the half block to the police station.

"Hello?" I called out. While the door was open, there didn't seem to be anyone inside.

"Just a minute," Henry called out.

"Henry? I just need to know where Ewan is," I said.

He came out of an office holding a bunch of files.

"He and Carl are checking out a break-in. Can I help you?"

"A break-in? Where?"

"I dinnae think I should say." He had a worried expression like I might press him on the subject.

"It is OK. Maybe, you can help me. I was curious when going through the victim's files, if you found he had any sort of life insurance?" That was only sort of a lie. I hadn't thought about the life insurance until a few moments ago.

"I can check the case notes. Let me put these down, and I'll take a look."

He looked through a number of pages.

"It says here, we are still searching the boxes and itemizing. He had so many files. It is not listed by the forensic accountant. She just sent in the first part of her report, but there is a second half to come."

"But so far, you haven't found anything pertaining to insurance?" That should have been the first place for me to look. But I was still a novice when it came to investigating.

"Not yet."

"Do you mind if I take a look through the files from his home and office?"

Henry blew out a breath. "Doc, I dinnae think the ACC would be happy about that."

"I'll take the blame. We can tell him I snuck into the station."

"I'm not one for lies," he said.

"Well, I've tried to text Ewan twice, and he hasn't answered. I have one of my gut feelings that Jacks's death might be tied to insurance or some kind of payout. As the coroner, I'd like to see those files. I adore you, Henry, but I'm fairly certain you have to let me look."

The color drained from his face. "Is that true?"

I nodded. "Ewan agreed to let me in on everything that was going on, so I didn't get myself into trouble."

"Well, I suppose that does make sense. Follow me," he said reluctantly.

He led me to the room where he'd come from earlier. "I've labeled everything home or office, and the desk drawer or cabinet it came out of," Henry said.

He was quite precise and careful about things. I had a feeling that was one of the reasons he and Abigail connected on so many levels.

After a half hour, I found what I'd been looking for, and I sat down in a chair to read it.

The insurance policy was for a million pounds, which gave everyone who had known him motive. The benefits were to be paid out to the sister, and a charity devoted to the restoration of old steam engines. Each party received half of the funds.

That was a lot of motive.

I wonder if the sister knows. She'd said she was owed some sort of payout. And the assistant and girlfriend had talked about the hidden money. Were those two things tied together?

I rolled my eyes. Of course, they were. And the sister had to know. That was why she kept pressing for the body and the death certificate. I took some pictures with my phone and put the files back.

When I walked back out, Henry was still the only one at the station.

"Have you heard from Ewan?" I asked. "I have something to tell him."

"No. He's not answering his radio, nor is Carl."

Well, that wasn't good. A knot of worry formed in my stomach. "Where did they go, Henry, and do not use protocol right now. They could be in danger."

"Do you think?"

"Just tell me where they are."

"At the murder victim's home. The neighbor, Mrs. Culbert, thought she saw a light inside the house. They went to check it out."

"You call in reinforcements. I'm heading over there," I said. And I ran out with the umbrella before he could say no.

* * *

The house was just down the street and over a block, and it was completely dark from the outside.

My hope was that Ewan and Carl had checked things out and gone back to the party. Maybe, he couldn't hear his phone or radio with all the noise.

When I approached the porch, Mrs. Culbert came out dressed in her house coat, an umbrella, and rain boots.

"Doctor, what are you doing here?"

"We haven't heard back from the ACC. Did you see them leave?"

"No, I assumed they were still in there. I could hear a bit of rumbling around through my walls. Paper thin they are."

Especially, if one kept an ear close to them.

"I'm going in to check on them. If you don't see or hear from me in ten minutes, call the cavalry."

I didn't give her time to answer. The door was unlocked. I shook out the umbrella and wrapped it closed. I held it like a weapon as I walked into the victim's home.

I hadn't gone far when I found Ewan out on the floor, his hands tied behind his back.

"Ewan," I whispered and shook him a bit. He was out cold, but he had a strong pulse.

"Carl," I called out. My voice warbling with nerves. That knot in my stomach tripled and bile burned the back of my throat.

"They can't help you," Kaitlyn said. "They are all tied up, Doctor."

She stood there holding the taser. It looked like a real gun.

"Why would you do all this? You'll never get away with it."

"I just have to dispose of one more body, and I'm home free. I take the insurance money and find a nice island that doesn't have an extradition treaty. All I need, Doc, is for you to sign that death certificate." She raised her arm with the taser.

I held up the umbrella, like it was going to help me somehow.

"I can't do that if I'm dead."

She laughed cruelly. "Oh, I won't kill you until the paper is signed. I've already shot up the ACC and his man with a cocktail of barbiturates. They won't be waking up any time soon, and they didn't see me. So, no reason to kill them. You on the other hand . . ."

Oh. No. I'd put myself in the middle of trouble once again. When would I learn?

Never, most likely. Especially, when others might be in danger.

"What happens if I refuse to sign?"

"I already have a copy of your signature, and I've become a fairly good forger," she said.

"You'll never get away with it." Then it hit me. "You're the one who broke into my office."

"I am. I wanted to destroy the evidence, but I had to settle for some papers that had your signature. All a part of my plan B. I also have another cocktail of slightly stronger drugs, in case someone saw my face, which you did. In a way I'm doing you a favor."

"What do you mean by that?"

"Your death won't be as painful as my brother's. You'll just die in your sleep."

"How did you get the venom into his lip balm? You said you hadn't seen him in more than a year."

She cackled. "Well, I lied, didn't I? I was here three weeks ago to drop off his birthday present. He'd called to tell me he was sorry. He wanted me to come for a visit. I pretended to forgive him. I had noticed the last time he came to apologize for losing my money that he used the balm constantly. That's when the idea came to me. So, while I was here, I used the bee venom I'd bought on all his toiletries. I'll be honest, I thought he would die much sooner. It took nearly two weeks for it to work."

"But you weren't at the train station that night."

"Oh, but I was. Just under a different name, and I left early. Well, once I'd pushed my dying brother into a cupboard. He had invited me, and everything fell into place that night. His face was swollen, and he could barely make out who I was by the time I found him. It was quite easy to guide him into that office and then the cupboard. And of course, I hid the EpiPen from him. Now, to finish my plan, we need to head down to your office so you can hand over that death certificate. My car is outside."

There was no way I'd be going anywhere with this one. But I had no idea what to do.

"Come along, Doctor."

"No," I said. "You'll have to figure out a different plan. I'm not going to help you."

She laughed. "Forgery, it is." She raised her taser at me. And then two things happened at the same time. I tossed the umbrella at her like a weapon, and Henry and the rest of Ewan's team burst through the door.

There was a scream, and I blinked as the lights flickered on. Henry already had her in cuffs. The taser had fallen to the floor.

I turned and hit the floor to untie Ewan. He was still out cold.

"Henry, I need Ewan and Carl to be taken to my clinic. They've been dosed with goodness knows what. We need to flush out their systems."

"Found him," one of the other officers said.

"Get the bus," Henry called out. "Boss is also down. Doc needs them transported to the clinic."

* * *

A half-hour later, I had them set up with IVs to help flush out their systems. Henry had found the syringes she'd used, and while they probably wouldn't do any permanent damage, I felt better making sure we did our best to figure out what was used against the men.

Abigail, who had shown up before we arrived, had taken blood samples to double check the barbiturates in their systems.

We had both men in surgical suites just off the lab.

I'd been taking Ewan's temp, when his eyes fluttered open. "Doc?" he questioned hoarsely.

"You're OK," I said. "We are flushing out your system. Kaitlyn drugged you."

"Kaitlyn?"

"The victim's sister. She hit you with the taser, and then shot you full of drugs."

He tried to sit up. "Have to . . ."

I pushed him back down. "Do nothing. She's in custody and was caught trying to kill me."

He blinked as if he couldn't quite believe what was happening to him. "Feel weird."

"It's the drugs. They'll wear off soon, though you might get a headache. Just let the IV do its job and stay still. She's in jail and isn't going anywhere. Henry will make sure of that."

"You OK?" he frowned.

"I am now. I was worried when I found you passed out."

The side of his mouth went up in a smile. "Worried about me?"

I touched his shoulder and squeezed. "Yes, Ewan. I was worried about you, but don't let it go to your head."

"I worry and care about you, too. Always," his eyes fluttered shut.

I swallowed hard. I was pleased, but also embarrassed. Would he even remember what he said?

Probably not. Drugs brought down defenses, and people often said strange things they didn't mean.

Henry came to take my statement. We stood just outside the room where Ewan slept.

"There is one thing I can't figure out," I said.

"What's that?"

"What were Davina and Catherine searching for in the office? And was the sister in on it? Was she the one who shocked Mara and Jasper?"

"Aye, she's made a full confession. She was working alone. But I questioned the other two after we took Katilyn Jacks to the station. They had been looking for a flash drive with secret accounts. The sister was waiting for them to find it, and then she was going to steal it from them. She'd given them the information, and they were all supposed to be working together. They're lucky you scared them that night. They might have ended up dead," he finished.

I shivered. "It is wild what greedy people will do."

"Aye," he said. "And to her own family. I dinnae always get along with my hard-headed sisters, but I'd protect them with my life, and I love 'em dearly."

I nodded. "Henry, you will always be one of the good guys and for that, we are all grateful. Thank you for saving me tonight."

He laughed. "Doc, it looked as though you had it well in hand. The umbrella was inspired. You hit her in the forehead. She'll have a good bump."

"Sheer dumb luck that I still had it in my hand," I said.

"I'll let you get back to the patients."

I smiled as he left and turned my attention to Ewan who had fallen asleep again. Rest was good for him, and the saline would soon flush out his system.

* * *

The next morning, I woke up to my favorite scent, coffee. After he'd finished his IV the night before, Ewan had stumbled uneasily to my living room and had passed out on my couch. He refused to let me take him home, so I stayed on the couch with him.

Abigail and Mara had looked after Carl, who had been taken home by Henry in the wee hours of the morning.

But when I opened my eyes, Ewan was no longer on the couch and the coffee scent had me headed to the kitchen.

Ewan stood there in sweats staring at the coffee maker as if his life depended on it.

"How are you feeling?" I asked

"Like a lorry hit me, but I'm fine."

"She dosed you heavily. Much more and there could have been serious complications.

"How is Carl?" he asked.

"Abigail and Henry took him home. He's fine, too. Though, like you, he probably will have a headache today."

"How did you know?" He squinted as if the light from the back window was too bright.

"I'm a doctor. We know these things. Caffeine will help."

He nodded. "Thanks," he said. "For everything, Doc. Henry told me what you did, and I read the statement he took last night. You could have been killed. Did you really use an umbrella as a weapon?"

I shrugged. "It worked. And nothing happened to me. I'm fine."

"But you put yourself in danger again, and this time it was for me."

I held up a hand. "Save the lecture, it won't work. If someone I care about is in danger, I'm all in. Period. Nothing you can say will change that."

He grunted. "I'm beginning to understand that."

Then he grinned and had a mischievous look in his eyes.

"What?" I asked.

"You just admitted to caring about me. I sometimes wonder if you can stand to be in the same room with me."

I laughed. "Well, it's taken a year, but you've grown on me. I'd be very sad if anything happened to you."

"I feel the same way about you."

Awkward silence.

And then the alarm on the front door went off.

Ewan and I rushed through the house to the clinic to find Mara, Jasper, and Abigail bringing armloads full of food inside.

"What is all this?" I asked.

Abigail was already shutting down the alarm.

"The town heard about Ewan, and they have been bringing food to the pub all morning. Abigail told them not to bother you here."

"That's enough to feed the whole town," I said. "And shouldn't it be going to Ewan's home?"

"They all knew he stayed the night," Mara said. And then she giggled.

I rolled my eyes. At the same time, my stomach grumbled.

"Looks like we made it just in time," Jasper said.

We made our way back to the kitchen.

The back door opened, and Tommy came through. "Food," he said.

We all smiled.

As my friends and I sat down to breakfast at my table, I understood just how lucky I was. These people would do anything for me, and I felt the same way about them. Never would I take for granted my wonderful life in Sea Isle, and the great blessing of calling these people my friends.

I was the luckiest woman in the world!

Acknowledgments

I always say it takes a village when it comes to putting a book out, and it is true. Thank you to my editor Tara Gavin and the team at Crooked Lane. You all do so much and I'm so grateful.

A big hug goes out to my agent Jill Marsal who is both brilliant and patient.

My friends Lizzie Bailey and David Faulkner, I could not do this without you. And thank you GayLynn Saari for cheering me on from the sidelines.

And dear readers, I dedicated this book to you because you've been so wonderful to me. You are all the best.